A Cold Assignation

A Cold Assignation

Joanna Spindler

JFJ Paperbacks

This book is a work of fiction. Names, characters, locations and incidents portrayed in this novel are either products of the author's imagination or are used fictitiously.

A Cold Assignation

Cover photo credit: H. Armstrong Roberts/ClassicStock/Getty Images
Cover design credit: Studio Trujillo
Author photo credit: From the Hip Photo
Proof reading credit: Maya Geryk

JFJ Paperbacks: www.linkedin.com/in/e2businessgifts

Printed in the United States of America.
ISBN: 1530565766
ISBN 13: 9781530565764

For CDJ, without question.

Chapter 1

AH, CANNES. THERE is nothing quite like an adult, late summer vacation to the South of France. The French know how to live well. To be able to pretend to live a life of leisure, even for a short while, along the Mediterranean Sea is simply heaven. Having grown up in the Midwest of the United States, drinking wine with our lunch of fresh baguette, camembert and curried tuna salads during the middle of the day overlooking large motor yachts moored in the bright blue sea is indulgent to say the least. Sitting alongside my husband Sam, I can't help but extend my wine glass for yet another toast to the glorious day.

"To the beautifully dressed brunette sitting at the table to our left," I announced. "To her poise, her Chanel sunglasses and her smile as she openly smokes her second cigarette, viva la France!" Sam is less impressed with my most recent toast. He is engrossed instead by the red, white and blue flags flying from the stern of many of the yachts in the water directly in front of our table on the café's terrace. Sam and I are relaxing at the grande dame of Cannes hotels, the Carlton. Specifically, the Carlton's amazing outdoor terrace café overlooking the sea, which has more or less been exactly the same since the day it opened just over 100 years ago.

Sam asked "Do you recognize that flag, the one on the pale yellow ship?"

"I see German, Saudi, English and French flags. The other flags look French, but not quite." I squint my eyes, to see the many small flags through the brilliant clear sun of the French Rivera, but I also do not recognize the nation of the flag in question. "Yes, it's close to the French flag, but not quite" I say. Sam, ever astute to the advantages of the one percent, says "It must be from a small tax-haven republic or country; that's why there are so many of them here."

Sam is my Jonathan Hart. We met at the most bohemian of coffee shops in the middle-sized Indiana town in which we were both born. I was seventeen and seeking more interesting characters than my public school classmates, plus the free nightly live acoustic music was a real draw. During this era, I fell in love with three things: murder mysteries, music and men. I consumed Hercule Poirot and Miss Marple paperbacks. The foreign locations and offbeat cast of characters, or should I say, suspects, held my interest for hundreds of pages. I relished attempting to discern clues from false leads, even though I was almost never successful in solving the mystery myself before it being disclosed by the author. Alfred Hitchcock also became an idol, as did his film's off-putting "MacGuffin" decoy plot lines. I watched PBS' *Masterpiece Mystery* mini-series along with my parents, as well as *Hart to Hart*, without my parents, on network TV.

The classic mystery stories I loved often took place in turn of the century European settings, but *Hart to Hart*, now this was a television show I could relate to! Jonathan Hart was a handsome, thoughtful, sophisticated and self-made man who was married to a clever and active wife, whom he truly loved to spend time with. The Harts always found themselves in the midst of a mystery at best, and a ruthless murder at worst. The Harts were not a stodgy old married couple, like all the parents that I knew. They did not have children and did not seem to miss them. Instead they had a trustworthy House Man named Max and an adopted mixed-breed dog named Freeway. They did not seek out murder, it found them. Mysteries in need of solving fell into their laps while they traveled and engaged in sport activities at exclusive resorts, while they met interesting people from all walks of life, and learned about foreign cultures and practices. This, I decided, is how my adult life should be.

During this time, my high school friend Liv and I would go to the Blue Mountain Coffee House and nurse cups of strong Jamaican coffee for hours, people watching, listening to the evening's live band and talking, like girls do, about everyone we knew. Often we discussed our futures. Future had a different meaning back then, more short term. Mostly we talked about which parties we wanted to attend the following weekend, and in lieu of an upcoming party, which of our homes we should sleep over at. We also recapped our recent dates; which men had made favorable impressions, which were jerks, and which new ones were on our prospect lists.

Liv and I were quite different on the surface, but always got along very well. Liv was intellectual and a bit shy which was often mistaken for stand-offish. She excelled in small groups, but became quiet in larger groups. She was petite and blonde with blue eyes and the classic feminine American perky nose. Her very large family was Republican and lived in the unincorporated suburbs, just outside the town limits. My reality was opposite of Liv's, but one personality trait we shared was the impetus to leave our small, shared hometown as soon as possible to ingratiate ourselves in the much larger (and we were sure, more exciting and sophisticated) world outside of the Midwestern United States. Liv and I both innately knew we would be successful in our adult lives. This was never a doubt for either of us. While I was outgoing and Liv was shy, we were both ambitious. We looked forward to the exciting careers that we would have after we finished undergrad and to the handsome and wealthy men we would marry eventually. One of the gems of being young, is that it didn't matter if our dreams came to fruition. What mattered was the here and now, how we brought out the best in each other, and how much we enjoyed one another's company.

On one such occasion at the Blue Mountain, Sam walked in. I noticed him immediately. He was, and is, the type of person that enters a room with presence. It doesn't hurt that Sam is very handsome, tall with bright eyes and broad shoulders. I was smitten from first sight. I watched him for several minutes before our eyes met. When they did, I felt my blood rush, straight to my stomach where deep down a tingle began. Teenage hormones are not to be messed with; I had to meet this man. I grabbed Liv by the arm and pulled her into the ladies room and began with "Did you see him?" followed by "Do you know him?" and after receiving negative responses, concluded with "I *call* him first Liv. Hands off." This may seem brash, but as I said, Liv was a beauty, blond and perky and thankfully, more shy than I. And so, after various durations of flirting from afar, flirting in close proximity, and then flirting on top of one another, here Sam and I are some 30 years later in Cannes.

Chapter 2

I TRY TO be diligent in my observations of the world around me. I do this for many (what I consider to be) positive reasons. I believe being aware of one's surroundings is the safest and most interesting way to live. I appreciate the free entertainment often provided by observing random people within my vicinity. I also appreciate how often I find things by simply keeping my eyes open: lost dogs wandering in a green space, spare change on the ground seemingly everywhere, unused gift cards in the middle of a crosswalk, and once, a wallet dumped just beside a trash bin in a public restroom. Warren Buffet once said that when he was child, his father had taught him to "stoop" at the horse race park. Stooping, according to Buffet, is to look for and pick up all the discarded racing tickets you could get your hands on. Buffet had said it was amazing how many of the tickets that he "stooped" as a youngster were unredeemed, winning tickets, so I too pay attention.

My name, by the way, is Lauren Hendrick, Mrs. Samuel A. Hendrick, and Lauren for short. My parents desired to give me a good strong first name, one that would suit well into old age. As

I've grown older, I believe I can learn things about our society, both good and bad, simply by watching how people interact and communicate. In the back of my mind, I strongly suspect that I pay attention to my surroundings so closely so that if ever I witness a truly nefarious going-on, I will be able to assist in the solving of a crime. Sam jokes that I am always looking for an old-school murder caper to entangle myself with and that I would be most happy being Hercule Poirot at a Cornish seaside resort.

Cannes is a perfect setting for such thoughts of mystery and espionage. The Carlton Hotel in particular, is not what one would a call budget-friendly destination for an American couple whose currency is the dollar. "You get what you pay for" is one of my frequent mantras. This is certainly true of the Carlton and it seems Sam and I are not alone in this belief, as the Carlton is busy with many long and lean, chiseled-faced guests who enjoy dressing to the nines at dusk and driving pristinely polished automobiles worth six figures five blocks to their evening's supper destination. With this kind of sheer natural beauty and man-made wealth in such close proximity, the Carlton seems to me to be a perfect setting for a jewel heist or a love-triangle murder. Alfred Hitchcock must have thought the same since he based his 1950s Technicolor film *To Catch a Thief* starring Cary Grant and the beautiful Grace Kelly at the Carlton.

Unlike many other historic hotels, the current service at the Carlton has remained fine, all these years later, in spite of its current full house of guests. Our staff at this temporary residence along Cannes' beach Croisette is unerringly attentive to their guests' needs and never appear to be too busy for one's special request. Sam and I love being referred to by name for example, by everyone from our chambermaid, to any one of the team of waiters and concierge.

"Madame et Monsieur Hendrick" is quietly spoken from behind our café table breaking my reverie. It's Steffan, the Carlton's most junior concierge. I assume this based on his age, not his capability. Steffan has seen us enjoying our wine on the Terrace Café and wants to inform us of his recent accomplishments. He has successfully reserved a BMW motorcycle to be delivered to the hotel for our following day's trip to Cap d' Antibes. He has also reserved two front row chaise lounges at the Carlton's private beach for us for the next and last day of our visit here.

"Merci Steffan. All is perfect, but what time will the motorcycle arrive tomorrow?" asks Sam.

"At 8 a.m. Mr. Hendrick, but we will observe it for you until you are ready to leave tomorrow." replies Steffan.

"Thank you again Steffan. Your help is appreciated. That will be fine." Sam has long since outgrown the habit to proffer a monetary tip at every interaction. He simply passes out envelopes with a stash of cash and a handwritten thank you note to all who have helped to make us comfortable, on the last day of our vacations.

"Look Sam, that brunette with the Chanel sunglasses, her first friend has left and now another, different man is joining her," I whisper. Sam turns to look and sure enough the dapper gentleman wearing the afternoon jacket is gone, his wine glass and napkin cleared already by the quick and efficient café staff and now another man of about the same middle age, but more deeply tanned, is kissing each of her cheeks and sitting down to join her. "I'll bet she is seeing them both Sam, and neither man knows of the other. It's an afternoon affair."

"Could be, we are in France, the land of love, after all" says Sam, inspired to give me a quick kiss himself. There is something in the air in this part of the world. I turn my attention back to the table in question, but I cannot make out the words from the beautiful French melody they are speaking to one another.

"Darn, the American school system Sam; I cannot understand what they are saying." Just then the tanned man proffers the brunette a small box. "Look Sam, he's giving her a gift. It looks like a jewel box from Cartier!" Sam looks just in time for her to accept and open the small red box. Her face falls as she sees the contents, but she quickly recovers her composure and smiles brightly. He stands, walks around their small table deftly avoiding stepping on the small dog resting on the floor beside her chair. He whispers something in her ear and then he leaves. Leaves. "How strange Sam. They didn't kiss. He didn't put the jewelry on her. He just left." I've got to find out what's in that box Sam."

Dogs and cigarettes are great. They both make easy conversation openers with strangers, I've found. After watching the woman tuck the box in her purse, reapply her lipstick and light another cigarette, I rise and slowly approach her table. "Bonjour Madame" I say. She turns, startled, her perfectly arched eyebrows raising behind her sunglasses. "May I say hello to your cute dog?" I ask in English. "We left our Olive at home and I miss her. Olive is the name of our dog" I say, as I gesture back toward Sam in explanation of "we". Sam nods his head and grins ever so slightly toward us.

"Oui" she says very quietly. I bend down and as is usually the case, dogs recognize dog-loving humans, her small, short-haired Terrier invites my affection by nuzzling my proffered hand and yipping twice.

"He's just lovely Madame" I say. "Young, I bet. Not more than two years old. Do you understand my English Madame?"

At this the brunette replies, "Yes, I understand. You are correct, little Vivi will be two this autumn."

"Oh, I just knew it. She is still so full of life. Our Olive, she is older now and has slowed down, so we don't bring her on such long travels anymore. She stays home with our dog-sitter. This is the worst part of having a dog, I believe, that we know we will certainly outlive them."

"Yes" she agrees as her brow furrows. I continue to pet her dog while trying to think of what to say next. But I don't have to. A moment later the woman coughs, then raises her hand to her face and begins to weep quietly. She lowers her face from mine and reaches into her clutch for a tissue. I take the opportunity to slide into the second-time vacant chair opposite her and gently proffer one of the fine linen cocktail napkins from the table to her.

"Madame are you alright? Is there anything that I can do?" I ask.

Chapter 3

"Please let me know what I can do to assist you Madame. It is far too beautiful a day for you to be upset." She said nothing, but also made no indication that I should leave. So I ventured further, in an effort to placate her. "May I order you a glass of Champagne? I know that I would love to have one and the tiny bubbles always make me feel better" I said. At that, the mystery woman smiled just a little, and tapped her knee to indicate that her cute little terrier should jump up onto her lap.

"Oui. Champagne is a very good idea indeed, as you see this is a happy day!" she said, dabbing her eyes with the cocktail napkin.

I motion to the waiter by saying "S'il vous plais," and caught Sam's eye. He smiled genuinely, telling me in a non-verbal way that "it's ok, take your time, have fun with the mystery of what is in the box." I order two glasses of Rose Champagne for Marie and me and then said "What breed of terrier is your dog?"

She replied, after taking a moment to refold the cocktail napkin which she had been using and placed it back down on the polished wooden table top, "She's a Boston terrier, her name is Vivi because she is so vivacious. Oh, and my name is Marie. I am sorry, I don't know what came over me. You see, I should be very happy: I am getting married next month."

"Marie, that is wonderful. A wedding on the horizon will make anyone a bit emotional, I understand completely."

Our Champagne arrived and Marie lit another cigarette, so I asked her if I could have one too. "Certainly" she said offering her box of Gauloises along with the smallest, daintiest silver lighter I had ever seen.

After a few sips, I ventured further inquiring, "Is your fiancé here at the Carlton with you?"

"Yes, he just left the café actually. He presented to me, what do you say, my engagement ring." I frowned. I have never had a poker face. Marie laughed lightly. "You saw him just now?" Marie asked.

"Yes."

"Then you see my problem, I feel strongly for Franco, my fiancé, but he treats our wedding like a business transaction. I lost my first husband almost four years ago." There Marie broke off and reached for another tissue from her handbag. I remained quiet, smoking. After a few minutes Marie said, "Thank you for the drink and the company. What is your name Madame?"

I introduced myself and my husband and then waved Sam over to us. "Sam, I would like for you to meet Marie and Vivi. Isn't Vivi sweet? She makes me miss our Olive at home." Sam extended his hand to Marie and asked her if he might join us for a glass of Champagne as well.

Marie, happy for the distraction I think, graciously replied, "But of course Monsieur Hendrick."

A round later, Sam and I had learned that Franco already lived with Marie in her villa on Cap d' Antibes. Marie had also shared that she had lived in France her whole life. She had been raised just outside of Paris and had moved to the Cote d'Azur with her first husband, Jan, over ten years ago and that she loved living in the Mediterranean region. Sam and I told Marie that we had been married for thirteen years and currently lived in Denver, Colorado, after a short stint in Houston, Texas. We told her we love Colorado and inquired if she had ever been there.

"Non" she replied, "but I have heard the Rocky Mountains are beautiful, much more expansive than the Alps, here." She then acknowledged that she and Franco were to be married next month, here at the Carlton, and that Franco was a good man. She just wished that he was more romantic.

I begin to get the impression from Marie, that she didn't trust that Franco loved her whole-heartedly. She didn't speak of Franco badly, just with a tinge of melancholy in her voice.

"When one has already enjoyed the love of one's life, does anyone else ever compare?" Marie mused. Upon hearing this, I reached for Sam's hand under the table and he squeezed mine back.

"I'm sure that is how I would feel as well Marie, but certainly you do not have to get married so quickly, perhaps you should wait a little while?" offered Sam gently.

"No, I feel that I must marry soon, Sam," replied Marie, "You see, my late husband left quite a bit of land here in the area to me, along with a wine distribution operation, and Franco will run it for me."

Sam and I were speechless.

When I was younger, I would have been inclined to tell Marie, someone I had just met, all the reasons that she did not need have anyone help her run her late husband's business and that she did not need to marry Franco at all, but now that I am older, I have learned that it is better to simply observe people and let them make their own mistakes. I'm also trying hard to be more optimistic about human nature, ever since I proclaimed this my New Year's resolution two years ago.

Just then Marie continued, "Franco has worked just under my late husband for many years, and during all that time, the three of us had always gotten along well. I love and respect Franco, and I feel that he genuinely loves me in return, but I suspect he keeps me at arm's reach due to some sense of honor to my late husband, Jan. I'm just not sure that Franco and I will ever have the intimate marriage like I had enjoyed before," she continued.

Sam thought for a moment, with a furrow on his brow, then said "Marie, in America we have an expression: 'It's always darkest before the dawn.' Perhaps you are just experiencing cold feet, which I certainly did in the weeks before Lauren and I wed, but as I hope you can see, we love one another even more now than we did then. Our love has grown since the day we said 'I do' to one another."

"Oh Sam, thank you," I said. "I agree Marie, for us, our love and trust has only grown. In time, it can certainly be the same way for you and Franco" said my optimistic side.

Sam then nudged my foot, imparting that he did not want to overstay our welcome and then turned his head to look for our waiter, who appeared next to the table immediately, seemingly out of thin air. "Our check for the table s'il vous plais" requested Sam.

But there was still one thing that I felt the need to ask Marie. "Marie, may I ask you a question" I began directly.

"Yes, of course, Lauren."

I began softly, a bit embarrassed, "Forgive me for being inquisitive Marie, but who was the other gentleman you spoke with here today? The one wearing the jacket."

Our check arrived on its silver tray, Sam signed for it and Marie replied, "That was my brother Jean Luc. He and I are close and he has been worried about me. He came to ask if I would consider postponing my wedding date. I feel I have burdened you both with too many stories, but sometimes life intervenes for a reason. I just want you to know that you both have made me feel so much better. More sure of myself somehow. How long with you be in Cannes? Can we meet again while you are here? After having spoken so much about him, I would like for you two to meet my Franco; to see us together."

"We would enjoy that Marie, but Sam and I only have two more full days here. Tomorrow Sam is taking me on a motorcycle trip, but the day after, Thursday, we will be here at the Carlton, on the beach. How about lunch at the Beach Club at 2 p.m. if you are both free and don't mind a little sand between your toes," I said.

Marie committed by saying, "We will be there! I look forward to it and I want to learn a bit more about what you two do at home, in the mountains!" Marie's enthusiasm was so nice to hear after her initial sadness just an hour ago, that I did not have the heart to tell her that Denver is not located in the mountains.

"The sky is blue, the sun is shining, and yet you forget
that everywhere
there is evil under the sun."

Hercule Poirot

Chapter 4

"SAM, WAKE UP. It's another beautiful day in Cannes. Is it really possible that the sun here is this sharp and crisp every single morning?"

"I doubt it" replied Sam, who I had just woken up and hadn't had his Nespresso yet.

Sam and I both became addicted to Nespresso a few years previously in Rome, where every television commercial and roadside billboard had had the funny, self-deprecating George Clooney hawking the brand. With good reason, as it turns out. Nespresso coffee is exceptional and highly additive to java lovers like Sam and me.

Today, our next to last day in the South of France, we were traveling to the nearby town of Cap d' Antibes for a little sightseeing. I leaned over Sam in bed, planted a kiss on his lips and a Nespresso in his left hand, as encouragement to rise. Sam smelled good and looked so handsome in the large four-poster bed with his tiny Nespresso cup in hand that I climbed back in with him.

Two hours later we descended the grand staircase into the understated front lobby of the Carlton and made our way into the sunshine at the motor entrance where Steffan the concierge had made sure that Sam's BMW 750cc rental motorcycle was waiting for us.

"Oh, it's a lovely motorcycle, Sam, this is going to be so fun!" I exclaimed as Sam walked around the bike, making sure everything was in order. "Do you miss your motorcycle?" I said next. Sam had given up his bike back at home in Denver a year previously to enjoy the open mountain roads of Colorado in a Porsche Carrera instead. The first step to middle age, he had said at the time.

"Every once in a while I do miss having a motorcycle, Lauren, but I always felt badly that Olive couldn't ride along with us like she does in the Porsche" responded Sam, then added "Plus, our trip today will be all the more exciting because it's become a novelty again."

When Sam says things like this, I fall in love with him all over again. I gave him another kiss and pulled on my helmet, threw my leg over the seat, hopped on, and adjusted my sunglasses. Sam started the bike, and off we rode along the Croisette, west toward Antibes with the sun sparkling off the calm Mediterranean Sea, which still filled with moored yachts, on our right side. We curved left along the coast and approached another beach at the far end of Cannes, with sunbathers enjoying the perfect early September weather. Next we ascended a hill, where Sam accelerated the large bike to pass a couple of motor scooters and a large tour bus. We rounded a sharp curve in the road and descended toward another small beachside village. This was a two-stop sign village, with both stops located right in the center of town and surrounded by the cutest, pedestrian-friendly independent shops and cafes. Nothing like the large corporate stores and strip malls back home. We continued on, along the coast, curving left and right, up and down for another 45 minutes or so, and then saw the first directional sign for our day's destination.

Having a motorcycle anywhere in Europe is the way to explore. Sam and I quickly figured this out on our first trip to France, thirteen years ago on our honeymoon. Simply stated, navigating the narrow streets in most European city centers, when one does not know where to go and therefore needs to make abrupt U-turns, as well as being able to park nearby tourist destinations, is much easier on two wheels than four.

The city center of Antibes was quite bustling, much like Cannes. It also was located along the sea. We followed the crowds walking along the sidewalks to the Picasso Musée and pulled up and parked the bike just across the cobblestone street from the main entrance of the museum. The Picasso Museum was housed in a centuries-old Grimaldi mansion where Picasso himself had once spent a summer season holed up on the top floor enjoying this lovely location and working. Before visiting this museum, I would have said painting, not working, but as it turned out, Picasso was a prolific sculptor and even made ceramic decorative arts as well as his more famous paintings and drawings.

The top floor of the museum was curated with photographs of Picasso working in this exact space overlooking the sea, which remained exactly as it appeared in those black and white photos from 1946, hung around the atelier. The lower floors of this mansion museum housed the largest assortment of Picasso works in one place that Sam or I had ever previously seen. The museum even had a sea-side terrace with a half-dozen of Picasso's dramatic life size female forms staring out toward the sea.

Another thing that I love about France is that it is perfectly acceptable to often stop for a refreshment break and actually sit down while doing so. This is the definition of café society for me and as Sam and I left the museum, Sam turned the motorcycle toward Cap d' Antibes, the very historic and residential neighborhood that juts northward, out into the Mediterranean from the city center where the museum was located.

"How does a drink and a rest at Eden Roc sound, Lauren?" asked Sam from the front of the bike. Sam, unlike many successful American businessmen, also relishes a slower café society pace.

Eden Roc was the subject of many vibrantly colored Slim Aarons photographs, which are reproduced regularly in the fashion magazines which I read. Slim Aarons found his artistic niche by shooting "beautiful people, doing beautiful things, in beautiful places." Eden Roc was developed in the late 1950s at the tip of Cap d' Antibes, as a destination resort for the ultra-wealthy and it certainly qualifies as a beautiful place. Sam and I had never been to Eden Roc before and I was very excited to see it in person and learn if the slightly retro mid-century modern vibe of the pool house that houses its Michelin-starred restaurant was still intact.

At the street entrance, as we pulled up on the BMW motorcycle, the uniformed gate keeper waved us to a stop and asked if we are guests at Eden Roc. Sam said "No, but we have a luncheon reservation." The tall, slim gate keeper noted the BMW's license plate number in a small journal pulled from his breast pocket, and asked us to park in the street side lot, just to his left. He then directed us to walk down the long, winding, single-track road to the pool house.

As we walked along the shaded path lined with plane trees, we saw the main guest house's patina copper roof above the tree tops, on a hill above the sea, to our left. It was huge, stately and timeless and I had the overwhelming feeling of being happy at Eden Roc. Sam and I walked about a half mile before the pristinely white, flat-roofed pool house appeared before us. It was situated on top of the rocky outcroppings that border the majority of this cape. Immediately to the left was the famous swimming pool, one of the original infinity style pools, with many guests in various stages of relaxation around its two landlocked sides.

We entered the pool house by the main entrance where we were welcomed by a very handsome man dressed in white uniform, with a hint of nautical flair to it. Sam asked him for a table on the outside terrace facing the pool and the sea. "All the better to view the guests," Sam whispered to me conspiratorially. We sat and were presented with menus, of which the first half dozen or so pages listed every cocktail concoction imaginable. Daytime drinking is still very much acceptable, and even encouraged, in France. Our waiter appeared, and Sam ordered a bottle of San Pel sparkling water, a Champagne cocktail called the Grande Dame for me and a perfect Manhattan for himself.

We settled in and begin to notice that many of the yachts moored before this resort also flew the same mystery nation flag Sam had observed yesterday in Cannes harbor. I turned my gaze toward the pool, lined on two sides by the natural rock walls; it appeared as though the pool had been cut into the rock cliff. Sam, I noticed, was looking at the many lovely women in Burberry & Eres swim suits, who all appeared to have been born with the lithe yet healthy bodies of tennis players or equestrians. Just then a young man with a golden tan and blond hair, which had a perfect wave texture to it, climbed high up onto the diving board that was located just below our terrace dining table. This diving board hung at least 15 feet above the clear sea water below it. He called out to his girlfriend, who was also stunning, puffed out his chest and then proceeded in a perfect swan dive into the blue water below us, with nary a splash.

"Sam, I love it here. Do you think we can stay here at Eden Roc, the next time we come to the South of France?" I asked.

"Certainly, Lauren. It appears to be as well maintained now as it was in its heyday, but this quiet, semi-remote location will be a vast difference from the up tempo of Cannes, which I know you love."

"Speaking of Cannes, Sam, I've been dying to ask you your opinion of Marie and her fiancé from yesterday. Sam, Marie seemed sad to me. How can one get married and appear so dismal about it?" I asked.

Sam turned his head toward me from the pool view and responded, "Marie did seem sad, anxious even, but very genuine, if you ask me. I think it will be very interesting to meet Franco. Do you think they both will actually turn up for lunch with us tomorrow?"

Chapter 5

As we entered our suite back at the Carlton that evening, an envelope was laying on the carpet just inside our door. "I love receiving communications slipped beneath our door, Sam. It seems such an old-school way to receive a message," I exclaimed as Sam picked up the envelope which had our names handwritten on the front.

Sam tore open the left edge of the envelope as he teased me by saying, "Don't get your hopes up Lauren." Then, unfolding the thick, cream colored stock of the Carlton's stationary read the letter aloud:

Dear Mr. and Mrs. Hendrick,

My fiancée Marie has expressed her delight at meeting you late yesterday afternoon, after my leave-taking, at the Terrace Café. She has conveyed her desire for me to visit with you both as well, before your departure from Cannes. I have taken the liberty of making reservations under my name for the four of us for luncheon tomorrow. We look forward to meeting you at the Carlton's Beach Club at two in the afternoon.

À bientôt,

Franco Alix

"Wow Sam, that's a very nice note. I feel better about Marie's fiancé already. A man who handwrites such a thoughtful note and has it delivered to us can't be all bad. I like Franco better already, Sam" I said.

"Well, it seems our lunch date is definitely on, Lauren. I have to say, I am looking forward to meeting this Monsieur Alix tomorrow, but first, how about we freshen up and share a bottle of Champagne on the Croisette together under the moonlight?"

"I love you Mister Hendrick. That sounds wonderful."

Sam retrieved the unmistakable yellow-orange bottle of Veuve Clicquot that we had purchased in a small wine shop a few days before from our small refrigerator as well as two wine glasses from the bar top above it, as I pulled on my warm cashmere sweater. We slipped out of our suite and tiptoed down the hall toward the staircase, feeling slightly like teenagers with a stolen bottle of booze. We crossed the beautiful lobby, thankfully virtually empty at the moment. Sam nodded confidently to Steffan, bottle and glasses in hand, as Steffan wished us bon soir.

We crossed the street directly in front of the Carlton after waiting for a few motor scooters, an Audi, and even a navy blue Maybach to pass. As we approached the Carlton's private dock, we turned right and walked along the Croisette beach path a few hundred yards until Sam saw an available bench, where we stopped. Sam bowed toward me, the bottle behind his back like a waiter and I sat. The moon was high and bright, reflecting in our eyes, as Sam opened the Clicquot and poured us each a drink. Our glasses filled with tiny golden bubbles magnified in the moon's light.

"Lauren" Sam said a few minutes later, "I love you more than ever. I wouldn't want to be here under this moonlight drinking Champagne with anyone else in the world."

What can a woman say to that? Nothing I suspect, so instead of talking, I wrapped my arm around Sam's waist, pulled myself closer in to him and kissed his neck softly under the clear South of France moonlight.

Later, back in our suite, with our shoes off, the French doors open, and with tipsy grins on our faces, Sam picked up his laptop and got comfortable on his chair. I took this as a sign that he wanted to check in with his office, so I left the room and went into the bath to get ready for bed, in order to give him some space and quiet.

He's been so great this holiday, I thought, barely working at all and really relaxing. It's really true, I mused as I brushed my teeth, I wouldn't want to be here with anyone else either.

As I finished up in the bath, my hair brushed and slathering my hands and elbows with lotion, Sam called out "Lauren, you're never going to believe this. I got online because I wanted to see who we're having lunch, with so I Googled Franco Alix. Guess what? His first wife is dead too. Only eighteen months ago, in Antibes. It says here, she died of natural causes, a heart condition apparently, nothing criminal, no charges filed."

I walked back into the living room. "So Marie and Franco are both widowers. The plot thickens. Sam, can you look up how Marie's husband died?" I asked.

"I have already tried. I knew that would be your first question, Lauren, plus great minds think alike" said Sam with the wink which he only uses when he's had a drink or two. "But we don't know Marie's last name and I don't see any obituaries from four years ago in this area, which seem to be applicable to his given name of Jan."

Chapter 6

DIRECTLY ACROSS THE street in front of our hotel, Sam and I were led to our reserved chaise lounge chairs on the Carlton's private beach by an attractive young attendant who tucked fresh, perfectly white cotton towels around the Carlton monogrammed chair cushions. He then introduced himself as Paul and asked me where I would like our umbrella positioned. Have I mentioned that the service here is exceptional?

"Please shade us for now Paul. Merci," I responded.

Paul's tanned arms thrust the umbrella into the sand. He tilted the canopy expertly to provide shade over both Sam and me, and asked if we would care to see menus.

"Not just yet Paul. The wife and I will begin today in the sea." responded Sam. "But please check back with us in an hour."

"I will monsieur." Paul adjusted the table between our two sets of knees, placed an ashtray upon it, and bowed ever so slightly before retreating.

It was eleven in the morning, the water was calm and the temperature felt about 85 Fahrenheit. Perfect. We had privacy screens, also monogrammed with the Carlton logo in white on the light beige canvas fabric, to protect us from the breeze and from seeing too much of our beach neighbors, some of whom were bathing in various stages of undress.

"Viva la France!" I whispered to Sam, for the first time today, but for the umpteenth time this week.

"Lauren, I want to dive into the water from the end of the pier. Are you game?"

"I cannot think of anything that I would rather do, Sam" I responded.

Sam and I both love swimming, not competitively, but often and whenever possible. We walked through the sand, past a handful of other sunbathers and up onto the Carlton's pier. The pier was already set with umbrellas, linen covered tables and cushioned chairs for the day's luncheon crowd. We walked along the length of the pier, in between the tables, where already a few diners in casual beach attire were enjoying their meals. At the end of the pier, parked just underneath the classic Carlton sign (just as it appeared in Hitchcock's *To Catch a Thief*), two small boats were docked. These motorboats were only about 25 feet in length, so I assumed they had taxied visitors from their much larger nearby yachts into the Carlton for dining and onto dry land for shopping, for the day. Sam and I stood at the very end of the pier with our toes dangling just off the wooden edge. The water was glorious, clear and clean with the most gentle of waves. One could see straight down into its depths. In spite of this, I asked Sam to dive in first. He obliged after doing a few gratuitous stretches for show. He surfaced some 20 feet forward. Sam shook his bobbing head and exclaimed that the water was warm.

I dove next. I hit the surface of the water, descended into its depths and there was absolutely no shock. The water was temperate, but not so warm as to feel like bath water. I could feel the sun through the top few feet of it, near the surface. I swam quickly to catch up with Sam, who was heading off toward our left, out and away from the pier.

"Damn the torpedoes, full steam ahead!" cried out my husband with a broad grin. This was not the first time that I have heard him use this expression. Over all the years together, I've come to learn that this is one of his happy expressions; when Sam desires more of the same and will not be diverting from the activity at hand. The last time he had used this expression, I remembered him dragging me through a crammed rummage sale or an "antique store" as he called it, looking for a 1950s era set of skis to decorate his office. Today, I appreciated his exclamation more.

We swam out away from shore for about twenty minutes or so with Sam leading the charge before we took a break to float on our backs then dog paddle and turn around to appreciate the view of the Croisette from our new vantage in the Mediterranean Sea.

As we swam back in to shore, letting the calm waves push us toward land, I swam into Sam's arms just as soon as I thought he could touch ground. I love the feeling of floating in Sam's arms. I suspect all women do: there is something wonderful about the feeling of being weightless in the arms of one's lover, with warm water and sunlight all around.

Hours that seemed like minutes later, at one thirty, I rolled over onto my side and brushed Sam's arm, lying on his chaise lounge beside me.

"Sam, I'm going to the changing room to freshen up for lunch. Will you please tell Paul that we will be lunching, but that we will return? Please also ask him how long the beach will remain open today."

"Will do Lauren. I'll just put my shirt and sandals on, my shorts are already dry." he replied.

Even the beach changing room here is magnifique, I thought to myself as I blew dry my hair and applied fresh mascara and lip gloss. I pulled my yellow sundress over my bikini and spritzed on a bit of my favorite D&G scent. I returned to Sam at just two o'clock. We made our way to the beach restaurant's host stand and were informed our party had already arrived. We were led to a table toward the far end of the pier, near where we had jumped into the ocean earlier. Marie and Franco were sitting quietly. Today, Marie donned a chic alabaster sun hat with very light green accents and a darker grass-green shirt dress which looked to be Celine, based on its very simple clean lines. Franco, who was sitting just to her right and looking at his phone, had on a pressed white linen short sleeve shirt and slim-fitting dark blue jeans with a cognac-colored Hermès belt.

"Hello, Marie" I said in greeting. "What a lovely chapeau."

"And you must be Franco" said Sam extending his hand to the deeply tanned Franco who placed his phone face-down on the table. "I am Sam Hendrick, but please call me Sam, and this is my wife, Lauren."

"It is nice to see you both again" said Marie as Franco shook Sam's hand and then pulled out the chair on his left for me.

"Merci, Monsieur Alix. We also are pleased to see Marie again and to meet you today. Thank you for the nice note. Unfortunately Sam and I will depart for home tomorrow already. With fair weather like this and lovely people like you, we really do not want to leave." Then, "May I call you Franco?" I asked.

After a few more pleasantries, the ordering of our drinks as well as, a fresh oyster plate for the table. I said "Congratulations Franco. Marie told us yesterday that you will be getting married here at the Carlton next month."

"Yes, I, rather we, are greatly looking forward to it, I think. I have only just proposed to Marie, but we have known one another already many years, and at our age there is no time to waste," Franco said while reaching for Marie's hand, now adorned with a diamond and emerald engagement ring.

"Oh Marie, your engagement ring, it is beautiful." I exclaimed enthusiastically. "I see you are wearing it on your left ring finger too, in the American style. I have to say, it is just beautiful."

"Thank you, Lauren. I am actually very happy. I love this charming man dearly and am looking forward to our wedding party. I do, however, wish that you and Sam could attend. It will be an informal affair, but we will have many guests and colleagues at our celebration. Will you, by chance, be able to be here in Cannes again next month?"

"I'm afraid not Marie. But best wishes, we are happy for you both. Lauren will enjoy hearing me say this; married is a wonderful way to live," said Sam.

"I agree absolutely Sam. I love your and Lauren's positivity. Is this the spirit of all Coloradans?" Marie teased us with a small grin. Marie then continued by saying "I told you yesterday that I have been married before, but this will be a second marriage for Franco as well. He, also, how do you say? Lost his wife just a couple years after my husband..."

With very poor timing, a cell phone chirped and Franco excused himself. He pushed his chair a few inches back from our table and began to read a message on the phone which he had placed on the table as we arrived.

"Well Marie, you have that in common. I can't imagine how difficult it would be to lose one's spouse at such a young age and continue on. I'll bet Franco has been a great support for you and you for him."

"Yes, we share a deep grief but are lucky to have found one another."

I wanted to know more. I wanted to ask Marie how Jan and Franco's first wife each died, but I knew that would be too personal plus I always become a bit uncomfortable talking about death, probably because I had been lucky enough not to have experienced much loss in my life. Frankly, I didn't know what to say, so I changed the subject by saying, "I'm curious to know, what type of industry are you and Franco in? You mentioned that you work together." I noticed Sam sneak a quick glance toward Franco who was engrossed texting and I continued, "Did

I hear you are involved in the famous wine making business of this Cote d'Azur region?"

"Non. My late husband Jan started the business with help from his family when he was in his twenties. It is not a vineyard at all, rather it is a wine distributorship, the second largest in all of France, of the local wine varietals grown all throughout the South of France. We do not make the wine. We just sell it all over the world. I don't enjoy the business as much as Jan did while he was alive, but it is mine now. I do a bit of marketing, throw parties for the exporters and the store buyers mainly, but Franco, he also has a head for the business, like Jan had. Jan hired Franco over eight years ago and they always worked very well together. I believe in many ways Franco helped Jan grow the business to the level we enjoy today. Franco took more risks than Jan would have on his own, and most of them paid in, what do you say, spades?"

Placing his phone down again on the table and pulling his chair in, Franco rejoined our conversation by saying "I'm so sorry for my rudeness. It was a work matter."

"I understand completely," said Sam, telling the truth. "We were actually just talking about work. Marie was just saying how well you and her late husband worked together. Tell me Franco, how do you find it making a living here in paradise, if I may ask?"

And easily as that, I recognized that businessmen the world round have at least one thing in common; they love talking about work.

Chapter 7

ALL THAT REMAINED on the four small plates on our water-side lunch table were twelve empty oyster half shells glistening in the sun like the jewels on many of the guests. The oysters in this part of the world are plump but small, much smaller in diameter than the Pacific Northwestern oysters Sam and I often enjoy in America. Perhaps because the French prefer fresh-caught oysters, not the farmed style so often found in the States. Grown either way, oysters are delicious. I have never found them to be an aphrodisiac per se, but it is nice that one often speaks of love while eating oysters due to this commonly held belief.

As we four waited for our lunch entrees to arrive, Sam and Franco were happily engrossed speaking with one another about work and business, which allowed Marie and me to learn more about each other as well.

"Where is Vivi today Marie?" I inquired. "I was hoping to see her again, as kind of a stand-in for our doggie Olive, whom I miss desperately."

"I left her at home today because we are eating al fresco on the pier. Vivi, she has developed a bad habit of barking at the waves, which does not make for a quiet lunch. She loves the water, which is strange for a small dog, and when she sees the waves but cannot go into the sea, she barks incessantly."

"That is hilarious Marie. You certainly gave her the appropriate name of Vivi, for vivacious," I said. Then, "Sam and I do not have children, so our dog Olive plays a large part in our lives back home. Thankfully, Colorado, much like France, is very dog friendly. I am always happy when Olive can accompany me on my errands and to my appointments, but you're right Marie, this setting, here on the pier, it would be hard for Olive to lie down quietly also."

"Lauren, I do not have children either, which is unusual here in France. Perhaps in America too? I like children; it's not that I do not like them, but I never truly desired to have a baby of my own. Sometimes I think it is because I come from a small family, so I am not used to it. I just have one older brother. Jan felt ambiguous about raising children too, so he didn't pressure me. And then when Jan died so unexpectedly, I felt relieved that we had not started a family. It would have been easier for me at first, I think, to grieve with another, and to have a remembrance of him, but that is selfish, I feel. I am relieved we did not have a child who had to mourn his father. I will miss Jan forever, but I find that having only a dog is enough for me, still."

"Yes, and a dog can be just enough of a cute, little, furry being to receive and give one's love to. I have often thought that taking care of Olive; training her, feeding her, bathing her and snuggling with her, is just the right amount of extra love, above and beyond Sam, to fulfill my desire to take care of another," I agreed. "It is however, an interesting point that you bring up Marie. I come from a small family as well. I am an only child, and no one on my side of our family ever had more than one or two children. Perhaps it is simply that one generally does not desire what one has never had." Marie took a sip of her drink and nodded her head in agreement, so I continued, "I feel the same way as you Marie. I enjoy our friends' children, but I have never yearned for them myself, perhaps because I had no younger siblings to make it seem important?

"On the other hand, Sam comes from a very large family yet feels the same as we do. Sam and I both are very content with our relationship as it is, without children, and with just our furry Olive."

"Plus, dogs, they do not speak, and are always happy to see you, even if you come home late and a little bit tipsy," laughed Marie.

At that I raised my wine glass to Marie, in appreciation of finding a kindred soul. As one ages, it seems to become more difficult to find a new friend where the relationship quickly extends further than showing feigned interest, smiling and being pleasant. It's easy to meet new people and to be social, to play golf, meet for book club or play bunko for example, while keeping it light, being friendly and upbeat. It is much rarer to meet a new friend with whom you each truly share some of the same core feelings about life, can look one another in the eye and let each of your guards down enough to speak what you genuinely feel to one another without either party being uncomfortable by full disclosure. Friendship like love, I feel, is heavily weighted by chemistry and risk-taking between two people who meet. Unfortunately, all too often, as one becomes older chemistry and taking risks is overruled by being polite, being too consumed with other obligations, and probably also by being afraid of being disappointed.

Marie tilted her head toward Franco, who was still in conversation with Sam. Franco turned and smiled at her. I noticed that she reached out to hold his hand under the table, which made me feel relieved, in an odd way.

I twisted in my chair to look away from them and down toward the beach. The Carlton's beautiful white stone Neoclassical façade could be seen above the sunbathers in the foreground, lying on the private beach. I looked up at the two large curved copper domes, covered in patina with age, which flanked the far east and west corners of the hotel. It has been said these domes were modeled after the voluptuous breasts of the wife of the hotel's original owner. What a sight, I thought to myself, these two copper breasts permanently on display above the many real breasts enjoying the sun and sand just below.

Our luncheon entrees were served, our glasses refilled, and between bites of my Caprese salad, I looked back toward the beach. In between the water's edge and the first row of umbrellas and chaise lounge chairs, was a very tall, slim woman with long thick hair dressed in a colorful, sheer caftan. She paraded back and forth in front of the sunbathers. Walking back and forth, perfectly erect, knees raising slightly high, she looked just like a model on a runway. I watched and after a few minutes, she bent down to her tote bag lying in the sand, pulled out a different flowy, sheer cover up and quickly put on a replacement of the previous one. This was a shorter version of the caftan in a different color, but also very sheer. She then began to walk back and forth again, at water's edge. Was it a photo shoot? I looked to see if there was a photographer nearby, but I did not see one.

"Marie, do you see that pretty woman walking back and forth on the beach?" I asked. "What is she doing? Do you think someone is taking photos of her for a magazine or website shoot? She's been modeling herself like this for quite a while now, and changing outfits too!"

"Oh no, she's just trying to sell her bikini cover ups to tourists on the beach. Cannes does not allow unlicensed beach vendors, unless they happen to be very discreet and very beautiful. She is beautiful, non? I have seen her here for many seasons and last year I finally purchased one of her silk wraps. It was rather expensive I must say, but such is life, one must always pay extra for a beautiful view."

Laughing I said, "You are too funny, Marie, and a bit snarky too. Oh, do you know what snarky means? It is one of my favorite words."

"Non, what is snarky? Does it mean like a snob? I do know what snob means."

"No Marie, snarky is an American slang word, but not as bad as snob implies. It describes one who has a dry, observant, slightly cynical sense of humor. I appreciate snarky humor, but to be frank it is not for everyone. For some it goes straight over their heads, they do not understand because a snarky comment is usually not so obviously funny and is usually dark in tone." Waving my hand toward the beach, I continued, "I must say, Marie, she is the most elegant beach vendor that I think I have ever seen. Just another example of how magical, unreal almost, the Cote d'Azur is! You are so lucky to live here."

"I am, but I am also very glad that I do not have to sell silk wraps half-naked on the beach every day."

Like magic, this comment coming from Marie, abruptly ended Sam and Franco's lengthy conversation. To men, words such as half-naked spoken by a woman with a French accent works like Pavlov's bell with his dogs.

After a few moments, and after Marie and I grinned at one another at both having noticed the men's conversation-interrupting reaction as a result of what she had just said, Franco stated rather abruptly, "It's been a true pleasure meeting you and Lauren, Sam. I'm afraid we will have to call our lunch short today however, as Marie and I have much wedding planning to do and must be going."

I looked toward Marie, who nodded her head in agreement, but not before her left eyebrow shot up quizzically at Franco's somewhat hasty request to leave.

"Franco, I hope you won't mind if I exchange email addresses with Marie." Then, "I would love to try to keep in touch with you Marie and I will simply love to hear all about your wedding," I said.

"Yes Lauren, I will truly enjoy an email friend from Colorado."

Chapter 8

Back in our beach chairs, in our wet bathing suits, the late afternoon sun felt wonderful drying my skin after our après lunch swim. Sam and I sipped the cappuccinos that he had ordered from Paul, our beach attendant. On the small table between us, Paul had also deposited a small plate of petite, pinky finger-sized biscotti in assorted flavors and two lightly lemon-scented moist real linen hand towels.

"Have I mentioned today, that I love you and that I also love it here, Sam? If Olive were here with us, I would kidnap you tonight and not allow us to travel back home tomorrow."

"Does your kidnapping involve tying me up with silk scarves and blindfolding me Lauren?" asked Sam, whom I realized just then had been unduly affected by *50 Shades of Grey*, which I had encouraged him to read several months before.

"Certainly Sam! What's a good kidnapping without a little erotic intimidation? Plus I'll have to keep you tied up until after our plane departs at least, to be successful in my mission."

"Can we compromise? Perhaps you can kidnap me only until eleven a.m. tomorrow, when we need to depart the hotel? You know I'd like that, Lauren."

"Me too. Just wait until I get you back to our suite and into that glorious shower Sam. But first, I have to ask you, what did you think of Marie today and of Franco? Marie was forthcoming that both of their previous marriages ended because their spouses died. But, that's quite unusual, isn't it Sam? I mean how often can it be, that both people, who are not elderly, each have previous spouses who passed away? And so close together, it sounded like Franco's wife died only shortly after Marie's Jan had passed. I mean isn't that unusual?"

"Lauren, don't be so cynical."

"I'm not cynical Sam, just suspicious."

"Well, regardless, I found Franco to be quite normal and savvy actually. Do you know that their wine distributorship is the largest privately-held business of its kind in all of France? Franco told me their sales have grown an average of twenty percent each year since he's started managing the firm, what did he say… eight years ago. He said that he's fielded two acquisition offers already this year. That's a pretty big deal Lauren."

"What I find interesting Sam, is that you say 'their' wine business. Is that how Franco expressed its ownership? Marie, she referred to it today as her late husband's business and only later in our conversation, as her company."

"I did get the impression that Franco is industrious, Lauren, and men generally are more likely to take ownership in their conversations regarding work and career, especially when talking with another male, more than women tend to do, I think."

"You're probably right about that. And, yes, from what I heard from Marie, it does sound like a very successful and large company. Do you know the name of it?"

"Yes, Franco said it was named after Marie's villa in Antibes, Azur du Cap Distributing."

"Sam, I really like Marie. She's quite confident and funny but I'm not sure I'm as fond of Franco. I can't quite put my finger on it, but I can't help but thinking Marie can do better than him," I mused.

"It takes all kinds, plus we've only just met them, we hardly know them at all. I did however, notice one suspicious thing Lauren, if it can be called that."

"Really? What?"

"Now don't get too excited, save that for my kidnapping, but I did notice that when Franco was texting at the table, he deleted his whole text history before laying his phone back down on the table, which I thought funny. I mean he had said it was business hadn't he? One usually needs to keep the history of a work communication via text, just in case a reference of the conversation is needed down the road. I thought that strange."

"Maybe it wasn't work at all, but rather an assignation already, and they are not even married yet."

"Now you're jumping to conclusions Lauren. You shouldn't say that. We really do not know anything substantial and they will soon be getting married. You know that its bad luck to bet against love, Lauren."

"There's another thing that I noticed as well Sam. Did you hear when he said that he and Marie had 'no time to waste', when he was referring to getting married next month? What do you suppose Franco meant by that? I mean, Marie told me as much as that they aren't in a hurry to have children, if at all, plus they've only been engaged a couple of months. I still think a one year engagement, at least in the States, is considered quite normal. Frankly, Sam, I'm thinking he may be after her company, her money, her chateau. It sounds to me like her first husband, Jan, was quite well off and they didn't have children Sam, so I imagine his whole estate went to Marie. I just hope there is nothing to worry about with Marie, but I can't help but think of the three most common things in life that bring out the worst in people which are revenge, passion and money."

"As usual Lauren, it sounds to me like you are trying to make this into an Agatha Christie mystery. I do agree however, that our entire experience with Marie and Franco has been a bit unusual. From our initial meeting yesterday when she appeared so melancholy and then told us that her brother had asked her to postpone the wedding, to lunch today and those little idiosyncrasies you just mentioned, it does seem odd that they will be marrying next month."

"I agree, Sam. I know that I don't know her very well, but there is something that I just really like about Marie. You know how I am. I do often judge a book by its cover, and I plan to continue to keep in touch with Marie after we get back home. In addition to liking her as a person, I have a nebulous feeling that I need to keep in contact with her, just to make sure she'll be ok."

"You should Lauren. If nothing else, she might just need a friend."

"Agreed. And I can always use a new friend too, but we'll see where it goes. I may never hear from her again. I really am sad to have to leave Cannes tomorrow Sam. I will miss this beautiful place. Everything is just exquisite here. It's heaven. I mean, just look at this view!"

"I think I'm going to miss seeing all of these statuesque Russian beauties in their bathing suits the most," said Sam, waving his right arm open wide.

With that, I rolled over on my side to face Sam. I pulled my sunglasses off slowly and waited for Sam to look at me in the eyes. Then, I slapped his thigh with a quick snap and say in my lowest, most commanding voice, "Ok, that's it Mister Hendrick. You are a very bad man. Sam. Rise. Now. It's time for your kidnapping."

Chapter 9

APPROXIMATELY TWENTY HOURS, several trains, two planes and one Uber Black car later, Sam and I ascended within the elevator forty-two stories up to our home located in Denver's first, now historic, residential high rise. Named Brooks Tower, this mixed-use residential skyscraper takes up a full city block of Denver's central business district, commonly referred to as "LoDo" by locals. We love living in downtown Denver and are fortunate to have an expansive view of the Front Range of the Rocky Mountains from both our master bedroom and living room windows.

We exited the elevator with our suitcases in tow, and walked down our hallway, which is shared with three other neighbors, to number 42B. Home again. "It's good to be home, Sam. I can't wait to see Olive. I miss that dog tremendously when we travel without her."

Sam unlocked our door and we immediately heard the very familiar sound of fifty pounds of female dog jump down from on top of our bed and land on the rug beneath. Then the rhythmic stride of four legs ambling, toe nails clicking, toward the entry where Sam and I both set down our suitcases and dropped to our knees. Around the corner came our smiling Olive and as soon as all of our eyes met, her tail began to wag in full circles, her extra-happy wag. Our dog is fairly unique with her canine greeting skills as she not only has the ability to swing her tail in full, complete circles, but she also is able to smile big toothy grins, usually at the same time. For fear of sounding like a braggart dog parent, I will admit that Olive is not able to smile on command. This dog simply has to *feel* it. Sam and I have tried for over six years to figure out how we could get Olive to smile on command, with absolutely no success whatever.

"Snookie! How's my Olive? We missed you," I coo as Olive smiles, dances and kisses my chin with her timid, dry little kisses.

"Miss Olive," Sam says attracting the full attention of our short-haired mutt. "You are looking well. Lauren and I are both happy to see you again. How's my second-favorite girl?"

In addition to Olive, I also love it tremendously when Sam speaks to our dog as if she is human. Sam does not use a soft babyish tone when greeting Olive. He literally speaks to her in the same tone and cadence as he does to me. I admit that I am biased, but it is extremely endearing and sexy. It makes me fall in love with Sam all over again.

We all ambled together into the living room and I drew open the draperies as Sam plopped down on the sofa. It was a little past four in the afternoon and the sun was just beginning its descent behind the mountains to our west. Daylight is particularly intense in the late afternoon during September in the Denver region. We even had to have tinting added to each of our west-facing windows, like one would do in a car, to prevent our furnishings and art from being damaged by the strong Colorado sunshine. Even with the tinting, I could tell that the sunset would be particularly gorgeous. The robin's egg blue sky was beginning to turn amber and pink over the mountains. My parents had always told me that a red sunset was a sure sign of nice weather arriving the following day. "Abendrot, schonwetterbot" my mother would announce in her native German tongue, back in the Midwest when I was growing up, during a fall sunset like this.

Our landline rang and I answered. It was our neighbor and dear friend, Rose, who lives with her husband, eldest daughter and their dog next door to us, in number 42D.

"You're back! Everything alright over there Lauren? I brought Olive over after our lunchtime walk today, as I knew you and Sam would be happy to see her just as soon as you arrived home."

"Yes, Rose. Everything is perfect here and thank so much again for watching Olive while we were away. I hope she was a good dog for you."

"Of course she was. No trouble at all. Lennox loves having a playmate. Well, I'll let you go. I know how exhausting it is when one travels through time zones. I just wanted to make sure you were back, and all is well."

"More than well. In fact this trip rated as one of our best ever. I have a few stories I'd like to share with you Rose, and a little thank-you surprise also, for watching Olive. Do you have time to come over to visit tomorrow afternoon or the day after?" I asked.

"How does two o'clock tomorrow sound?"

"Perfect Rose. I'll see you then, and bring Lennox over too."

Sam and I awoke the next morning to the sound of Ella Fitzgerald's distinctive voice crooning *Summertime* at six thirty a.m. Sam quietly got out of bed and into the shower. I knew he needed to go into his office today. I rolled over and called Olive up onto the bed with me. Sam enjoys decadent, lengthy showers and I wanted to snooze for as long as possible. About twenty minutes later I heard the shower shut off, so Olive and I rose and headed into the kitchen together to start the coffee. While it was brewing, Olive eyed the front door and then led me to it. I opened the door and she stepped out into the hallway to pick up the morning newspaper with her snout, she then carried it back into the kitchen in exchange for a biscuit. Our morning routine. I poured two mugs of strong coffee just as Sam walked in.

"Wow, perfect timing, Sam," I said as I turned to look him over and give him a good morning kiss. He looked dapper and ready to work with his blue Hugo Boss suit on, a mixed-color checked shirt open at the neck and his vacation tanned skin. "I think your hair is blonder from swimming in the sea under the sun, Sam. You look happy and well rested and handsome. Are you at all jet-lagged Sam? You surely don't look it."

"No, I feel really well this morning, but I'll bet this afternoon will be another story."

"Will it be a busy day for you Sam?"

"Not too bad. I'm going to spend the morning catching up and then I just have two conference calls with my two proposal staffs to work on the IAH and SEA-TAC RFQ's." Then turning to Olive who was waiting patiently, "Are you ready to go outside with me Olive?"

Sam took his mug and our dog and headed out to the elevator to descend to the small grassy park outside directly across the street from our lobby entrance, where we take Olive to relive herself first thing in the morning and last thing before bed. During this time, I looked to see what I could make for Sam to eat, but I realized that I neglected to order groceries for delivery before our return and our food stock was dismally low.

"A breakfast burrito it is Sam!" I exclaimed as he and Olive returned. I placed a multi-vitamin on the plate next to his Cholula-covered frozen steak and egg burrito. "So tell me, I know Houston's IAH airport is bidding to expand their international terminal, but what is see-tack Sam? I've forgotten about all of your pursuits during our two weeks away." Sam's business vernacular includes a lot of acronyms and even after all our years together, I still didn't know them all and he seemed to keep producing new ones.

"Sound Transit is planning a major extension to Seattle-Tacoma's light rail line and the proposal for its design portion is due in three weeks. I expect my team has made good progress on our proposal while we've been away and I didn't receive any frantic calls, but today will tell." Then after swallowing, "Mmm. This burrito tastes good after all those croissants and fruit."

Olive hustled to the front door barking at the sound of the doorbell. It was two o'clock and Rose was right on time as usual. I greatly appreciate the people in my life who are punctual; it keeps life simple and staves off the flurry of last minute texts which often accompany the tardy.

Rose was accompanied by her huge male dog Lennox, who bounded inside happy to see Olive again. As the two dogs trotted together toward the kitchen, I welcomed Rose in. Rose and her husband are a little older than Sam and I. They have lived at Brooks Tower for about twenty years, about twice as long as we have. They are the best neighbors one could ask for, and after all these years we have become very good friends as well. I often hoped that they never move away.

"So glad you're here, Rose," I said as we each made ourselves comfortable in the living room. "Tell me, what have Sam and I missed over the last couple weeks?"

"Not too much Lauren. Everything, I'm happy to say, has been status quo." Then after thinking for a minute, she added, "But I did hear that the unit down on the 22nd floor, the one with all the noise complaints over the last few months? The owner finally evicted the tenant who was living there. Turns out he was a drug dealer and the police actually came here to arrest him while he was at home."

"No kidding. When was that?"

"Last Tuesday. Cindy, at the front door, she said the police showed up, at least four of them, at six thirty in the morning. She had to take them up with the unit's door key. She watched as they knocked and the tenant, who looked like he had been sound asleep, answered the door. She said she didn't know that the arrest was for drugs exactly, but figured what else would it have been? She called the owner. Two days later the owner, who lives in Austin, had the management office post the required eviction notice on the front door and change the locks."

"Wow, that's pretty big news for Brooks Tower Rose. I never met the man living there, but I surely remember how heated up some of the Board members were about him at the last meeting. I understood he was the source of many loud, late parties, with people coming and going at all hours while parked in the building's loading zone."

"That's right. I know they just legalized marijuana here in Colorado, so that can't be it. He must have been involved with something more serious, plus I guess people don't really sell marijuana anymore do they Lauren? What with being able to walk right into a store nowadays and purchase it legally, it kind of cuts the dealer aspect out, I suppose."

"I suppose that is right, Rose. Well I'm glad he's gone, if for no other reason than to not have to hear about him at every Board meeting," I said laughing. Then, "How about some tea, Rose? Do you prefer green, black or herbal? Or maybe coffee?"

"Green tea would be perfect."

As the water boiled, I remembered to retrieve Rose's little thank-you gift from our guest bedroom, where I had placed it while I unpacked last night. I brought the heavy canvas bag to Rose and placed it on the coffee table before her.

"This is just a little something from France for you, Rose. To thank you for taking such good care of Olive while we were away. You know I wouldn't leave her with just anybody."

As Rose opened the burlap bag containing two bottles of wine that Sam helped me carry all the way home from France, I told her the story of how this particular Lambert and Chardonnay were made organically and by hand by a group of southern French monks. The twenty or so monks who made this wine live in complete silence on their tiny island called Saint Honorat, just off the coast of Cannes. They have inhabited their tiny island since the middle ages and in recent years their winery produces about 30,000 bottles of wine per year which are of the best quality and served in some of the finest restaurants in France. I regaled Rose with the story of how Sam and I took a ferry only two or three miles off the coast to their Isle St. Honorat. This island is completely uninhabited except for the Abbey of Lerins Monastery and a café for income from tourists. The original stone monastery, built during the B.C. era, sits atop a rocky cliff on the island's north coast. The newer, but still more than one hundred-year-old monastery where the monks currently reside is surrounded by the plane trees indigenous to the area, and is located closer to the center of the island. There are hiking trails around the circumference of the island, as well as through the middle, where all the vineyards are located and many varieties of grapes were growing. I told Rose how it was a terrific day of quiet nature walking so close, but so far removed in ambience from Cannes. The food and wine that Sam and I had ordered at the café were both exceptional and it was then that we had decided that we needed to bring a couple of bottles home for Rose and her family so they could also experience the taste of this outstanding wine made by French monks.

Chapter 10

SAM AND I quickly, too quickly, fell back into our real-life routine over the following weeks back home in Denver. Sam worked long hours and traveled to Houston, San Diego, Phoenix and Seattle in pursuit of new environmental study, construction and engineering contracts. I kept myself busy volunteering with the local animal shelter one day per week, managing our handful of residential rental properties, socializing with my bunko and bridge clubs and, most importantly, attempting to be a decent wife to Sam by providing breakfast and dinner at home on most evenings when we are in town. I've never been a natural in the kitchen but I've grown to enjoy preparing meals. I have always deeply hated the task of grocery shopping, however. This hatred has not changed over the years, so I'm an enthusiastic user of the online grocery shopping with home delivery that our local supermarket offers. Unlike me, Sam is an artist in the kitchen. I define artist as being able to create visually appealing and delicious meals by simply looking through our pantry and refrigerator's stock. I, on the other hand, must follow a recipe to prepare anything other than spaghetti Bolognese with packaged noodles or a fresh salad.

We try to eat out for dinner once or twice per week, with friends or on our own. On the other evenings, when were are home together, we always take Olive on a post-dinner walk along the nearby outdoor 16th Street walking mall, rain or hail, snow or cold. We enjoy these walks just as much as Olive does. Often on these walks we run into neighbors we know. Sometimes we run into groups of rowdy twenty-year-olds, who have imbibed a bit too much within the many restaurants, bars and pubs located on the mall. Once in while we have to dodge large groups of conventioneers, who seem to travel in packs while visiting our city on business at the nearby convention center. The thing about Denver is, the general population that one encounters downtown is remarkably friendly and laid-back. Due, I've always said, to Colorado's average of over three hundred days of sunshine a year. After our nighttime promenade, when Sam doesn't have work to do, he practices playing guitar while I read one of the many glossy magazines that I subscribe to. Sam has been noodling with his acoustic guitar for several years. He has an excellent singing voice with a low but strong timber. Sam's guitar playing is the running joke of our household. Frankly, try as he does, he'll never play like any of his idols: Ben Harper, Johnny Cash or Chris Martin. He can sing as well as any of them, but whew, that guitar! When it comes out, Olive and I look at one another. Then she will retreat into our back bedroom, the one furthest from our living room. Unlike Olive, I stay put as I enjoy listening to Sam sing and am secretly happy that he is a terrible guitar player. It's one of the only skills which Sam is not a master of, and this makes me feel better about my many more numerous shortcomings. I'm glad Sam is a lousy guitarist.

The following month, Denver received its first snow of the season. Large, wet flakes fell straight down past our windows all day long and into the evening and descended upon the streets below. A muffled quiet fell over the city and I decided to email Marie in France. I had not heard from her since we last saw one another at the Carlton. I figured a respectful few weeks had passed since her and Franco's wedding and I was curious to learn how their fête was, and curious to learn if she would reply to me.

Dear Marie,

It is Lauren Hendrick here in Denver, Colorado. Sam and I so enjoyed meeting you and Franco in Cannes. I wanted to send you a quick email to say Bonjour!

Sam and I miss your lovely part of the world very much, but all is well on our end. It is becoming cold here already. Our city of Denver just had its first snowfall of the season. Sam is busy working long hours. (I suspect Franco is also a bit of a workaholic; so maybe you can relate?) I find myself back in my daily routine as well: cooking, taking long walks with our dog Olive, playing with my Bridge group, spending time with my good friend named Rose, and watching Downton Abbey on television. Do you know this TV show?

I'm eager to hear how you are and especially all about your wedding. I'm sure it was wonderful. Reply anytime. I'd be pleased to hear from you.

All the best,
Lauren

A week later, I rang Rose's doorbell. She was expecting me. She opened her door looking very Audrey Hepburn-esque in slim black capris and a tissue-thin bright pink cashmere sweater. I greeted her dog Lennox and followed her inside.

We had lunch reservations in thirty minutes at our favorite nearby sushi restaurant called Hapa. Rose collected her cell phone and purse, slipped on her coat and gloves, and then said goodbye to Lennox. We left the building together and walked north one block to catch the free 16th Street Mall Ride bus which would take us the several blocks west to Hapa.

"It smells delicious in here!" Rose exclaimed as we approached the hostess stand.

Indeed it did. How raw fish can smell so good I will never know, but every better sushi restaurant has a similar, distinctive smell of fresh sweet fish combined with the pleasant aroma of starch from the rice cookers. Once we were both seated comfortably at the bar, I couldn't wait any longer to tell Rose about Marie. I had received Marie's emailed reply yesterday.

I began by telling Rose about first seeing the chic but downtrodden Marie at a nearby table in our hotel's terrace café with a very handsome man and how after that man departed he was quickly replaced with another distinguished looking man who proceeded to give a jewelry box to Marie, but that she didn't appear pleased by it. I told Rose that at the time my curiosity had been piqued because it appeared as though Marie might have been having an affair or was involved in some sort of jewel theft because she looked remorseful. She was very sad, I felt at the time, perhaps because she felt guilty or maligned in some way.

"Ooo, that's just like you Lauren, to imagine a romantic femme fatale involved in a jewelry theft ring right before you in the South of France!"

"I know. I know Rose but let me continue, I promise, I am not exaggerating this story at all."

With that I recapped Sam's and my conversation with Marie that day and how she had told us (accompanied with tears) that the second man at her table was her fiancé, who had just given her her engagement ring, and that the first man had been her brother who had asked her to postpone the marriage. I then detailed to Rose that her fiancé had simply handed the Cartier engagement ring box to her, not placed the ring on her finger, and left her by herself at the table shortly thereafter. I told Rose how I had approached Marie by asking about her dog and how that had led to a couple drinks and over an hour of conversation between Sam, Marie and I. Then a couple days after that, we had met both Marie and her fiancé for lunch and that she had seemed in much better spirits, but shared with us that she and Franco's previous spouses had both died. Also, that Marie is most likely very wealthy as she had inherited her late husband's wine distribution company and that Franco had actually just been and is an employee there. Finally, I relayed my impression that while Marie was interesting, humorous and I truly enjoyed her company and conversation, Franco left me feeling skeptical. Specifically because he texted during our meal together and that Sam had seen him immediately delete his text history, which in my mind is not a sign of trustworthiness. Also, he had off-handedly said that he and Marie had "no time to waste" when referring to their short engagement.

"Rose," I then concluded, "it's not likely that Marie is pregnant, she is our age, so why is there no time to waste? Marie had seemed to have more than just last-minute cold feet to me."

"The thing I find most interesting about your story is that both of their previous spouses died. I grant you that that fact alone is rather unusual. Do you know how they died or if they were much older in age than Marie and this fiancé of hers?"

"Marie said her husband had died unexpectedly. She didn't give me the impression that he was much older, but she did impart to me that even though they had not had children, he had been the sole love of her life and that Franco, her fiancé would never compare. As for Franco's previous wife, according the Internet, can you believe it ... Sam actually Googled them, she died of a heart condition a mere year and a half ago! According to all the crime novels that I read Rose, heart condition-reported deaths are often a result of vague autopsy reports, and can often mask much more nefarious causes of death. Frankly, it's suspicious and I'm sure I'm jumping to conclusions, but what if Franco killed Marie's first husband, waited a year and then murdered his wife as well, with the goal of marrying Marie for what would then be her very successful company and assets?"

"Not much you can do about it now though Lauren. Didn't you say they were to be married shortly after you and Sam departed Cannes last month?"

"Yes, but guess what? I emailed Marie earlier this week and she just replied to me! The good news is that she is still alive, I say that jokingly for effect Rose, and she did in fact marry Franco. I was so happy to hear from her. Frankly, if you can't tell, I am genuinely a little worried about her. Not necessarily because I think Franco will actually plan to murder her for her money, but that he may just be a common gold-digger and that Marie perhaps deserves better."

Chapter 11

I FELT AS though I had a pen-pal, which I had never had before. I remember having a few childhood friends who enjoyed pen-pals, some ongoing for years, with remote and exotic sounding friends who were located across the country and even overseas. This was back when pen-pals actually wrote letters and posted them to each other by dropping them into the large blue metal collection boxes which used to stand on the street corner at almost every busy intersection across the country. My childhood friend Liv, I remembered, had a pen-pal who lived somewhere in Europe, Austria, I believe, while we were both in middle school. I remembered her enjoyment of showing her letters to me during period breaks at school, which she received with distinctive foreign postage stamps on the envelopes.

Marie and I have never written one another an actual mailed letter, but we have begun an almost bi-weekly correspondence via email. She has shared stories of her daily life in the Riviera, tales of her friends' as well as, employees' foibles and triumphs, and even her personal political bent. All of which has endeared her to me even more. Frankly, it's been fun to write to her with regularity. The sensation that I felt when I powered up my iPad and saw that a new email had arrived from Marie, made me giddy with expectation of her news from afar. This was the same feeling that I expect Liv must have experienced when she found a letter had arrived in the post box hanging on the front of her parents' home, from her childhood pen-pal. I wondered if Liv was still writing to a pen-pal these days.

This week's communique from Marie told me about a charity benefit event for blind children which she and Franco had attended last weekend at the Hotel Majestic in Cannes. Sam and I had enjoyed afternoon tea in the Majestic's formal tea room when were in Cannes. I can vividly remember the glitz: multi-layer crystal chandeliers, golden wall sconces, thin, almost see-through fine bone china, and chintz everywhere. I wonder, I thought to myself as I read, if the benefit had been held in a room or area of the hotel as over-the-top as what I remembered? Instead, Marie's email described the notable people who were in attendance as well as, the gowns, hairstyles and minaudières that she had found most beautiful. Apparently, according to Marie, the finest of the female attendees had moved to a marine theme with their jeweled clutch evening bags this season in France. She described her favorite minaudière of the evening as a shiny black acrylic clutch topped with a golden highly-detailed coral reef, a koi fish sparkling with emerald eyes as a topper and with four finger holes in which to hold the clutch. "Looked like Alexander McQueen to me," she wrote and I could visualize her awe as well as how stunning that evening purse must have been. Marie also shared that she and

Franco had had a bit too much to drink (she Clicquot and he Bourbon) and that they had bid on and won a week's stay in a private four-bedroom villa in the Alps mountain town of Courcheval. Like all good Europeans, both she and Franco are avid skiers. I learned next from Marie's email, that they enjoy the same winter adventures that Sam and I do when we head up to Vail, Winter Park or Breckenridge for long weekends of snowboarding, dining and hot-springing in Colorado's quaint high-altitude mountain towns.

To date, Marie has remained quite frank with me, expressing her true opinions and sometimes, snobbishness. I find it refreshing and enjoy her sarcastic point of view. With my most recent reply to her, I waxed nostalgic about the state of Chardonnay wine in the United States. Specifically, the lack of proper aging in oak barrels as of late. It's a travesty, I wrote in my reply to Marie, the way that so many vineyards are not barrel aging their Chardonnay varietals. My definition of Chardonnay, I typed, is a smooth and rich texture with a butter and oak finish. I'm sure they are only doing this because it's cheaper, a cost-saving measure, but they've actually started to brand it as "un-oaked" here in the States, as if this is a good thing. What they should do, I typed further, is call it something else, like white table wine! I mean, Chardonnay should be full-bodied, otherwise it's just Pinot Grigio and if I wanted a Pinot Gris, I would order one, I lamented. I then described to Marie a recent visit Sam and I had taken to a new upscale restaurant in downtown Denver. There were two Chardonnays on the menu, neither described specifically as being oaked. Because of this unfortunate trend, I had asked our waiter which one was a traditional oaked Chardonnay and he had replied neither, but that the more expensive option had been aged in stainless steel and offered a refreshing citrusy palate. Bah, that's not a Chardonnay, I vented to Marie. I had felt as an India Pale Ale beer loyalist would, if the IPA menu selections were switched with weak, clear lagers that had been given the IPA name and price. I asked Marie, because I was dying to know, have you noticed this in France? And such began an almost bi-weekly email exchange with Marie all through the start of winter.

In early December, I received an unexpected message through Facebook from a dear old friend named Robyn who I had not seen in person for twenty-two years. I had been slightly aware of this friend's professional and family life from her status updates, since we had reconnected via Facebook approximately five years ago. Robyn and I had originally met during my first year of high school and became best friends. She was two years older than I, and in her junior year at the time. Robyn had pierced my ears; not my first piercings, but the third and fourth up my left lobe, in her bedroom with ice and a needle. Honestly, I don't remember if I did the same for her but I didn't think so as I've always been quite squeamish with needles and blood. Robyn and I had spent a memorable summer together in a sublet apartment in Grand Junction, Colorado after my sophomore and her senior year. During our three months living together in "The Junction" as we called it, we worked at the restaurant located within the Hilton Hotel where her father, who was divorced from her mother, was the general manager. Her father lived in a top-floor unit of the hotel, which was a short five-block walk from Robyn's and my apartment, which he had subleased for us that summer. We were expected to pay for the rent with our earnings from the restaurant gig and luckily found that we still earned enough extra to allow for spending money. Her father gave us plenty of freedom, perhaps looking back now, more than we should have had at the ages of sixteen and eighteen respectively. Nevertheless, we didn't get into too much trouble that summer in spite of the fact that Colorado's age limit for drinking at the time was only eighteen.

Robyn's Facebook message said simply that she would be in Denver the following week attending a work conference. She said she would only be in town for three days and was staying at the Hyatt Convention Center Hotel downtown. She asked if I would be available to get together with her one of the two evenings that she would be here. I immediately checked my calendar and saw that I was free the following Thursday and suggested we meet at the Peaks Lounge on the 27th floor of the hotel where she would be staying. This would be a convenient location for both of us I explained, plus it has an amazing view of both downtown and the mountains where we could enjoy the sunset, if we met there by six p.m. Robyn responded with her cell phone number and said she would look forward to seeing me again then and there.

I emailed Marie again a few days after hearing from Robyn. Excited about our approaching rendezvous, after not having seen one another in over two decades, I told Marie about it and shared some of my memories of Robyn. I wrote to Marie how excited I was to reconnect with Robyn again, now that we were practically middle-aged and in Robyn's case a mother with two teenage children that were currently about the ages we were when we had been close friends.

"I'm glad you will see your long-lost friend again," Marie responded a few days later. "One of the most beautiful aspects of getting older is that the world becomes smaller."

I have often used this expression myself and totally believe it to be true. It's odd how similar Marie and I are, I thought while reading, even though we grew up in totally different environments and countries.

Marie's email then went on to say she had just developed a cold or a flu and was planning to stay home and rest for the next few days. She concluded by asking me to write to her again immediately after my meeting with Robin as she would most likely be bored at home by then and would enjoy to hear stories of our reunion.

Chapter 12

AT FIVE FORTY-FIVE on Thursday, it was beginning to become dusk as I exited my lobby with a wave and nod to our doorman. I walked out onto the street and into the brisk evening air. The day had been quite warm for early December because it had been sunny. I am still amazed by the dramatic temperature swings that Denver experiences from day to night. The sun shines strongly here, keeping even our winter days warm while it shines, but as soon as it sets behind the Rocky Mountains the temperature frequently drops by thirty and sometimes forty degrees within the same day. I buttoned my coat up around my neck and began to walk the four blocks toward the Hyatt Hotel. Many people were out on the sidewalk with me and we clustered at each crosswalk waiting for our turn to walk across each intersection. One has to be careful walking near the convention center as the light rail commuter line traverses this dense downtown area and the electric-powered train cars are virtually silent. I passed the iconic big blue bear sculpture, officially titled *I See What You Mean*, which stands about one hundred feet tall and peers directly into the convention center atrium windows along 14th Street. I turned left and entered the Hyatt using the side entrance. I checked my wrist watch, which had been a birthday gift from Sam a few summers ago and saw that I was five minutes early. I pride myself on being on time for any and all of my appointments and I grinned to myself in anticipation of seeing Robyn again after so many years punctually. I entered a hotel elevator and pressed the express button for Peaks Lounge on twenty seven.

Peaks was busy with many people still wearing their expo lanyards. I removed my coat, draped it over my arm and walked slowly into the fray. I began to look for Robyn as well as for an empty cocktail table. Just as I reached the far corner of the bar with its floor to ceiling windows facing due west, I felt a tap on my arm. I turned, and there she stood with a big smile on her immediately familiar face.

"Lauren! It's so good to see you. I recognized you as you walked in. You look just the same, but I didn't remember you were this tall!" said Robin standing back to give me a friendly once over. "Follow me. I have already been here for a little while, catching up on email, and I have a table for us."

Robyn did indeed have a table, a prized table within the room. Located smack in the middle of the lounge but against the windows, with a terrific view of the sun which was beginning to set behind the Front Range, and right beside a table filled with three attractive men who appeared to be in their forties and were dressed finely. Based on their attire, I immediately assumed the men were from Chicago or New York. None of them were wearing rubber-soled shoes, which men from Colorado wear frequently, unfortunately.

"Robyn, before we sit, I need to give you a hug!" I exclaimed. "Is it really possible that it has been twenty-two years since we last saw one another?"

"Actually, I believe it's been twenty-three!" she said hugging me back.

"Where do we begin? I'm so pleased to see you in the flesh after all these years! Let's sit, order a drink and start by you telling me what you're doing here in Denver."

"Sounds good Lauren. Do you feel like sharing a couple of appetizers too? I glanced at the menu while I was waiting and there seem to be a few nice vegetarian options," said Robyn. "I'm a vegetarian now, have been for about the last decade."

"It's working for you Robyn. You look wonderful. Just as pretty as I remember you, but with even better hair."

"Thank you. My daughter who's a senior now, older than we were when we met Lauren, can you imagine? Well, she decided to stop eating meat when she began middle school and frankly, she made such a compelling argument, that I decided to join her and become meat free as well."

"You have two children though, right Robyn? A boy who is older as well? I enjoy seeing photos of them in your Facebook posts."

"Yes, my boy, he's actually a man now. He stands at least a foot taller than I do and is halfway through college already. For the record, he's still eating meat though," she said laughing.

"How are you handling them becoming adults and going off to college? Many of my other friends who are parents say it's a difficult time in their lives, between the letting go, the missing them compounded with worrying about them and even the sheer cost of schooling? I know you've been raising them both on your own for many years now Robyn."

"That is part of why I'm in Denver now. I'm here attending a technology conference specific to the international nonprofit industry. I had to start working again after Paolo and I divorced."

Such began an hours long catching up of two old girlfriends' lives. Robyn told me about initially meeting her husband, the father of her children, in college at UCLA while she studied social justice and lived with a deadbeat, lay about roommate. She had fallen for Paolo, a fellow student who was from Brazil and in California studying on a student visa. She told me how he was paying for school with a merit-based scholarship but that he had been selling weed to other students for extra cash. He was caught a year after they began dating, jailed and then quickly deported. They had kept in touch after Paolo's deportation, Robyn said, because she had fallen in love with him and because she did not have any moral qualms about his criminal activity and resulting deportation. He was not a violent offender and frankly, was simply an example of what was wrong with our criminal justice system especially as it applied to men with dark skin and marijuana, she said. Shortly after graduating UCLA (this had been in the nineties), Robyn moved to be with Paolo in his homeland. She found herself in the large city of Salvador located on the water, where she married Paolo, and also fell in love with his family, the culture, the climate and the food. They had two children which she raised while he worked in a software development firm. Paolo was intelligent, Robyn said more than once. After about ten years together in Salvador, Robyn told me she became sorely homesick and asked Paolo to consider moving back to the States. Perhaps understandably, said Robyn, he vehemently would not consider moving back to America and so began the slow dissolution of their marriage.

Back in the States in the mid-2000s, Robin and her two children moved to Rhode Island where she had been offered a job with a philanthropic organization that works toward securing and enhancing the rights of minority children around the globe. A perfect fit with her social justice degree, social networking experience (of which she had taken courses during her last year in Salvador) and her fluent Spanish language skills. This is how Robyn described this new chapter of her life to me. Rhode Island had been a comfortable environment to raise her children unmarried, but now that her son had already left her home and with the second child soon to follow, she decided to take another big risk and move to New York City, where she had always wanted to live. It said a lot about Robyn, and about the Midwestern work ethic that we both were raised with, that her employer encouraged her to move to New York and continue to work for them remotely. Robyn said her relocation was smart for both her and for her Board of Directors. She traveled so extensively, she said, that it was quicker and less expensive to commute through JFK or Newark airports than from Warwick, Rhode Island.

With our appetizers finished and our second glasses of wine on the way, we segued to stories from the past. Back to high school and specifically to our summer together in Grand Junction, Colorado. We commiserated about how neither one of us had ever been able to work in the service industry again after that summer's job when Robyn waited tables and I delivered room service meals for the on-site restaurant at her father's Hilton Hotel property.

"It's still amazing," she said, "how easy it was to make friends at that age. Do you remember the group we so quickly connected with and spent the whole summer hanging out with? You dated the tall dark-haired boy with the 280ZX."

"I can't believe you remember that! I haven't thought of him in years. He had the best rims on that car!" I practically shouted in the middle of Peaks Lounge. Catching myself, I made a mental note to lower my voice. I always get loud after a few glasses of wine. A habit which I'm trying to break.

"You know what else I remember, Lauren? I was leaving for UCLA that coming fall and I was fretting about still being a virgin. I remember you telling me that summer in Grand Junction, that there was a perfectly nice and healthy boy right in front of me. Remember him, the slim blond one? You said that I should just get it over with, with him! So I did."

"Wow, I haven't thought of that in years either. Frankly, I think I'm mortified Robyn. Imagine me talking you into having sex for the first time. Will you join me in a toast to that summer together?"

"Yes," she said, laughing.

With both of us holding up our glasses, I looked Robyn in the eyes again for the first time in twenty-two years and said simply, "I'm so glad to see you again Robyn. To being young again in your presence, and to young love!" Sighing and picturing the two young men in my mind's eye, we drank. After a moment I said, "You were with me when Sam and I first met. Do you remember that Robyn? Sam was always my first love, none of those other boys compared. I'm happy to report he still is. Speaking of which, Sam is very sorry to miss seeing you tonight Robyn, he sends his regrets and made me promise to fill him in with all the details of our reunion. I think I'll leave that last bit from Grand Junction out though."

"You can tell Sam everything, but I suspect that after all these years together, you would anyway, Lauren. So tell me, are you really still happy with him and is he still as attractive as I remember?"

After honestly assuring her positively on both fronts, I asked which of our mutual high school friends she was still in touch with. She told me that the previous year she had visited our friend Jen in Portland and had met her husband and family. She had been there for a work trip. During that visit she learned that Jen's youngest child was born with Down's syndrome two years ago, but that the whole family of five rallied and were making the best of a tragic situation. "Inspiring" was the word Robyn used to sum up her visit with Jen.

Next she relayed to me that she connected over dinner with our other school friend Liv while Liv had been visiting New York a few months back. Without any umbrage in her tone, Robyn relayed that Liv looked amazing; younger, blonder and thinner than ever.

"She is still unmarried and was dating a very wealthy man from the look of it," Robyn said. Liv's lover had joined them both for a nightcap after their supper together. Liv currently resided in Chicago, in the Golden Triangle area, and had just started dating the man, who Robyn told me was named Harry and was stunning, possibly even more beautiful than Liv. During their visit, Liv had confided to Robyn that she wasn't sure that she was head over heels for Harry yet, but that she was enjoying the here and now with him, and was hoping for the best. "They looked great together," summed up Robyn, "and Harry seemed very kind to Liv. If it was me, I wouldn't let a gorgeous and rich man like that Harry slip through my fingers."

After a casual appreciative glance to the group of gentlemen seated at the table beside us, it was my turn again for storytelling. I told Robyn that I still returned to our hometown a few times a year because both of my parents still lived there and were thankfully, each healthy and well. I regaled her with the much-deserved success of another mutual friend Tom, a painter and former classmate, who had become the talk of the town with his new eponymous art gallery and regional corporate painting commissions. We both agreed that was no small feat, particularly in the Midwest where often the fine arts are under-appreciated and under-valued. I told her next how happy and proud I also was of Melvin, who is not only still directing live theater productions full time, but has also written his first original play based on Ryan White, the teenager from Kokomo, Indiana who was diagnosed with AIDS in the eighties and was expelled from his public school because of it. Lastly, I told Robyn how sad I was that our friend Ania, who now lived in Cleveland with her very sweet and thoughtful husband, were divorcing after about fifteen years together.

"It came out of the blue," I said. We had learned of their separation when Sam and I had rendezvoused with them at Del Mar Horse Race Park early this past summer. We are still quite close with them both, as the four of us would meet up around the country to attend horse races at different racetracks. It was an interest that all four of us shared. I told Robyn what a shock the news of their divorce had been to Sam and me and that we were both quite saddened over it.

"It just goes to show, Lauren, every individual human is different from everyone else and when any two unique humans enter a relationship, that relationship can take infinite forms. I'm not convinced that both people in any relationship ever know most of what is going on with their partner." She then stared at me quite pointedly and said, "Don't take your relationship with Sam for granted, Lauren. You never know what might happen next in life."

Chapter 13

The evening following my reunion with Robyn, Sam and I ate dinner together alone at home sitting at our large oval dining room table with Olive lying quietly beside me. Olive was touching and therefore warming my left stockinged foot; a little furry foot heater. Sam was on my right-hand side. We often sat like this, side by side facing outward, so we could both enjoy the expansive skyline view. Large, dense snowflakes had begun to fall and the nearby lower rooftops were quickly turning white. The outdoor temperature had dropped quickly as the sun set, and the bottom edge of our windows had begun to turn opaque with light grey frost.

"It was a bit ominous Sam," I said, "the way that Robyn had warned me not to take our relationship for granted. I'm sure she was coming from a good place. There was no ribaldry to her tone, and what she had said about human relationships being a mystery is certainly true, but it was almost like a warning to me, Sam. I haven't been able to get it out of my head all day. So I have to ask you outright now, are you still happy with me? Do you still like our relationship as it has become after all these years? Is there anything that you want or need?"

Sam put his fork down and turned to face me head on. He did not say anything for at least a full minute. In my head, in that minute of silence, I feared the worst. I thought of the many hasty, unkind comments that I had made to Sam in the past months. I thought of how often he traveled for work, alone on the proverbial road by himself. I thought of how handsome he is and how infrequently I had complimented him as of late on his many attributes.

But Sam is an intelligent man, and he knows that he should collect his thoughts before answering loaded questions like the ones I had just put forth, seemingly out of the blue.

"Lauren," he said, "it is always a good idea to be reminded not to take anything that feels natural, comfortable, and easy for granted. That is what Robyn did for you and that is what you are now doing for me. It's a favor she did for us, Lauren. I sometimes wonder at our good luck in life. At how young we were when we found one another and how we've so successfully made our lives together, happily. Frankly, I do take you for granted because you make my life enjoyable. I'm going to take our long-lost friend Robyn's advice for what it is: that we both need to take a step back to really appreciate each other, our fortune in life and our loving relationship which comes so naturally. I think that Robyn has not had it so easy, frankly most haven't, and she most likely just wanted to remind you, and us, of how damn good we've got it."

Exhaling and taking a sip of wine before I responded, having learned from Sam's example, I thought of how important what I said next was. Important not just to Sam, but to myself.

"I can't imagine this life without you in it, Sam. You're exactly right. We've had it so easy together that Robyn's comment has made me think that I do take you for granted, to our detriment. She's right, of course. We do take each other for granted. Which, if I've heard you correctly, we wouldn't do if there was trouble in paradise. Sam, I love you. You are my happiness. What you just said is an example. I feel like I am a better person because of you and I intend to fully appreciate you every day."

"Yes, and this is simply another one of life's reality checks. To make us stop for a minute and realize consciously again, that we naturally slip into taking one another for granted, as all old couples do. But by realizing this, and speaking of it aloud now, we will both try to truly appreciate one another as if our relationship is not a given, not so easy, and as if we both need to continue to prove our admiration and love for one another."

The following evening it was still snowing in Denver. It had snowed on and off throughout the previous night and most of the day. Despite the five or six inches which had accumulated in the city and the dozen or so inches that had piled up in the foothills west of town, Sam's flight that early afternoon had not been canceled or delayed. Denver is one of those cities that a little snow does not stop, and five or six inches only counts as a little snow. Coloradans are a hearty people. Additionally, the majority of voters in this state understand that we all need to share in the expense of city services and infrastructure, like snow removal, and Coloradans, Denverites in particular, usually vote to increase taxes for increased service. We feel it's equitable.

Sam had flown out to beautiful Tucson, Arizona for a conference to be attended by most of Arizona's executive-level Department of Transportation staff. Sam had told me, while packing his suitcase that morning that Arizona was about to release many requests for qualifications for engineering, project management and design work for the many transportation improvements the state would be making over the next decade. He felt that his firm was well positioned for several of the projects and he was eager to attend the conference to learn more of the project specifics and meet, in person, some of the staffers who would eventually be on the RFQ review committees.

After our conversation last night about not taking one another for granted, I reset our bedside alarm fifteen minutes earlier than Sam had set it while he was out of sight in the bathroom brushing his teeth. When it had sounded this morning, I rolled over and whispered to Sam that he had an extra fifteen minutes of which we would be taking full advantage. It had been a good idea, which we both had enjoyed fully. I still had a grin on my face now this evening, from the sheer vigor which Sam had displayed as well as, from my pleasure at having successfully instigated our morning tryst after our previous night's slow leisurely burn.

The television news I had on was reporting the day's crime as Olive and I sat on the couch together. I picked up my iPad, opened my mail and composed a message to Marie.

Hi Marie,

Tonight I'm home, sitting on the sofa with Olive by my side keeping me warm. It's cold and snowing. Winter is here! I have the TV turned on and the evening news is filled with story after story of dumb people doing criminal things. It seems the freezing cold weather does not stop the stupid here, Marie!

Last week there was an interesting crime reported, but not tonight. Last week I watched a news story, not from Colorado, but from the Westminster Dog Show which takes place in England, that one of the top-prized competition dogs, an Irish setter, had been killed with poisoned meat. Apparently, according to the dog's owner, the dog had only been left alone during the exhibition part of the show and that an insider, most likely an unknown competitor, had fed the dog the poison. A toxicology report had confirmed this by uncovering several undigested cubes of beef that had been stuffed with poison, in the poor animal's stomach. Can you believe such a thing? I wish that I had been there. This is just the type of murder mystery that I would like to solve. Imagine how fun it would be to play Miss Marple and search the show grounds for clues as to whom had committed this crime? I could have questioned the other contestants as well as the show ground employees, and would have enjoyed trying to uncover the Westminster dog murderer. But alas, I missed it, Marie. I only heard of the crime when it was broadcast here in the States, days afterward. That's my problem, Marie, I'm never around when the good crime mysteries happen.

Anyway, and more importantly, let me fill you in on seeing Robyn last night. As I told you before, it's been forever since she and I have seen one another in person. I am happy to report my old friend looks happy and healthy. We had so much fun reminiscing about old times; it really was like we picked up just where we had left off some twenty years ago. Robyn is living in New York City now and has an interesting-sounding job using social media to connect with at-risk children in developing countries. She told me about her husband, the father of her children and their subsequent divorce. She's still single and her kids are almost through college. She seems to be relishing her "single in the city" phase. We also caught up on a few mutual friends. It was a great night, but toward the end she kind of freaked me out by asking about Sam and my relationship and then warning me not to take him for granted. In hindsight, I'm sure it was an innocent remark, but she had said it with an alarming tone while staring at me directly in the eyes. In the moment it made me feel like she knew something that I didn't, but that's silly, we haven't really been in touch in over two decades, so she couldn't.

The next night I mentioned Robyn's warning to Sam over dinner. He took it much better than I had and said, in short, it was good advice. That I shouldn't take him for granted! Ha-ha. Well, he ended up showing me twice exactly why I shouldn't take him for granted, so I'm feeling much better now.

Hope to hear from you soon!

Good night,

Lauren

Dear Lauren,

It is nice to read your musings. I've never known someone who wants to solve a dog murder! If you had been there, and found the dog's murderer, you could write a book and call it the "Harrowing of the Hound"!

I'm glad to hear you enjoyed seeing your old school friend again, too. I was glad you felt that you and she had picked up where you previously left off. I know that feeling well, and it is a good one. I have a school friend also with whom I get together every few years, and it is always enjoyable. We both get along just as well as we ever did, in spite of not seeing one another often.

As for your concern about her telling you so directly not to take your marriage for granted. I think perhaps Robyn had felt she could be direct with you. And you of all people, Lauren, should be able to take it. You are quite direct with others yourself, you know.

As for me, I have nothing much interesting to tell this week. I am still feeling poorly. I've been staying home and resting. It's been a week already since I came down with this, how do you say, annoying cold?! I will visit my doctor next week to get a proper medicine of some kind to make me feel better, but for now I'm trying not to smoke so much and eating many fruits and vegetables. The good news is that I've lost a few kilos!

Till later,

Marie

Hi Marie,

I do hope you are feeling better now. What did your doctor say? Please write to me again and let me know.

Wishing you well,

Lauren

P.S. Harrowing of the Hound…what a title! I love it.

A week went by and I had not heard from Marie, so I picked up the phone to call her. It was early morning in Denver and early evening in Antibes. A woman answered on the third ring with a crisp bonjour.

"Bonjour Marie. This is Lauren Hendrick. Is this a good time to talk?" I said.

"Ooo, this is not Madame. This is the housekeeper, Maeve. I'm sorry but Madame has asked not to be disturbed. Do you care to leave a message?"

I am always impressed by a household that has a staff and am even more awed by a staff who are able to answer the phone so professionally, even in a foreign language.

"Maeve, I am a friend of Marie's. Calling from America. I'm sure she will want to speak with me. Please let her know that it is Lauren Hendrick phoning. I will hold."

"Oui. I will check. Please wait a moment, Madame Hendrick," she replied.

I heard the phone handset placed down and Maeve's footsteps retreating on a hard surface. I envisioned the beautiful wood or tile flooring that Marie and Franco must have and

Maeve dressed in a classic black and white maid's uniform with a crisp white apron tied around her waist. After a few minutes, I heard footsteps returning. It was not Marie but Maeve again, who told me that Madame Marie was pleased to hear that I was ringing but did not feel strong enough to speak. Maeve informed me that Marie had instructed her to tell me that she would call me in a few days' time, when she would certainly be feeling better.

"Merci, Maeve. Please tell Marie to phone me back anytime and that I hope she will be feeling better soon."

I immediately rang Sam on his work number. "Sam, remember how I told you that Marie had told me that she had come down with cold or flu or something a couple weeks ago? I just tried to phone her as she has not responded to my emails since then. Her housekeeper told me that she was not feeling well enough to speak on the phone. It's been weeks, Sam. I'm worried about her. I know you'll think I'm silly for saying this, but what if Franco is poisoning her? You know his first wife died unexpectedly: what if Marie is in danger? What should I do?"

"Hmmm," said Sam. "It does seem like she has been ill a long time, Lauren, but what can you do?"

Chapter 14

What could I do indeed? Nothing. Marie was in France, a grown woman, who could take care of herself. So I went about my normal routine, distracted by gift shopping, card writing, a couple of holiday soirées that Sam and I had been invited to and our building's annual resident holiday party as the Christmas season approached. I had not heard back from Marie, even via email, and in the back of my mind I was worried that she was going to die and that Sam and I would only hear about it weeks later, after her death had been deemed a result of natural causes just like Franco's first wife.

After my unsuccessful phone call to Marie, I had mailed a holiday greeting card addressed to her and Franco at their home address in Antibes. I had not written much, just that we hoped they were both enjoying the start of the holiday season and that we hoped that Marie would be feeling better in time for Christmas. I closed with "Please phone me, Marie. I'm worried about you and miss hearing from you." I intentionally wrote that I was worried hoping that Franco would also read the card and know that Sam and I were paying attention and that we knew that something was amiss with Marie being ill for such a seemingly long time.

On December twenty-second, just as Sam was coming back inside from having taken Olive out for her morning constitutional, the phone rang. I answered it and I heard a soft familiar voice. I had not heard her voice since we had been at lunch in Cannes in September, but her beautiful French accent gave her away.

"Marie!" I exclaimed, looking at Sam, "I am so relieved to hear your voice. How are you?"

Sam smiled at me and walked over. He was about to leave for work, and he kissed me on the forehead and said gently into the phone receiver while I was holding it, "Marie, it's Sam. Pardon my interruption but we are *both* happy to hear from you. I am leaving for work now, but I trust you are feeling better and Lauren will certainly fill me in this evening about what you ladies have to catch up on. Please also send my regards to Franco." He winked at me at the mention of the name Franco, patted Olive on the head (who as usual was at my feet), reached for his briefcase from the kitchen counter and headed out for work.

Marie and I talked for three quarters of an hour, but it seemed like twenty minutes. She sounded upbeat but I detected some tiredness in her cadence. She told me that she and Franco were looking forward to Christmas, which they would be spending with his sister's family. Franco's sister, she said, was a real Martha Stewart-type. I laughed at her American reference, as she explained that the sister's home would be fully decorated from top to bottom and that she was also an excellent cook, so there would be an abundance of delicious Noël-themed, hand-cooked food. "I expect plenty of gros souper, which usually involves five or six courses in Franco's sister's home," Marie said with a chuckle.

She told me that the doctor had not found a specific reason for her stomach cramps and queasiness. She had not had a fever or any other traditional flu symptoms. She had just felt exhausted, weak and dizzy. Marie described it as having food poisoning for almost three weeks.

"I'm so glad it's over with now, Marie. It is, isn't it?" I inquired hesitantly.

"Yes. I've lost weight and I am not back to full energy just yet, Lauren, but the worst is behind. Frankly, I don't know what came over me. I have never been so sick before."

"Have you tried any new vitamins or supplements, Marie? Or any new foods or drinks, with Franco perhaps?"

"Lauren, I know what you are getting at! You make me laugh. Franco is not trying to poison me, Lauren!" Marie said laughing.

It was good to hear her laugh. "No, of course not, Marie. That is the furthest thing from my mind," I lied. "I just wondered if it could have been something new in your diet that you are allergic to or had a bad reaction to."

I was relieved that Marie concluded the subject by saying she had thought of that, but that she had not remembered anything foreign which she had consumed. She was just glad to be feeling better in time for Noël. I took the hint and dropped the subject. Marie next segued into an idea which was music to my ears. She said that she and Franco had spoken and they both wanted to come to Colorado to visit Sam and me in the new year.

"Sam and I would love it Marie. You've just made my day," I assured her. "I can't remember, have either of you ever been to Colorado before?"

"Non," she replied. "The closest I have been is to Texas. I went to Dallas about fifteen years ago and even saw the Ranch where *Dallas*, the television show, was filmed."

"That's South Fork! Marie, I used to love that TV show. I still have a crush on Larry Hagman, who played JR. Going to South Fork is on my bucket list."

"What is bouquet list, Lauren?"

"Oh, it means that virtual list that we all have, of places to visit, people to see and things to do before we die," I explained. "It's pronounced buck-ett, like a pail to fill full of all these aspirations. My bucket list contains many things that I would like to do that are not particularly sophisticated. Did you like South Fork Marie? Should I go to see it too?"

"From what I remember, it was quite small. Smaller than it appeared in *Dallas*. But I was there for a fundraiser and they threw an amazing Texas meat party on the lawn and we were allowed to walk through the estate as well." Considering for a second, she said, "Yes, you should go there, Lauren, before you die."

"Ok. South Fork will remain on my bucket list, Marie. In the meantime, let's get you and Franco out to Colorado, which is very different from Texas, as soon as possible. I miss you, and feel we have become friends. I very much want to see you again. In the meantime have a joyous Noël Marie! Continue to feel better and we will plan your trip here after the holidays."

Sam, Olive and I stayed home for Christmas and New Year's too. Sam travels so often that it is a luxury to stay in our forty-second floor condominium home alone together, with no work to do, no one to call on, and no place to be. We drank wine, listened to the 24/7 holiday music playing on the radio station that broadcasts nothing else (much to Sam's chagrin) and made Cornish game hens and pork loin dinners. The holiday week flew by.

Sam and I discussed what I should suggest for Marie and Franco's visit. After debating staying in Denver with us or going up to Vail or Aspen, we decided a quaint and easy journey to Estes Park in February would be best. Estes Park is a short, about two-hour, and breathtaking switchback-filled drive from Denver's airport. Most of the journey would be via the two-lane Peak-to-Peak highway which has dramatic rocky outcroppings on one side and a creek down below which ripples along the opposite roadside. Sam and I would rent a larger vehicle; we'd always wanted to try out the Mercedes G-Class. We would pick Marie and Franco up at the airport and drive us all up to the iconic Stanley Hotel, with its historic lobby, panoramic views and Michelin-starred restaurant. Sam and I figured we would all stay at the Stanley for four or five nights and then invite Marie and Franco to our home for another night or two, before we returned them to the airport for their seven-hour flight back home.

On Monday during the second week of January, after Sam left for work, I sat down at the desk in our home office to turn on my laptop and email Marie with the plan for their visit. While the old PC warmed up, I looked at the light maple wood of the desk, which we'd had since the eighties, and thought to myself that it was time to call my friend Karen, an interior designer, to help me update our office. Karen had designed our living, dining and bedrooms a few years back, with wonderful results. While I have always prided myself of having good taste, I also realize that when one finally lives at an expensive address, cookie-cutter Pottery Barn furnishings no longer cut the mustard.

Switching gears mentally, I opened Outlook to peruse my unread messages, none of which were time-sensitive or particularly important. My inbox contained two committee meeting reminders, several junk mails, a few Facebook notifications (which are never urgent) and one vet appointment reminder for Olive. I ignored them all, and composed a new message.

Happy New Year Marie!

Sam and I are over the moon at the prospect of your and Franco's visit. How does mid-February sound for a trip to Colorado? February is a quiet month here in the States, before Spring Break begins in March, and would be a good time for a relaxing trip and stay up in the mountains.

Here's what I suggest: book your flights into Denver International Airport (DEN) on the dates that work best for you and plan to stay about one week with us. (Sam has assured me February looks like it will be a slower month work-wise for him.) We will pick you up from the airport and will whisk you both about two hours up into the mountains by car. We will stay for four or five nights at the historic and dog-friendly Stanley Hotel in Estes Park. I will book two suites for us at the Stanley, our treat. Estes Park is NOT a ski resort, simply a charming mountain town with many fine restaurants, hiking trails, horse-back riding and little shops. We will relax, we will drink and we will walk up mountains! Then we will drive us all back to Denver, where we hope you both will want to stay in our home for a night or two before we return you to the airport.

Colorado is a very casual place. You will not need fancy or formal attire. Jeans and a jacket for Franco is all that is needed at even the nicest restaurants. Please bring warm sweaters, hats, gloves, sunglasses and snow boots for walking outdoors. It will surely be snowy and cold in Estes Park, which sits one and one-half miles (about 7500 meters) above sea level!

I hope this arrangement sounds good to you. Please let me know what you think. Sam and I are happy to change anything. This plan is just a starting point. I cannot wait to see you again.

Ciao! Lauren

Marie's reply came through on Friday. She said that she had checked with Franco and they both loved the whole itinerary. She said they would not, however, allow us to pay for their accommodations at the hotel, and said simply that they would pay for their suite, if I wouldn't mind making the reservations. She said the trip sounded lovely and that she would enjoy calm winter nature walks instead of skiing as she was still a bit weak. She asked about snowshoeing, which I love to do with Olive. I took this as further indication of our mutual similarities and as affirmation of how well we all would travel together for the first time. She said that after reviewing their calendar and work schedule, she and Franco would like to fly out on February 10th, arriving Denver February 11th at 10:15 a.m. They would return via an 8 a.m. flight on February 16th. Marie closed by saying I should confirm that these flight dates and times would work, and then she would immediately purchase the plane tickets.

Chapter 15

I HAD RENTED the G-class and paid for a second parking space in our Brooks Tower underground garage to park the gleaming silver behemoth. It dawned on me as I made a six-point turn to park in the assigned narrow parking space, that I was not all practiced in driving such a large, tall vehicle. I was grateful that Sam would be driving the four of us and Olive to Estes Park the following day. I had packed our suitcases two days before and had had them delivered via courier directly to the Stanley, so that the Mercedes would have adequate room for Marie and Franco and their luggage. I didn't know them well enough yet to know if they packed lightly or if they would be arriving with a full regalia of accoutrements.

As I took the elevator from the garage up to our condo, I thought to myself how pleased I was that the weather was clear and cold with no forecast for snow the following day when our French friends would be arriving to Denver and we would all drive up into the mountains together. The thought of seeing Marie and Franco again in person was exciting to me, but also a bit nerve wracking. I hoped that Marie and I would again enjoy a natural, unforced rapport in person.

Sam had stayed at the office late working each night this week, to make himself feel better about playing hooky at the Stanley for the next five days. When he arrived home the night before Marie and Franco's arrival, it was almost 9 p.m. I made him two fried egg sandwiches on rye toast with some hot decaffeinated green tea. Sam sat down at our kitchen bar and asked for a Manhattan instead of the tea. I poured him a couple of fingers of Maker's Mark over ice, and added a dash of vermouth & bitters to it. This is Sam's favorite drink. Sitting down next to him at the bar, I placed his drink beside his untouched tea cup and gave him a kiss.

"Are you feeling caught up at work, Sam?" I asked.

"Yes, for now. Amazingly the Sound Transit RFP that should have been released last week, has been pushed back to late next week, which is a stroke of luck. I can relax until that comes out."

"Fingers crossed it doesn't release while we're up in Estes. That would surely distract you from all the fun and relaxation we're going to have with Marie and Franco," I said trying to cover up my own last minute nervousness. What was I thinking by inviting people we'd only met briefly, to fly all the way to Colorado and stay with us in a small hotel, in the middle of nowhere, in a very small town for five days?

"You know how these things go, Lauren. If they say it'll come out in a week, it'll most likely be a month. That's how these P3 projects go," said Sam before taking another bite from his "there's nothing in the kitchen" dinner.

"Delays have certainly happened before, Sam. I hope your theory proves accurate this time. You know, I'm counting on you to entertain Franco. I'm still not sure I like that man."

"Then why on earth are we spending five whole days with him in the mountains Lauren? I swear, sometimes you bewilder me."

"Oh, come on, Sam. We'll have a great time. We'll *make* it a great time," I said, trying to project a self-fulfilling prophecy. "I just meant that I care for Marie. I feel she has become a person whom I genuinely enjoy and care for but Franco I don't know very well and he hasn't grown on me yet. I'm hoping he will on this trip, but I'm counting on you to entertain him, until he does. Initially I plan to spend more catching up with Marie during their visit. I hope she's feeling better. Remember, I told you, she was quite sick last month."

"She wouldn't be coming all this way if she was sick, Lauren."

"No, you're right. She emailed me last week that she's all better now, but she also said she was glad we wouldn't be skiing, as she still felt weak."

"This sandwich is very good, Lauren."

The alarm rang early and it woke me, which it usually doesn't on the first ring, but I was half-awake already. I had been in a space of slumber where one is totally relaxed, but not fully unconscious. I hurried to use the bathroom and get the coffee brewing before I roused Sam and Olive from bed. Olive is a deep sleeper, like me.

"Sam," I whispered rubbing his shoulder. I've always loved Sam's shoulders. "Time to wake up." Sam responded with a "merrumph" sound and I gave him a coffee-scented kiss on the forehead. "I've got your coffee here on the nightstand Sam. I'm getting in the shower."

After my shower I walked back in our dark bedroom and saw that Sam had curled up with Olive, both still sleeping soundly. I opened our draperies and tilted open the blinds. It was quickly approaching eight, and the sun had just started to rise, illuminating the room with crisp light. "Good morning, sunshine! It's almost eight, Sam. You and Olive really need to wake up now."

Sam turned his head, opened his eyes and said, "Do we have to go?" with a curl on lips, which showed me that he was teasing.

"Yes, we have French people whom we barely know arriving at the airport in two and a half hours!" I teased back.

"That's just enough time for a quickie. Come on, Mrs. Hendrick, we'll start our holiday off right. And I promise I'll be the perfect host all day if you give me a little of this right now," Sam said while pulling open my bath towel. Olive, who's no chump, jumped down from the bed and tottered out of the bedroom, leaving a nice warm spot next to Sam for me to crawl up into.

Traveling frequently in and out of Denver International Airport has advantages such as knowing exactly where a few close-in short term parking spots can almost always be found. Today we were lucky. "It must have been the nookie Mr. Hendrick; look at this front-row parking spot," I exclaimed as we pulled the rental G-class in directly across from the international baggage claim doors.

Sam turned off the ignition, told Olive to stay put in the back seat, that we'd be back soon, and said to me "Here we go, Lauren. Let's go find Marie and Franco."

I checked the visor mirror quickly to make sure I didn't have lipstick on my teeth or mascara flakes around my eyes; both minor annoyances that I seemed to acquire more frequently with each passing year, precipitating more frequent mirror checks. I dabbed each of my eyes, got out of the vehicle and noticed how softly, yet solidly, the G-class' door closed shut. "I told them we would meet at baggage claim, so let's go check the board first, Sam," I said taking hold of his hand as we walked across the three lanes of one-way traffic in between our parking space and the airport doors.

Lufthansa code share United flight #44 from Frankfurt had arrived into DIA and its passengers' baggage was to be routed to baggage claim conveyor number six. "Look at that Lauren, their flight has arrived on time. That's sure to be a good sign for our trip."

"We have clearly been together too long, Sam! I was just thinking the exact same thing."

We made our way toward international arrivals. I pulled out my phone and composed a text to Marie stating that we were at the airport and waiting for them just outside of customs.

She replied almost immediately saying they had arrived and were just waiting to pass through the immigration line and pick up their luggage.

"Just so you know, Sam, I plan to make this a romantic vacation for us, in spite of visiting with Marie and Franco," I said looking him in the eyes. Then, with a smile, I laid a big kiss on his lips.

"Music to my ears, Lauren," said Sam smiling back at me. Then his eyes flicked past me and he said, "I think our friends are here."

We both stood and immediately recognized Marie and Franco walking side by side in our general direction. It's true what they say about French women, I thought as I waved to them. Even at a distance Marie looked chipper and pressed, not at all like she just been on an international overnight commercial flight. She wore bronze metallic pointy toe flats, dark slim jeans (not stove-pipe skinny like American women tend to do) with an eggplant collared shirt unbuttoned quite low and a tailored, shrunken jacket. Her dark hair was a bit longer than before, now touching her shoulders in loose, but not messy, waves. In short, she looked well put together and very, very French, almost like she hadn't tried at all to appear well coiffed. For his part, Franco also looked well in light brown leather shoes with a matching belt, chocolate slim cut flat-front trousers and a bright magenta cashmere V-neck sweater. I've always found it appealing that European men, even middle-aged ones, are not afraid to wear bright colors. I enjoy men who are comfortable wearing colors other than black, grey, khaki and blue.

Grabbing Sam by the hand, I beelined toward our French friends and called out "Welcome to Denver, Colorado, Marie and Franco!" They saw us then and I was pleased to see them both smile broadly in our direction. Marie and I immediately embraced in greeting. Following her lead, we then air-kissed both of each other's cheeks. A one-cheek kiss is simply not enough for the French. Up close, Marie looked much slimmer and smaller than I had remembered. Sam and Franco shook hands and then we changed partners to exchange the same greetings.

"Marie, I am so happy to see you again in person. You look rested, not at all like you've been flying all night." Turning toward Franco, I continued, "Thank you both, so much, for coming all the way here to visit with us. Franco, Marie told me she has not been in Colorado before, have you?"

"Non, I cannot say that I have. I've actually only been to *Amerika* once before, to New York City. Marie, she has traveled more than I. I've always had to *travailler,* and Marie, not so much, she's had more time than I to enjoy exploring the world outside of Europe."

And there it was. I remembered exactly why I didn't care for Franco as much as I did for Marie. He was a grouser. So quickly he gave me the impression of being jealous of Marie and of her money, her lack of need to have to work.

"Well, I think you are both going to love our fine state of Colorado," said Sam, "and I know Lauren has planned a wonderful few days for us together in the mountains. Why don't you ladies use the powder room and purchase some drinks for us for the drive. Franco and I will load the luggage in our vehicle."

We fit in the Mercedes just fine, with Sam driving, Franco in front and Olive nestled in between Marie and me in the backseat. Franco and Marie's luggage fit easily in the rear of the vehicle and I was pleased to note that they shared only three Rimowa roller suitcases, two in black and one in silver, along with one fine leather carry-on duffel which looked like well-worn Gucci. I admire people who pack lightly; like being punctual, it makes everything easier.

It was late morning and traffic was light as we headed north toward the college town of Boulder along commuter highway 36. Sam had the radio on for us. It was tuned to a station that played a mix of acoustic singer-songwriter, blues-oriented jams and classic rock. I told Marie this music mix is the most typical and popular in Colorado, but that I personally preferred cheesy, bass-heavy hip-hop. Marie responded that she preferred "old lady" music like Celine Dion and Mariah Carey. She said it's like she was stuck in the 1990s music-wise.

"I'm stuck in the nineties also, but my nineties are Dr. Dre and The Roots," I said laughing.

"Where are we now Lauren?" asked Marie, changing the subject.

"We're just passing through some of what I call our suburban sprawl, Marie. What I mean is this whole area was open plains with horses and cows and farmland when I first moved to Colorado. In the past twenty years all of these next-to-the-highway residential neighborhoods, strip malls and low-rise office space has sprouted up. It's because both Denver and Boulder have quite expensive housing and this is the main thoroughfare between the two. It's less expensive to live here and to drive either to Boulder or into Denver for work."

"We have this too, especially outside of Paris and Lyon. There used to be open space between the cities and neighboring villages, but now the land is filled in with development."

"Same thing here Marie, but Boulder is unique. You'll see it for yourself in a minute. Just at the top of this hill, you'll see how Boulder has protected its green space all the way around the city. Sam, let's stop at the scenic overlook and show Marie and Franco the view of Boulder."

Sam pulled into the small parking lot just beside the highway at the very top of the hill which descends down into Boulder. There is nothing like this particular view, right off the highway. Frankly, the views all over the state are glorious. Colorado is truly beautiful. It's one of the many reasons that Sam and I had not moved anywhere else since arriving here so many years ago. We all got out of the car and I leashed up Olive, so she could stretch her legs too. It was getting cold and I asked Marie and Franco if they would like to get their coats out of their luggage. Marie replied yes and Franco no, so Marie and I walked to the rear of the car and the men walked toward the benches facing directly down into the Boulder valley which lay before us. Marie struggled to pull out one of the black suitcases and I reached forward to help her pull it out.

"How are you feeling, Marie?" I asked as she unlatched the hard case and opened it.

"Quite weak actually, Lauren. I seem to have lost my strength with my illness and I have not regained it yet, even though I am feeling better otherwise. My doctor says to eat more and has put me on a vitamin regimen that would choke a horse, but I can't seem to gain any of my strength back yet. They haven't found anything wrong with me, but I had pneumonia and it's taking a long time for me to bounce back."

As Marie removed her blazer and pulled on her black shinny Montcler down jacket from the suitcase, I said "We'll do our best to feed you well this week, Marie. To start we're going to have lunch in Boulder, just down there!" Watching Marie fold her blazer and lay it within the open suitcase I noticed a deep emerald green sweater on top and several pill bottles tucked in the corner, which may or may not have been vitamins. I helped Marie reposition her suitcase back among the others, closed the trunk and we walked over to the bench that the men were now sitting on. Olive jumped up on Sam's knees, acting as though see hadn't seen him in a week, and I laid my hand on his shoulder. The Flatirons flanking the west side of Boulder reflected the sun on their smooth, flat rocky fronts. Sam pointed out that all of the terra cotta colored roofs in the valley before the Flatirons are the University of Colorado campus, and that just behind those is the central business district.

"There in the heart of the valley, where you see the straight tree-lined street heading straight out from the mountains, is Boulder's Pearl Street Mall. It's one of the first outdoor areas in the country to be enforced completely smoke free."

I heard a small "ugh" from Marie, but she said nothing further. "Boulder prides itself on being one of the healthiest and fittest cities in America," I said. "And it's true. You will see fewer obese people here in Boulder than almost anywhere else in our country. But I also think the outdoor smoking ban is a bit excessive. I think Boulder just needed to give its police force something to do, because there is not much crime here, above and beyond normal college student shenanigans."

Sam continued by pointing out the small, blue body of water to the east of town which is the Boulder reservoir where college students swim and boat in the summer and also do a Polar Bear Plunge on each New Year's Day. From this vantage, it was easy to see all the undeveloped grassland completely surrounding the small city. If we looked closely, Sam said, one could see the many miles of trails for all to use, meandering throughout this huge protected green space.

Comfortably back in the G-class, as we descended into to Boulder, the four of us decided Mexican over pizza for our lunch. Sam pointed the car downtown and we headed straight for the Rio, a Boulder institution, located just off the Pearl Street Mall in the heart of town. After giving her some water and a biscuit, we left Olive in the car and were happy to be seated right away near the front window. The restaurant was almost full with a luncheon crowd that looked like a cross between stay-at-home moms and unkempt software engineers taking lunch breaks, with a few bohemians thrown in for color, literally, like the picante in our salsa.

Before ordering, Sam shared the restaurant's secret to its success. The Rio has been open in Boulder since the 1960s and is famed, and still popular today, for its two-margarita drink policy. The Rio's margaritas are so potent, no one is allowed to order more than two. It went without saying, that after an introduction like that, the four of each ordered a margarita with our respective lunches.

Franco seemed in good spirits and regaled us with a story about the American couple who had sat across the aisle from Marie and him on their flight in. "Marie said it was a sign, but I disagree," said Franco. "You see, this couple told us the story of how they had almost *died* on their last vacation."

Chapter 16

"MARIE AND I have a small catamaran boat cruise planned for this summer," said Franco. "We plan to sail with a group of friends; three boats total, each with three berths plus a captain and a cook. This has always been a dream of mine, you see. To sail on a very small boat through the Caribbean Sea. Marie is not convinced and feels a bit scared of spending a whole week at sea on such a small vessel. Is that fair to say?" Franco asked turning to Marie.

"Oui. I have never spent the night, let alone a whole week, on a small boat. My father had had friends with yachts upon which my family would often weekend, but they were much, much larger than what Franco has in store for us. I am a bit leery of the open seas already, and don't like the idea of being on such a small boat, which so few people aboard, if a storm or turbulent weather should arise. Franco has always wanted to do this, probably for the exact reasons that I am hesitant: sailing on such a small vessel is more daring and dangerous."

"Apparently it can be!" chuckled Franco before eating a salsa-laden chip. He dabbed at his lips with his napkin and then proceeded, "So this couple sitting across from us in the plane, they were Germans and visiting Denver to spend time with their family. Their daughter and her husband live in Denver. Anyway, out of the blue, we had not mentioned our summer sailing plans, they began to tell us about their last vacation, which they described as having almost been their *last* vacation! They told us they had chartered a small sailboat, 50 feet, I believe they said, from a website. They flew to Tortola and met the other couple whom they would be sailing with and the boat and crew. Everything was lovely for the first few days: they got on well with their companions and the on-board food was simple but delicious. Then on their third night at sea, the sailboat began to rock violently, waking them both up. They awoke and literally staggered, due to the boat's violent rocking, to locate the captain. He was at the wheel sweating profusely and did not appear to be calm at all. He told them he did not know the strength or size of the storm that they had found themselves engulfed in because the sailboat's radio had gone out. He asked them to get dressed and wake the others. That's when the seasickness began. This couple said they had never experienced seasickness before and it was horrible, indescribable, incapacitating."

Our server returned then with our margaritas and replenished our chips and salsa with a smile. Never having been able to forgo an opportunity to propose a toast, I quickly lifted my glass, before the others were able to take their first sips and said, "Cheers! Sam and I are so happy you are here, Marie and Franco. To becoming better friends and to absolutely no seasickness in Colorado!" The others raised their glasses and we all drank. I noticed shared appreciative glances around the table between Sam, Marie and Franco for the perfectly mixed proportion of tequila and fresh lime, or perhaps for my succinct toast.

"Merci, Lauren. We are also happy to be with both of you. Sam you are right, these margaritas are excellent."

"Please go on with your story, Franco. I can't wait to hear what's next."

"Well, apparently the women on board began to panic when a few hours later, keep in mind this was the middle of the night, the sailboat began taking on water. All four of them had to use buckets and whatever they could find, to bail water out of the boat as it continued to rock violently. Just then they all heard a loud crash and the mast broke and fell on the starboard side! It dragged into the water and tilted the small sailboat precariously. Can you imagine? The radio and internet navigation was out, they were in the middle of a violent storm and the mast broke!"

"Exactly why I think having perfect strangers tell us this story is a sign from the heavens not to go on our catamaran trip this summer Franco," said Marie through thin lips.

With a glance to Marie, Franco continued, "So the couple told us that this went on for *days*. The storm, the sea-sickness, the continual bailing of water, no form of communication. Then when they thought it would never end, a commercial tanker ship spotted them and rescued them. They said they had never been so happy in their lives. They were on the cargo tanker with Portuguese speakers for three more days before they finally made it to land. And the sailboat they had chartered is still at sea, maybe completely capsized, they said. It has not yet been found!"

It's impossible to top a story like that so we all concentrated on finishing our lunches.

The second half of our drive to Estes Park from Boulder was uneventful, with only the occasional small gasp by Marie at the steep forty-foot drops on the left side of the two-lane highway which we were taking up into the Rocky Mountains.

"See the river way down there?" I said as our vehicle turned through one of the switchback curves that proffered a particularly dazzling view of the roadside drop straight down to the rushing, shallow water. "That is Boulder Creek. It's usually quite dry here. We're in an arid climate. That creek is usually as you see it now, charming and only a few feet deep, but four years ago this whole area experienced a torrential rain storm that lasted for days. This creek turned into a raging white water river from all the mountain run-off, and washed out this whole valley and the highway we're driving on. It also flooded the town of Estes Park, which was practically cut off from the rest of the area due to this road being washed out. This is the only paved road in and out of town. In the four years since the flood, thanks to federal disaster funding, this highway and the town of Estes

Park have been completely rebuilt, most would argue better than it was before."

"Impossible," said Franco. "You are telling me that there is only one road in and out of the whole town and that this road we are driving on has been completely rebuilt in such a short time? In France, we would have train service in addition to a road, but the reconstruction would take at least a decade. Highway construction is a notoriously corrupt industry in France."

Laughing, Sam replied, "We were all impressed at how quickly Estes Park was rebuilt too, Franco, especially considering there is no real industry here. The only real source of revenue in Estes Park is tourism: you see, the town is situated right at the base of the entrance to Rocky Mountain National Park, which is one of the largest and most popular national parks in the country."

"And guess what was practically the only thing *not* damaged in that flood?" I asked as we made the last descent into the small mountain town of Estes Park. "Our hotel! The Stanley Hotel. Look, there it is." From the backseat, I stretched my arm between Sam and Franco pointing to the front windshield of the Mercedes. In the distance we could just now see the gleaming all white hotel with its four large rooftop turrets surrounding the largest center turret with a bell tower in the center, and its bright red shingled roof.

The Stanley hotel is situated atop a grassy hill overlooking the whole town, out of water's way, at about 7,500 hundred feet above sea level. Estes Park lies in the valley below, directly in front of the hotel. Just behind the hotel, by about three hundred yards, are dramatic, very tall rocky outcroppings rising above the roofline which perfectly frame the white and red Stanley hotel with shiny grey stone and dark green foliage, mostly pines, growing from crevices in the rock. "The Stanley was built in 1909, three years before the Carlton Hotel was, where we met you two," I said. "When it was originally painted, Mr. Stanley's wife chose a mustard yellow color for the whole hotel, because apparently at the time, yellow was the most expensive tint to add to the white paint base. I do hope you will like it here. Sam and I have always enjoyed our stays at the Stanley, but it has been at least five years, prior to the flood, since we've last been here ourselves."

As we turned off the highway, and drove up the long narrow private drive leading to the hotel's entrance, one could see the beautiful covered veranda along the entire front of the main building. Several guests were sitting out front on the cushioned white wicker chairs and settees. The sun shone brightly and most of the guests wore sunglasses with their brightly colored bubble-goose jackets. Passing the grassy meadow in front of the Stanley, Sam exclaimed "Look!" and slowed the car to a stop. In between the outdoor pool situated at the very front edge of the property and just past the large brass ornamental sundial where the property's terrain begins to slope down toward town, were three young elk grazing on patches of grass where the snow had melted away. We all sat quietly in the car, agog, watching these mammoth wild animals enjoy their snack.

"We called ahead and asked for an elk viewing," joked Sam. "Actually, I was wrong before, Estes does have a major industry. It's called elk bugling. I believe the season is normally in September and October, right Lauren?"

"Yes, I think that's right."

"So in September and October you can't throw a stone without hitting a bull elk. They're literally all over the place bugling and looking for a mate. Elk fanatics and tourists are all over the place at that time of year too. The whole area books up to capacity and all night one hears them bugling. Lauren and I were here during the season once; I couldn't get any sleep at all. The bugling is loud and very strange sounding, like nothing I have heard before."

"These elk look quite young. Don't the males usually have much larger horns, Sam?" asked Franco.

"Yeah, these were probably born last season. They look like adolescents don't they, quite lanky with small antlers? They haven't put on their middle-age weight yet."

Grabbing her cell phone to take a picture, Marie said "They are beautiful. I have never seen real elk before."

Quietly, in my head, I was patting myself on the back. I was proud of myself. The visit with our new French friends was starting off well indeed. As Sam put the vehicle into drive, Marie glanced at me and caught me smiling. She grinned back, waving her phone in an I-got-a-great-photograph kind of way. French women have such a casual chic, both in looks and in attitude.

We parked and walked with Olive along the sidewalk, up through the front veranda and into the main lobby of the hotel. Immediately we faced the grand staircase in the not overly large, historic room. On each side of the ornate mahogany staircase, on both far ends of the lobby were huge stone fireplaces with seating areas in front. Each identical sitting area was outfitted with four Colorado-style oversized leather arm chairs and a long dark wood coffee table. There were a few guests reading and relaxing in front of each fireplace as well as a few people walking around, tourist-style, taking in the hotel's displayed artifacts and the amazing views of Estes Park down in the valley below, from the large lobby picture windows.

Before we checked in, I motioned for us to walk to the far right side of the lobby. "Look at this," I said. As we walked to the right, tourist-style ourselves, away from the front desk, Franco gasped as he saw the real American automobile which had been assembled for display inside of the hotel's lobby. "It's a *Stanley Steamer*," I told Franco. "The man who built this hotel in the middle of the Colorado mountains, made his fortune manufacturing these cars at the turn of the 20th century. They were steam engine cars, pre-gasoline, hence the name."

"Here's a plaque. It says 1910 Stanley Steamer Runabout and it's only ten horsepower," read Marie.

"I'm impressed," acknowledged Franco taking in the Kelly green paint, the tall thin tires and the buggy-style passenger carriage of the classic automobile. Franco, I noticed, had not checked his cell phone yet on this trip. "Death-defying drives, beautiful scenery, real elk wandering around town and now a genuine steam car from 1910 in the middle of a hotel lobby. I had no idea that Colorado would be so interesting."

"There's more," said a man who had also approached the Stanley Steamer. "This hotel is supposed to be haunted. Did you know?"

"What? Are you joking with us?" said Marie in her cute accent.

"No, I am not. The Stanley is haunted, some rooms more than others, but definitely that old 1909 Otis elevator over there. I wouldn't use it, if I were you," he said smiling genially.

"It's true that they made a very scary movie about this place back in the 1970s called *The Shining*, Marie and Franco, but the story was just inspired by the Stanley. It did not take place here. I can assure you that Sam and I have stayed here several times and it's not really haunted," I said to everyone.

"Correct. *The Shining* was inspired by a stay that the author Steven King had made here to this hotel, but my partner and I came here especially because it is reported to be haunted to this day according to a very reliable paranormal website that Kip follows. Oh, how rude of me! My name is Jarvis Peterson. My partner Kip and I are here visiting from Fort Collins for the weekend."

Sam extended his hand and introduced himself by full name and then each of us in turn by our first names. Franco followed suit, also shaking hands with Jarvis, I gave him a quick head nod and Marie asked, "Where is Fort Collins, Jarvis?"

"It's north and east of here by about three hours. You have a lovely accent, my dear. Where are you from?"

"We are visiting from France. Antibes. Our friends here, Lauren and Sam, invited us for the week."

"Oh how exciting! My Kip will just love to meet you all. In addition to loving the paranormal in life, he is a true Francophile. He just can't get enough of the country and its wonderful people. We've been there vacationing three times together so far. I keep asking Kip to go somewhere new, but he insists that 'it's France or nothing! Why would anyone want to go anywhere else?' he always says. I love France too, so my resistance to Kip is mostly for dramatic effect, I must say."

"Sam, my husband, and I also love France, Jarvis. The four of us met in Cannes, when Sam and I were there last."

"How fun! Was this long ago? How long have you all known one another?" Jarvis asked.

"Not very long actually. We just met Marie and Franco this past September. Sam and I started talking to Marie one afternoon at the Terrace Café in our hotel, just a few days before we had to return home to Denver. Marie and I have kept in touch since then, and we just planned this trip to see each other again, this time in Colorado, on a lark, for lack of a better word. Marie and Franco just flew in today, and we came straight here," I replied.

Jarvis then gave Sam a friendly pat on the upper arm and said, "Well you all get my prize for being the most adventurous people I've met all week! I feel I'd better excuse myself so you can catch up with one another. It's been a pleasure to meet you."

"Will you be dining here in the hotel tonight Jarvis? Perhaps we could meet for drinks in the Whiskey Bar afterward?" asked Sam.

"Kip and I will be going into town for dinner. I have a taste for Italian tonight, and there is a wonderful little place with homemade noodles right on Main Street. Would ten o'clock be too late to meet for a cocktail? We will be back by then and I know Kip would enjoy meeting you all."

"It's a date. We'll meet you in the Whiskey Bar at ten, Monsieur Jarvis," chimed in Marie.

"What an accent! So charming. Will you promise to say my name like that again tonight, Madame Marie?" With that Jasper made a little bow, one arm bent in front of his slight paunch, turned on his heels and walked back toward to center of the lobby.

"Such a nice little man. I like Colorado so far, Lauren," said Marie when Jasper was out of earshot.

"I'm so glad to hear that, Marie. I also liked Jasper, and I really can't wait to meet Kip." Turning to Franco and Sam, who were pointing to various parts of the Stanley Steamer, I said, "Gentlemen, would you mind checking us in while Marie and I get some tea on the veranda? What can we order for each of you?"

Sam and Franco agreed and requested beers and a dish of cashews, if possible, so Marie, Olive and I went back out the front doors and onto the huge covered porch. To my great relief, there were a few vacant seats on the smoking half of the veranda and we sat down, each facing outward, toward Lake Estes and the town nestled beside, in the valley below. Olive lay down beside my chair. We placed our order with the polo-shirted server, amazed that she was not cold in her shirtsleeves.

"Marie, are you still smoking?" I asked.

"Yes, but I have cut way back since my sickness. I am simply not able to quit completely; it's a weakness of mine."

"May I have one, Marie? Would you mind?"

"Not at all. We're on vacation. Let's smoke, drink and eat without remorse."

Chapter 17

"ARE THESE SEATS free Mademoiselles?" joked Sam as he and Franco approached Marie and me on the hotel's veranda.

"Oui, Sam" said Marie, not taking the bait but smiling widely at him. "Here are your beers and some mixed nuts, as requested."

"We're all checked in," said Sam sitting down next to Marie, leaving the seat next to me, with the better vantage for Franco. "Lauren, Stephanie, the assistant manager from our last stay, is still working here. She remembered us after all these years. Can you imagine?"

"She probably remembered your bar tab Sam. As I recall, there was a boxing match on TV that weekend, which you had had a bet on. When your fighter won, you bought a round for the entire bar!"

"You have too good a memory, Lauren," said Sam. Turning to Franco, he continued, "That's right. I won two thousand dollars that night on Lennox Lewis. Before the bar tab." To me Sam said, "Anyway, Stephanie asked if we brought the same dog with us again and I told her certainly, that Olive is outside with you and Marie right now. She said she would have the Stanley's in-house baked dog biscuits waiting for her in our room. Oh, and all of our luggage, ours arrived yesterday Lauren, will be taken up to our rooms for us. We should be all set in about thirty minutes, she said. Marie and Franco are located on the top floor corner here in the main hotel, suite 515, right Franco? Lauren, you and I are also on the top floor corner, number 420, but we're in the Lodge, the separate building just down this sidewalk, next door."

"Oh, that's too bad. Why couldn't we be in the main hotel too?" I asked Sam, trying not to sound whiney.

"Because of Miss Olive here," Sam replied scratching Olive's chin, who had walked over to lie down next to him. "Apparently, since we've been here last all dogs with guests have been relegated to the Lodge only."

Returning his pint glass to the table, and taking a handful of nuts, Franco said, "Thank you again, Sam and Lauren, for planning all this for us. The hotel and town look promising and your company has been outstanding. But you Americans like your beer served too cold."

"You're most welcome, Franco," I responded simply. "It's about two o'clock now and I've made dinner reservations for us here at the hotel, in the Crimson Room just off the main lobby, for seven. The in-house restaurant is highly rated and Sam and I remember it having many delicious Colorado game-inspired entrees and a nice wine list."

"Yes, seven o'clock for dinner. That sounds perfect. I think I'll take a nap until then. The jet lag is catching up with me, I'm afraid," said Marie. "Franco, how are you feeling, shall we retire to our room after you finish your *le froid* beer?"

"I could also do with a rest, Marie, and there is no one I'd rather rest with than you."

"Lauren, do you still want to go for a short trail ride today before dinner at that nearby stable?" Sam asked me.

"Ooo, that sounds fun Lauren. I love to ride," interjected Marie. "Do you think we can all ride another day during our stay?"

"Yes Marie, we'd love to, although I am by no means an experienced horse woman. I was hoping to go a few times while we are here, since the stable is open to the public for trail rides and it's so close by. It's just there on the left side of the Lake Estes," I said pointing to the stable roofs one could just barely see on the near left side of the calm blue lake water. "It's called Sombrero Stables. This will be perfect, Sam. We can go today for a short one-hour ride as practice, to get my horse legs back, before we ride with a real equestrian like Marie. Franco, how about you? Do you also like horses?"

"I prefer attending horse races as a spectator. Leave the riding to the professionals, I say."

"We also enjoy attending the races." said Sam to Franco. "Attending the Kentucky Derby, dare I say, was one of the highlights of Lauren's life. Perhaps someday we could all attend a race together? Which race parks do you go to in France?"

"Nearly half of all the European racing venues are located in France. We, as a nation, love the sport, Sam. One of the closest, we call them *Hippodromes*, is located right in the Cote d'Azur in a small village called Cagnes-sur-Mer. I have invested in a few colts over the years who have raced there."

"A man after my own heart," I said. "I hope one day to do the same, even if only in a very small way, by joining a racing syndicate of independent investors."

Yawning, Marie stood up and Franco did as well. "Have a nice ride and we'll see you later at dinner, Lauren and Sam."

"Enjoy your siesta, and don't forget about drinks with Jasper Peterson and Kip after dinner tonight. Let's all sleep in late tomorrow morning, ok?" said Sam, shaking hands with Franco and kissing Marie on the cheek.

Upon Marie and Franco's retreat to their suite, Sam scooted over into the chair next to me and I patted the cushion on the chaise beside my legs so Olive could jump up and hunker down beside me. "This visit is turning out well, don't you think Sam?"

Just then his cell phone must have vibrated, because Sam patted his thigh and reached into his front pocket, pulling out the phone. "This is Sam," he answered without looking at the screen. Sam stood up; he always paces when on the phone. He looked at me, made the one moment hand signal and walked down the stairs off of the veranda and onto the front lawn to focus on what must have been a work issue.

I placed my hand on Olive's rump. She seemed tired from the busy morning. I began to entertain myself by looking more closely at the other guests around me on the Stanley's front porch. There were about a dozen people outside on both ends of the long veranda. I noticed an elderly man and woman, both with shocks of silver hair, who looked like a long-married couple, sitting in the seating area directly to my left. They sat quietly, bundled up in matching Burberry patterned cashmere scarves, hers a dusty rose with burgundy and his in the classic camel and charcoal grey plaid. They were not speaking, just gazing out toward the quiet lake. The gentleman, who appeared in his eighties, had his wedding ringed hand resting nonchalantly on the woman's thigh. So sweet, I thought. People tend to feel sorry for couples who are not talking to one another in public, but I prefer to think of these silent couples as having already had a long life together, with many shared experiences, and that idle chit chat at this point in one's relationship can be just superfluous. In this couple's case, his hand so comfortably on her leg, their silence made me think they were contented. Their overly cute matching scarves didn't hurt either. I wondered what Sam and I will be like at their age. I hoped we'll make just as comfortable a couple as these two.

I glanced out toward the front lawn and true to form, Sam was pacing back and forth on the sidewalk immediately in front of the hotel's grassy front lawn. He was gesturing calmly with his right hand while holding the phone to his ear with the other. Sam is left-handed, a sign of creativity, I've always thought.

Walking up the same sidewalk, momentarily blocking my view of Sam, a very handsome couple dressed top to bottom in sleek black approached the hotel. Both were slim and tall. I guessed that they must be from the east coast, based solely on their appearance. They turned slightly toward me as they ascended the stairs, making their way to the hotel's entrance in the center of the porch. I continued to observe them, hoping to make eye contact so that I could smile to them in a 'Welcome to Colorado" way and also to see how attractive each was in the face. The woman was somehow familiar looking. She had long blond shiny hair and an expensive looking handbag, the brand of which I couldn't quite make out. I wondered if she was an actress or celebrity, but couldn't quite tell. I still had not seen her face straight on. The man beside her was handsome from what I could tell. Dark in both hair and complexion. His black leather collarless motorcycle jacket appeared rich looking in its lack of adornment and it fit him like a buttery glove. They passed to my right, entering the hotel's lobby and then I noticed the fragrance that one or both of them was wearing. The scent was pleasant to me, like pepper, sweet plum and tobacco. It smelled expensive, and familiar.

Turning my focus back toward the front lawn and to Sam, I saw that he had returned his phone to his pocket. He climbed the ten or so steps up to me and smiled at the elderly couple and then at me. "Sorry about that. Just a last minute question about a chart we have in our proposal for SEATAC. The staff is having the red team meeting on it right now."

"No worries, Sam. I have just been sitting here with Olive and people watching. Did you see the couple in black that just walked into the hotel?"

"No, can't say that I did. What about them?"

"Oh, nothing. They were just really attractive and somehow seemed familiar. I wonder where I may have seen them before. They might be actors or something. Wouldn't that be fun to have a famous couple staying here?"

"Never can tell. It's a small world, especially the older one gets." Nonplussed, he continued, "Are you and Olive ready to go to our room and throw some boots on?"

Having heard Sam utter her name, Olive raised her head and hopped down off the settee. "Yes, I'm finished with my tea. Let's go. Olive will be happy to have a nap while we ride," I said standing up and handing Olive's leash to Sam. Sam signed for the check and we walked down the stairs and along the front side walk to the Lodge building on the left. It was just past the small front parking lot, beside the main hotel.

The Lodge turned out to basically be a mini version of the original hotel building. We climbed a few exterior stairs up to an identically outfitted, but much smaller veranda, and into a lovely intimate lobby. This lobby did not contain a Stanley Steamer car. It was designed with more of a chic mountain cabin esthetic, more modern. The antlers that hung above the entrance, I noticed, were not real, but rather hand carved from some varietal of hardwood. Nice, I thought, as I've never been a fan of dead animal parts as interior design elements. There was no formal front desk in the Lodge, and we were welcomed by a petite woman sitting behind a large antique steamer trunk which had been converted into a sit down front desk.

"You must be the Hendricks?" she asked gaily. "Stephanie, our manager, phoned to tell me you are here. Your luggage, which arrived yesterday, has been placed into your suite upstairs. It's number 420, one of our best guest rooms, with a view that I'm sure you will adore. I've set up your little canine friend here with a dog bed, bowls and some fresh-baked biscuits. By the way, my name is Molly and I run the Lodge. Please don't hesitate to let any of my staff or me know if there is anything that we can do for you during your stay."

"Thank you Molly. You can call me Sam, this is my wife Lauren and our dog is named Olive. Olive is very friendly and she loves the Stanley's biscuits. One question: does the Lodge also provide room service twenty-four hours a day?"

"Certainly. Just dial zero from your room phone anytime day or night for anything you might want. Like the main hotel, the Lodge is also fully staffed around the clock."

"Perfect. We're happy to be here. We can find our way up. Thanks again Molly," said Sam reaching for my arm and turning us toward the elevator.

We rode the small elevator (happily encountering no paranormal activity) to the fourth floor, and exited into a well-lit hallway. Olive's nose was to the ground, eagerly sniffing all the scents the carpeting apparently offered as we walked to the far right end of the floor, where our suite was situated. Sam pulled the key card from his wallet, opened the door and handed another room key card to me.

"Oh, this suite is lovely, Sam. Look at those antlers above the fireplace, they're not real, they are carved wood, like downstairs in the lobby. Isn't that cool, Sam?"

Plopping down on our king-size bed with a rustic but smoothly carved wooden headboard, Sam agreed, "I didn't see the antlers downstairs, but yes, those are beautiful. I'm glad they are wood and not real. We'll have to ask Molly if they were carved by a local artist. I think they would look terrific in my office, and they're PC so none of my vegan clients would get upset."

I turned and saw that our luggage had already been placed in the dressing area of the suite. I walked over and counted out our four bags which I had couriered to the property the day before. Then I walked across the large room to the sitting area which contained two small couches facing one another in front of a gas fireplace and a desk facing toward the largest window. I saw a small paper sack tied with a purple ribbon on the desk and opened it to find four dog biscuits that smelled good enough to eat myself. "Olive, come here, sweet stuff," I said. She trotted over and I gave her one of the delicious treats after she sat down for me. While she ate, I picked up one of the bowls which had been placed on the floor next to the desk and carried it into the powder room to fill it with water for her. The bathroom was large with light grey and white Carrera marble wainscot high all the way around the room. There was a large sunken and jetted bathtub, separate dual-head, walk-in shower and double sinks accented with square-cut glass pendant lights hanging above the bathtub and each sink. I returned to Olive with her water bowl. She was just finishing her treat by licking up the last crumbs from the wood floor.

To Sam, who was still lying on the bed on the far side of the large room, I said, "I'm going to change my jeans and pull on a sweater and my boots and I'll be ready to go in a few minutes." I looked at the clock on the desk. It was just after three o'clock.

"We need to get over to the stable so we can beat sunset, which will be here in about two and a half hours," I said.

I changed quickly, while Sam pulled on his boots and we left Olive to nap. We headed back down through the lobby and out into the brisk mountain air. The sun was still shining, but our shadows had become longer since we'd first arrived.

"Do you want to drive over?" Sam asked me.

"I'd prefer to walk, if it's all the same to you, Sam. We've been inside the car already so much today and it's a short walk. Less than a mile, if I remember correctly."

"Fine. Should only take us fifteen minutes or so to get there."

We headed down the Stanley's private drive on foot and veered left on a multi-use crusher fine trail toward Lake Estes. We didn't see any more elk along the way and the traffic that passed nearby us on the road was light. We arrived to the stable quickly and saw a half-dozen horses tethered to their front hitching post. The rest must have already been stabled for the day. We entered Sombrero Stables' office and introduced ourselves to a young man whose name tag said *Geoff – Agoura, California*. Sam asked Geoff if he had two mild-mannered horses tacked and ready for us to take out along their main, close-in trail for just an hour's ride. Geoff sized us both up and asked "guided or un-guided?" Sam told him either, but that we would prefer unguided today as it would be such a short ride. Geoff affirmed and led us out of the office's side door toward the horse coral. He suggested a medium-size chestnut with a pronounced star named Pablo for me. For Sam he offered a larger, stocky draft horse that was almost black, named Charles. Sam liked large, calm horses, and I knew he was pleased when he smiled and rubbed Charles on the cheek. Both horses were already saddled, and we mounted with the help of a step that Geoff brought over to each of us. Geoff led us around back to the opposite side of the stable and to the main trailhead which began and ended there. He waved us off by telling us to have fun, not to let the horses graze too much, Charles apparently tended to be a glutton, and to be back no later than five o'clock as it would be getting dark by then and Geoff would want to be getting home.

Chapter 18

PABLO FELT GREAT underneath me. Strong, but nimble. Sam, on the towering and sturdy Charles, rode beside us on the wide dirt trail leading up and away from Sombrero Stables and Lake Estes, which was now at our backs. We rode our horses at a walk, and I patted Pablo's strong neck with my right hand while making sure to keep the reins even and relaxed in my left. I love riding a horse, particularly in the Colorado mountains with its never-ending picture worthy scenery. Every time that I have the opportunity to go for a trail ride, I ask myself why I don't do this more often.

"Sam, why don't we do this more often?"

"Because we have too many varied interests and hobbies, Lauren. We're always doing different activities and to ride more frequently would mean sacrificing something else that we also enjoy."

Always the voice of reason, I dropped the subject. Sam was right. As much as I, and we, love riding, we'd never be expert horse people as we didn't have enough free time to dedicate to riding and wouldn't want to take time away from golfing, camping, tennis, traveling, poker, bunko, snowboarding and the other sundry interests we enjoy. As Sam has often said over the years "we are good at many things, and experts at none."

Our horses smelled nice, particularly mixed with the fresh scent of pine sap and the dry, earthy trail dust in the air. I was just relaxing into Pablo's stride when Sam and Charles pulled out in front of us. Sam gave Charles a little squeeze and they trotted up ahead. I remained walking, concentrated on balancing in my saddle, and breathed deeply while enjoying the scenery. Sam was out of eyesight as Pablo and I climbed higher and rounded a bend in the trail. The well-worn path was beginning to narrow to single-track trail with scrub and boulders lining each side. Every now and again, I had to duck below a branch extending over the path, which made me smile. Just the right amount of hazard to make weekend riders pay attention, I thought. Next the trail began a descent into a pristine meadow. As my field of view opened up, I saw Sam on Charles in the middle of the meadow. Charles had his nose in the grasses beside the trail, undoubtedly grazing. I now gave Pablo a little squeeze with my heels and made a click-click sound, and we picked up our pace trotting the few hundred yards toward Sam. Even fully dressed, I felt like Godiva. I can only imagine how great it would feel to ride fully naked, alone through the mountains on a warm summer day.

"Good idea, Lauren. I feel like Gary Cooper!" exclaimed Sam as I gently pulled Pablo's reins, stopping a few feet away. Sam and I often shared uncannily similar thoughts at virtually the same time.

"Only thing that could make this better would be seventy degrees and naked, huh, Sam?" I laughed.

"Agreed, but I'd like to keep my shorts on if it's all the same to you." With that I got a wink, and Sam said, "Let's keep going to the top of the ridge there, check out the view and then it'll probably be time to head back."

"Deal."

With a bit of effort Sam got Charles to stop eating and to turn around. They trotted ahead of us through the meadow, which aside from the packed down trail that we were on, showed no signs of human life. I scanned for animals near the forests edge which surrounded the entire meadow but saw nothing. On the far side, Sam slowed to a walk for the trail's next steep slope up to the top of the ridge ahead of us. As Pablo and I caught up, the pine trees thickened again and the trail became softer and more silent due to the cushion of pine needles under hoof. We switched back and then traversed diagonally along the face of the ridge. I could not see the meadow we had just been in because already the foliage was thick. It felt like Sam and I, and Pablo and Charles, were the only living beings within miles. Living in a city, it's quite an ethereal experience to realize the quiet of absolutely no man-made sounds. We weren't far from civilization, but it certainly felt as if we were in a remote wilderness without any sound of cars or people.

The next switchback in the trail was even steeper and passed on the outside of some rough stone steps that had been carved into the slope, mostly likely by Colorado's Forest Service. There was a wooden handrail on one side of the steps.

The trail took a sharp turn around the steps and then flattened out toward what looked like our last diagonal stretch up to the top of the ridge. When we arrived at the top about five minutes later, we stopped the horses.

The rim where we stood was approximately as wide as a one lane street. We could see where the trail continued down the other side into yet another valley and then up to an even higher, rockier peak. The sun was beginning to set in the direction from which we had come. From this vantage on the rim we could see parts of Lake Estes far below. Patches of water glistened in the day's last light. From here it looked as if we had come maybe three miles up and away from the stable.

"Look Lauren," said Sam breaking my momentary nature inspired revelry. "Look at the hawk there, circling to the left."

"Geez, that's a large bird," I said. "He's circling. Do you think he's spotting his dinner?"

"Probably he has his eye on a squirrel or mouse and is just waiting for his opportunity to attack."

"I've said it before, Sam, but these animals have it hard enough. I've never understood why people need to hunt wild animals for sport."

"I'd love to argue the point with you Lauren, but we need to head back. As it is, we'll be a few minutes late getting these horses back to Geoff and I don't think Olive will let them stay with her in our room for the night."

"Promise me we'll get back up here again for a longer ride before we leave."

"I promise. Let's go."

I patted Pablo again, told him he was a good boy and followed Sam back down the same trail we had taken up. Walking down I realized just how far up we had climbed. The trail, even on the diagonal, seemed very steep going down and I leaned back in the saddle to help compensate for the angle.

"Do you think this is forty degrees?" I called to Sam. "It seems more dramatic going down."

"More like thirty degrees Lauren, but look at this."

We were approaching the same stone steps from above this time and they descended steeply. From this angle it looked like two stories worth of hard stone steps, all in slightly varying heights, due to the uneven rocks that had been used to forge them.

"Geez, I'm not sure those steps are any safer than the trail we're on, hairpin curve and all. I wonder why they even put them here."

"I'm only guessing, but maybe the trail gets too icy for hikers later in the winter or perhaps it floods-out here in the spring?" said Sam.

We continued walking down along the outside edge of the rickety wooden handrail. At the bottom, I sat up straight for the next, more gently sloping grade section of path. We switched back again, and I ducked at the crest of the curve to avoid a branch which I hadn't remembered being there on the way up. We approached the grassy, open meadow a few minutes later and Sam began to trot on Charles. More confident in Pablo, I followed suit at a quick clip, which Pablo seemed eager to do. We slowed the horses once more for the last section of our ride. As the trail widened and the trees thickened, daylight faded fast which it always does when it abruptly ducks behind a mountain range. I was relieved to see the stable a few minutes later, and Pablo was happy to see it also, as he ever so slightly picked up his pace and perked his ears.

"I'm so hungry I could eat a horse and the rider" said Sam as we walked Olive around the Stanley's lawn for her post-dinner constitutional.

"Not funny, Sam. But I'm starving too. It's all this mountain air. Let's order plenty of appetizers for the table, before we all decide on our entrées, ok? You know how long the French like to take for supper."

"Soup, calamari and Rocky Mountain oysters it is."

"We totally have to order Rocky Mountain oysters for Marie and Franco! Great idea, Sam. They'll probably love them and will also have a terrific story for their friends back home. Let's let them think they are regular oysters, until they are served to our table, ok?" "They are actually delicious, Lauren, crisp on the outside, juicy and soft within, and the Stanley prepares them exceptionally well, as I recall," said Sam.

I grunted as we turned back toward the Lodge. Sam threw Olive's waste bag away in a closed, bear-proof trash receptacle. I told Sam I would wait on the porch for him while he returned Olive to our suite.

When Sam returned to meet me without Olive, it was exactly seven o'clock. I stood and we walked hand in hand along the sidewalk to the main hotel lobby. Unlike the Lodge lobby, the main lobby was bustling with people. Sam waved to a woman behind the front desk, who must have been the assistant manager named Stephanie. I smiled and nodded toward her as we passed. We entered to a warm glow, emanating from the up lighting beneath the onyx surface of the bar top running the length of the Whisky Bar. The bar area is situated in between the lobby and the Crimson Room restaurant. A perfect location to meet one's dining companions. I scanned the length of the bar for Marie and Franco but did not see them, so Sam and I took seats at the far end. As I perused the drinks menu and Sam took in the hundreds of whiskey, scotch, bourbon, and rye bottles displayed on the wall behind the bar, I heard our names called out in Marie's unmistakable accent.

"Did you enjoy your rest?" I asked Marie and Franco as Sam stood to pull out the bar stool next to me for Marie. "You both look refreshed, I must say."

"Merci. I feel much better," said Marie giving me a small kiss on each cheek as she sat down.

"I do as well," said Franco as he and Sam shook hands and he bent to give me a quick kisses as well. "Our suite is very nice and the bed quite comfortable. Marie and I both approve," he said smiling toward to Marie with what I am sure was a glint of satisfaction in his eyes. "I am very hungry now though. Would it be alright with you two if we went right in to our table?"

"I couldn't agree with you more, Franco. Why don't you ladies stay seated for just a moment and we'll go ask the hostess if our table is ready," said Sam.

"They both clean up very well don't they, Marie? I think we are with the two best-looking men here," I said to Marie as they had moved out of earshot.

"We are lucky indeed," she responded. Then, "This trip was a good idea, Lauren. Franco has been so relaxed, so fun, since the moment we departed Nice. I just wish he would be like this at home." She sighed lightly and concluded with, "But I suppose this is why one vacations, to relax and remove oneself from the drudgeries of everyday life."

"Very common in men especially, I think, Marie. When they are able to detach from work and office, I think a large weight is lifted. No matter how much they enjoy their work, vacationing by definition is relaxing. And we all are our best selves when relaxed, aren't we?"

"Franco doesn't have to work you know Lauren. I am his second wife. The first Madame Alix was quite wealthy and left him a rather large sum, so money is not a problem."

"Marie, are you saying that Franco profited by his first wife's death?"

"Oh, yes. Franco's family is wonderful, but not well off financially. Hers was, and she had no siblings. She left everything to Franco. He does not need to work, but I guess I should be grateful that he's driven."

"Often men do need to work though, to feel useful."

"You're right, Lauren, but he just doesn't seem to really *like* me at home. He acts as if I am a distraction. He's all consumed with work. I hardly see him. Sometimes I just miss Jan so much. He started our distribution firm from the ground up, you know, but I always felt truly loved by Jan, even when he worked long hours."

Just then a young woman approached and told us that our table was ready and to please follow her. As we did, I said, "We can talk about this more after dinner if you'd like to, Marie."

The Crimson Room's dining room contained about twenty free-standing tables and four larger banquet tables. The room was about three quarters full and a din of diners' conversations filled my ears as we walked in. I wondered if Franco and Marie would notice how loudly Americans speak. Sam and I are rather loud people, but after returning to the States after our European travels, I am always sensitive to the sheer volume of Americans in public places for the first few weeks until I get used to the clamor again.

Our husbands were engrossed with thoughts of dinner, each of their heads buried in their menus, as we arrived to the table. The hostess pulled out a chair for Marie and then for me. She laid our menus on the table as we sat.

"I've already ordered appetizers, ladies," announced Sam. "Franco and I couldn't wait. Please just decide what you'd like to drink."

"Do you like Chardonnay, Marie? The have an outstanding one by a Napa vineyard called *Rombauer*. I first learned of it here during our last stay and have rarely had one better since, except of course for the one made by the monks living on the island just off shore of Cannes."

"The monks' wine is top-notch, no doubt about it. Sells out every season," said Franco with good humor, "But I'm willing to bet Marie would like a gin and tonic tonight, to start. Marie, they have Bombay Sapphire. I know you like that one."

"Yes, that is exactly what I'd like. Thank you, Franco."

A bread basket arrived, along with two additional glasses of water for Marie and me. I picked up the basket and peered under the cloth. It was filled with fresh, warm baked rolls and breads. "One of the signatures of the Stanley property are the scratch-made baked goods; everything from fresh morning scones to dog biscuits to the bread basket before us now," I said passing the basket to Marie.

"Did your Olive receive gourmet doggie biscuits? That is such a nice touch. Where is she now? In your suite?"

"Yes. I'm sure she's happily sleeping. This was a rather big day for her."

Our server, a mature man in white shirt and black tie arrived to inform us that our soups and appetizers would arrive shortly, and to take our drink orders. Sam ordered a perfect Maker's Mark Manhattan and a glass of the Rombauer for me. Franco ordered Marie's Bombay and tonic and asked our server which whisky he recommended. Unfazed, our waiter began by inquiring if Franco was visiting Colorado. Franco affirmed and was expertly advised to begin by trying a Colorado distilled whisky called Stranahans. Franco ordered one, neat.

"I believe you'll enjoy the Stranahans's Franco," said Sam. I think it is very good. I should have probably ordered it myself, but I sometimes find myself in the habit of ordering the same thing time and time again."

Our drinks arrived swiftly followed moments later by our first course. Sam had ordered warm winter squash soup for us all. It was topped with turnip shavings, which added color as well as a satisfying crunch.

"Delicious," pronounced Marie followed by appreciative murmurs of approval from Franco.

"What shall we all do tomorrow? After we sleep in, of course," Sam asked as our bowls were cleared and fresh plates placed.

Marie and Franco remained silent, so I threw out my idea of going into the town of Estes in the early afternoon to explore, window shop and scout out where we wanted to dine that evening. Everyone agreed that that sounded fun, after I further colored the town as having a real Western feel.

Our calamari and Rocky Mountain oysters arrived and Sam served one oyster and a small portion of the lightly fried squid to all of us.

"What type of oyster is this Sam?" asked Franco. "There is no ocean here. Is this farm-raised perhaps? I've never had a deep-fried oyster before."

Before Sam or I could answer, Marie had taken a bite and smiled pleasantly. I tried not to regret our little inside appetizer joke, since Marie had taken a bite before we could explain. I looked to Sam, leaving the proverbial ball in his court.

Rightfully, before answering, he cut his oyster in half and ate it. I did the same in solidarity. "Rocky Mountain oysters are a delicacy in the west, usually only served at restaurants that specialize in game meats, like the Crimson Room here. These Rocky Mountain oysters are not oysters at all, but rather sheep testicles which have been peeled, pounded flat, dipped in flower and deep fried."

"Oh my," is what Marie said.

"Amazing," responded Franco. "Why on earth would they be called oysters? Is it simply to trick foreigners?"

"No, Franco," said Sam laughing. "I believe they're called oysters because they have a very similar juiciness inside the fried, crispy outside. Don't feel obligated to eat one, if you'd rather not."

I love the way that grown men still resort to "I dare you" techniques in polite society. It worked. Sam took his second bite and Franco tried his oyster then as well, pronouncing it delicious, and yes, very similar to what he imagined a fried oyster would be like. I finished my oyster as well. Marie took a rather long sip of her drink, picked up her fork and said, "Sometimes in life, it's best not to know," before finishing her oyster too.

I raised my glass in a toast and said, "The calamari is going to be blasé in comparison!"

Chapter 19

After finishing our second course appetizers, we all perused the Crimson Room's menu. We weighed the pros and cons of almost each entrée. Moments like this make me think of the irony of my younger self's relationship with food. When I was in school, as well as, for several years after undergrad, I was literally hungry all the time and didn't often have enough disposable income for gourmet meals such as we were enjoying now. I often didn't have enough extra money for even an Olive Garden meal. Back then, when I would attend a party or social event, there was never much good food offered or served, just plenty of inexpensive booze. Now that I'm older, I'm rarely truly hungry, and have access to more good food than I need or sometimes even want. Every social event that I attend now as an adult practically revolves around copious amounts of food. Appetizers are passed, buffet tables are full of hot and cold options, cakes and desserts are served. Now that I don't want it or need it, food is everywhere and often free.

Sam chose the house specialty Colorado game meatloaf made with elk, buffalo and pork, Franco ordered the Colorado rack of lamb served with root vegetable couscous, and Marie decided on the seared scallops with cauliflower puree. When there was no more time left for me to vacillate, I asked for the pepper crusted Rocky Mountain trout with red quinoa. Our server asked if we would like another round of drinks and Sam and Franco decided instead to order a bottle of wine for us to share with our meals.

Marie leaned toward me after our waiter retreated leaving the men with the wine menu to decide on a bottle. She asked if I would like to join her for a cigarette before our dinner arrived. "Surely," I replied. We stood and excused ourselves. We backtracked through the dining room, which was now almost filled to capacity. The older couple who I had observed on the veranda that afternoon were eating at a table by the window. They were not speaking now either, I noticed. We strolled through the Whisky Bar and instead of heading to the right and outside toward the veranda, I motioned for Marie to follow me to the rear side of the lobby where I knew a lovely sculpture garden was located just outside. We found a table and chairs on the far edge of the garden beside a life-size bronze statue of a young doe.

Exhaling a plume of smoke into the chilly night air, I asked Marie about her outfit. As usual, she was dressed beautifully for dinner. I loved the current iteration of her Colorado wardrobe of cashmere sweater and slim trousers.

"Loro Piana makes the best quality cashmere I think," Marie responded. "They have a lovely little boutique in Cannes, filled with beautiful young Italian salesgirls. I found this outfit on sale just after Christmas, before I even knew that Franco and I would be traveling here, to cold weather."

"It suits you to a tee, Marie. I just love that color on you. I noticed you wore a similar shade when I last laid eyes on you in France. Is green your favorite color?"

"Always has been. I've always believed green is the color of good luck, plus a boyfriend many years ago when I was young once said green becomes me, so I've been wearing it ever since."

As we sat and smoked, the Stanley's clock tower sounded nine beautiful tones from the bell at the very top of the hotel. I wanted to ask Marie more about how she and Franco were getting along at home, now that they had been married for a few months. I wanted to ask her what she had meant, just before dinner, when she had said that he did not have to work any longer and inferred that he wasn't home much, but I thought it better to let her continue with her story when and if she felt like it. Instead, I took a couple more puffs of Marie's delicious French cigarette and then stubbed it out in the glass ashtray on our table. She did the same, then stood and said, "We'd better go to the powder room and get back to our table before Sam and Franco eat our meals."

After washing our hands and reapplying our lipstick, we exited the restroom together and walked through the lobby back toward the Whiskey Bar. As we approached the front desk area I noticed the familiar blonde standing at the desk speaking with the clerk on duty. I touched Marie's arm and said, "Just a moment, Marie." I pulled Marie back a few feet from the desk area, hiding slightly beside the Stanley Steamer automobile. We stood and I stared at the blonde woman's back, who still seemed familiar to me. I said, "Marie, I think that blonde lady there at the front desk might be an actress. I saw her earlier today with a most handsome man, and thought she looked famous, like I'd seen her before on TV or in a film or something. Do you mind if we wait for just a moment to see if she turns around?"

"I'd love to meet an American celebrity. Who do you think she is?"

"That's just it. I can't quite place her, but I know I've seen her before somewhere."

We watched for a moment from our vantage which was behind and to the right of the front desk counter. Her body language, I noticed, seemed aggressive. Both of her hands were on the counter, her shoulders pulled up and she was leaning forward. Just then she stomped her boot-clad foot. Her heel audibly clacked on the walnut wood floor.

"She seems upset," whispered Marie. "Are we about to witness an American reality star throwing a tantrum?"

I turned my head and giggled. "Maybe, Marie. Wouldn't that be something… so American. Maybe we should get out our cell phones to take a picture of her to sell to the gossip magazines when she explodes?"

"How dare you! How could this happen? Where is the manager?" came her voice loudly with another stomp of her foot as a sort of punctuation to her irritation.

That voice. Where have I heard it before? I pulled Marie a little further to the side, so that we would be more to the far right side of the front desk and less behind her.

"I am sorry ma'am, but I am sure we can work something out. Please wait here while I bring the manager," said the clerk before turning and disappearing into the office behind the counter.

She exhaled audibly, and said "This is fucking unbelievable," out loud to herself without turning.

No. It couldn't be.

"Liv?" I said aloud not expecting a response.

The blonde's head turned in our direction as soon as the name left my lips. We stared at one another for a few seconds, which felt like a full minute. Her brow was furrowed, her eyes sharp. She was clearly angry about something. Then it happened. She recognized me. Her eyes softened and grew wide, like in a cartoon drawing.

"Lauren?" she asked.

"Oh my god. Yes. Is it really you, Liv?" I said walking over to her.

"Lauren. I'm speechless. I don't know what to say. I'm so mad right now. The hotel has lost one of my bags and I was just arguing with the clerk here who has no explanation whatever."

"I can't believe it's you, Liv! You are the absolute last person I expected to run into up here in the mountains. I actually saw you this afternoon as you were walking into the hotel. I thought you looked familiar, but I did not recognize you until just now when I heard your voice as we were passing by! Oh, excuse me. This is my friend, Marie. We're up here for the next few nights with our husbands."

"Hello," said Marie. Then, "How do you two know one another?"

"It's been years and years, Marie. Liv, here, she was my best friend growing up. This is incredible," I said turning back to face Liv. "We lost touch after school. We haven't seen one another in what... twenty years at least? I knew I recognized you, Liv. I just had no idea it was you! What on earth are you doing here in Colorado of all places? Don't you live in Chicago these days?"

"Yes, I do." Her eyes darted around. "I'm sorry, I'm just so distracted right now, Lauren. It's great to see you, but I simply *must* find my bag."

"Oh sure. I understand. Will you be staying for a while? We have to catch up on the last twenty years! I have missed you. It's been so long."

"My fiancé and I are staying through Sunday. Oh, where is that damn manager?" she said next, turning back toward the front desk.

Not exactly the warm reception I would have expected from Liv after all these years, but then again, I had possession of all of my luggage, so I said, "We have so much to catch up on. I had no idea you were getting married. Sam is here too, Liv. He will also be happy to see you. Perhaps we can talk tomorrow?" I took a step forward and gave Liv a tentative hug. She was tight. She felt wound up like a top, but she lifted her arms and returned my felicitation.

"Yes. Tomorrow. I'm really am pleased to see you, Lauren. I'm sorry, this is just a complete surprise. Once this *damn hotel* locates my bag, I'll be less distracted. We'll visit tomorrow, Lauren. I promise."

"Nice to have met you, and good luck for your bag," said Marie. We turned and walked back through the bar and toward our table in the dining room.

"Marie, that was my absolute closest friend growing up. I simply cannot believe that she is here in this hotel right now too. I'm silently freaking out; it's like my very oldest and very newest friends are both here, in the same place at the same time. It feels like an altered reality. I love it."

Having seen us approaching, both Franco and Sam stood. "What has taken you two so long?" asked Franco justifiably.

"In the lobby, we just ran into an old friend that Lauren recognized," answered Marie.

"No kidding? Male or female?" joked Sam. "Who was it Lauren?"

"Guess."

"I'll give you a clue Sam!" chimed in Marie. "She's a she. She's very blonde and very angry."

"Hillary Clinton!" gamely guessed Sam.

We all begged off dessert opting instead for one more drink in the Whiskey Bar after we had finished our dinner. I had filled Sam in on running into Liv, of all people, here in the middle of the mountains. I told him she was distracted, stressing over a lost piece of luggage, but that she was here with a man whom she was going to marry. Regardless of her bad temper at the front desk, we've all been there, I was happy to have seen her.

At the bar, I told Marie and Franco the story of Liv's and my long-ago friendship. I told them how we were inseparable during school and how we attended our first live rock concert together. The concert had been of a one-hit-wonder band called *Quiet Riot* and we had stolen booze from our parents to sneak into the show. Liv had poured her parents' vodka into a Jean Naté fragrance bottle (a popular eau du toilette for teenagers at the time). I'll never forget how it made our illicit drink smell and taste like the inexpensive scent.

Sam already knew all the stories and I realized I was monopolizing the conversation with the many memories of Liv that had come rushing back, so I was grateful to see Jarvis enter the bar with another man. Jarvis was dressed in a boldly patterned shirt and freshly polished shoes. He wore a genuine smile and flashed perfectly un-genuine teeth.

"Jarvis," I called, waving to him and his friend.

"Good evening. Let me introduce my partner, Kip," he said putting his arm around the more conservatively dressed man in a beautiful cobalt suit.

We each introduced ourselves and the two men bellied up to the bar alongside the four of us. Jarvis and Kip were a hoot right off the bat and I was starting to feel my drinks; an excellent combination. They told us stories of a year they had dropped out and lived off the grid in an artists' colony outside of Flagstaff, Arizona, and of getting married in Hawaii by a world-class surfer who was also an ordained minister before gay marriage had been legalized in most other American states. We were all feeling good and talking freely. At one point Franco almost slipped off of his bar stool laughing at the yarn Jarvis spun about his coming out as a gay man during a college break in Jamaica, one of the most un-gay-friendly countries. Kip was quickly enamored with Marie, as Jarvis had predicted, and engaged her with many questions about all things French. I heard him exclaim more than once "My dear, with your accent you could talk the fuzz off of a peach." I didn't know exactly what he meant by that, and I'm quite sure Marie didn't either, but Kip and Jarvis were both so ardently charming that we all ordered a second round at the beautifully up-lit onyx bar, not wanting the evening to end.

Chapter 20

Olive, who is a late sleeper, woke us up at the crack of noon. She was ready to go outside and do some exploring of her new environs. Sam pulled on some clothes and took her outside promising me to bring back a few freshly baked scones, if they were any still available in the breakfast room. I finished the water from my glass on the nightstand and walked around to each window pulling opening every drapery. I gazed out toward the town of Estes Park down below our hotel. It was another bluebird day but I noticed a few guests, outside near the front lawn, had hats and caps on.

Colorado, particularly in the mountains, can be deceptive. It looks warm from indoors with the sun shining, but the outside air can be very, very brisk in spite of the sun. I looked left, toward the lake, and saw two runners coming up the trail. A moment later, as they got closer to the front lawn, I recognized Liv. She was dressed in skintight black running gear and had her bright long hair pulled up into a high pony tail. The handsome man beside her was also in black workout gear. He wore it only slightly looser. It must have been the man I had seen with Liv yesterday, but I could not quite tell as he had a knit cap pulled low on his forehead. They were running together, not jogging, and appeared to be in excellent shape, not winded at all, even at this altitude. They slowed to a stop in the middle of the hotel's front lawn and then both began an elaborate stretching routine to cool down.

I thought of Liv while I brewed a cup of coffee in our room's Keurig machine. I was looking forward to catching up with her and also to meeting the man she was with. Would his personality live up to his good looks and his excellent shape, I wondered? I recalled that when I had last seen our mutual friend Robyn in Denver a couple months ago, she had said that Liv was dating a rich and very handsome man. Was this him?

I wandered into the bathroom with my coffee and eyed the huge jetted tub. Sam had not showered before taking Olive out. I betted that if I ran a bath instead of taking my normal shower, and if I was inside of the beautiful tub upon his return, I would be able to get him to join me in the hot, soapy water.

Bathed, dressed and smiling like a schoolgirl, I walked along the sidewalk with Sam and Olive to the main hotel's veranda to meet up with Marie and Franco for our day's excursion. They were already there, sitting on the beautiful porch with empty espresso cups in front of them.

"Bonjour," called Marie when she saw us. Olive pulled toward Marie at the sound of her voice, tail wagging. Marie immediately petted Olive and cooed over her arrival which garnered Marie several kisses on the hand, as well as Olive's signature propeller tail wag.

Becoming more comfortable with the custom, Sam and I also greeted Marie with cheek kisses. Franco smiled and asked how we had slept.

"Very well, thank you, Franco," responded Sam. "I'm so glad we slept in late today. I needed it. How about you? Do you feel jet lagged at all?"

"No. I'm fine. Marie, on the other hand, did not sleep so soundly and I'm afraid she has a headache today," said Franco frowning.

"Oh Franco, don't be so dramatic. I am fine. This espresso has perked me up."

"Marie, have you been drinking water?" asked Sam, turning to her. "At this altitude, it is very common to experience altitude sickness, especially as we were all drinking at dinner and well after, last night. A headache is the most common first symptom."

"Sam's right, Marie," I chimed in before she could answer.

"That's probably what it is. That and all the travel. I finally fell asleep around four this morning, but once I did, I slept right though until noon."

"Do you need some aspirin, Marie? I have some back in our suite. I'd be happy to go get it for you."

"No, no. I am fine. Franco, see what you have started?" said Marie, now frowning back to him.

Sam motioned to the waitress who was just on the other end of the porch. "Would you prefer sparkling or still Marie?"

"Thank you Sam. Sparkling please. San Pel, if they have it."

Sam ordered a large San Pellegrino bottle and asked for four glasses and some lemon wedges on the side. Even in very small ways, Sam is a man of action and I have always loved that about him. We sat in silence for a few minutes waiting for our water to arrive. I felt a bit awkward and was reminded again of why I hadn't understood Marie's decision to marry Franco in the first place. He had shown no compassion, even in front of Sam and me, for her possible jet lag, dehydration or altitude sickness. I can't imagine how it must have been for her at home while she had been truly sick over the holidays.

Franco broke the silence first by asking what we should do this afternoon and then added to Marie, as an afterthought, "If you feel up to it, of course, my dear."

The Stanley's clock tower bell rang two and Sam suggested that we all take Olive on a leisurely walk down into Estes Park.

My newest favorite word is promenade, which we did, down toward and around the quaint three-stoplight town of Estes Park. The men walked ahead. Sam held Olive's leash as she trotted alongside of him, happy to be outdoors exploring new smells and sights. Colorado is a dog-friendly state and most of the charming boutiques and shops had water bowls set up near their entrances; universal code that well-behaved dogs are welcomed inside that establishment.

As we walked behind and just out of earshot of Franco and Sam, I asked Marie if her first few months of being married to Franco were going well.

"It's just not like the first time, Lauren. I don't quite know how to answer you. Franco can be kind, charming and loving, but he also has an independent streak. Sometimes I'm not sure I can trust him as completely as I trusted Jan. When I was so very sick this winter, I felt he distanced himself from me. I felt like my illness was taking up too much of his time and energy, even though he had stayed away from home a lot."

"Do you think he was just giving you space to rest and recuperate, Marie? Some people, like me for instance, prefer to be alone when sick. It might just take more time for the two of you to better learn and understand one another and to develop more trust Marie."

"That's true, or maybe it's as good as it is going to be with Franco now and that should be good enough. Maybe we each only ever have *one* true love in life and we should be grateful for a second opportunity to merely have a partner to carry on with."

"As long as you feel safe and loved, Marie. You deserve that, we all do. Sometimes that is simply enough."

"Yes, we're all adults now and I'm committed to making this marriage work. Frankly, I feel badly that I've not been my usual picture of health for much of our marriage, so far. It's not like me to be so weak and ill, but I'm sure that's behind me now, as long as Colorado's thin air doesn't kill me!" she joked.

Laughing, I responded, "Don't even say that, Marie. You just need to drink more water than normal up here. You came all the way from sea level after all. Please make sure to drink plenty of water while you're here and just know that Sam and

I are in your court. You can call upon us anytime, even when you're back home, for anything, Marie."

The men had stopped in front of a restaurant bordering the pedestrian Riverwalk which ran through town. We quickly caught up to them as they perused the menu displayed near the front door.

"It's French Marie," said Franco. "I love French food. I wonder if it will be authentic. Shall we try this restaurant for dinner this evening?" Franco asked us all.

"Looks fine to me, if it's ok for Lauren and Sam," replied Marie.

"Absolutely. This is Bistro Vendome, one of the best restaurants in town. It's run by two female chefs, very notable, but I'm afraid I've forgotten their names right now," said Sam.

"I'd love to eat here tonight," I said. "It will be fun to learn how well you like their French cuisine, way up here in the mountains of Colorado, Franco. Why don't you and Marie go inside and look around though, before you decide? If you still like it, make a reservation for us. Sam and I will wait out here with Olive."

Franco opened the door and held it for Marie. They entered the dimly lit foyer together. Sam and I turned back on the Riverwalk sidewalk in order to sit down on the bench opposite the doors of the Bistro.

"How's it going with Franco?" I asked Sam and gave him a quick kiss.

"Well, I'd say. He's an interesting character. Quite a gambler from the sound of it. Do you know he currently owns six race horses?"

"Really? No, I didn't know that. That's so cool, but it sounds expensive. Did he tell you how they fared this racing season?"

"He said two are winners, one is breaking even, but still young, and the other three he's planning to put into claiming races next season. I'm actually learning a bit about the industry. It's quite interesting and I'm taking notes for you, for when you retire and become a gambler too, Lauren."

"It warms my heart to hear you say that, Sam. Makes me think that you think I'm serious about getting into a horse racing syndicate myself someday."

Sam knows that too much indulgence of my many fancies will go straight to my head, so he then changed the subject by asking, "How's it going with Marie? Is she feeling better now, I hope?"

"I think so. She was actually just telling me about her first few months married to Franco, Sam."

"Don't tell me anything more, Lauren," said Sam frowning. "And I advise you not to get too involved. It's best not to know too much about one's friends' marriages. No good can come from it and knowing too much can come back to bite you."

"You're right, Sam. For the record, I did ask Marie, I started it, but I will keep it light from now on. I remember what happened with my former friend Stacey when she got divorced like it was yesterday."

"Thank you."

When Marie and Franco regrouped with us outside, Franco informed us all with a big smile that they had perused the wine list and the menu, that Marie had visited the ladies room, and they found the Bistro very acceptable and that we had a dinner reservation for eight p.m. "It'll be our treat tonight," announced Franco with a friendly clap on Sam's arm.

"Excellent," I said. "That'll give us plenty of time to shop, return Olive to the hotel and freshen up before returning here for dinner. Speaking of which, let's walk along the Riverwalk. I remember a few cute shops near here which we should check out."

As we turned the corner, toward the water, a sharp cold wind hit us face on. The creek, fed from snow melt up in Rocky Mountain National Park and which cut through the center of town, clearly also acted as a wind tunnel much like the city blocks of high rise buildings in downtown Chicago do. The Lake Michigan effect in miniature.

"Liv!" I exclaimed. Liv and the dark haired man from yesterday were holding hands and walking directly toward us. "I was hoping to run into you again today!" I grabbed Sam by his free hand and pulled him and Olive forward the forty feet toward Liv.

She smiled her dazzling smile. I recognized it as if we had still been close friends, seeing one another regularly during the past two decades. She dropped the man's hand and reached out toward me. We hugged, which truthfully felt very nice to me, not awkward at all. Liv had been my first and best friend for many, many years.

"Lauren," she said. "I still cannot believe I've run into you here, but I am so glad to see you again. Holy shit! Is that you Sam?"

"This is like a very pleasant time-warp, Liv. Lauren told me that she saw you in the Stanley last night, but I could hardly believe it. I thought maybe she had had one too many, but here you are. It's very good to see you after so many years," said Sam before also hugging her.

The man with Liv cleared his throat.

Liv stroked her long hair, which now hung free, to straighten it and pull it forward over her right shoulder, while saying, "Sam and Lauren, you have to meet my fiancé, Harry Ross."

Harry extended his hand and Sam shook it introducing me as Lauren Hendrick, his wife and a very long-time friend of Liv's. He then expressed our happiness at their engagement and of running into Liv so unexpectedly here in Estes Park.

Harry shook my hand next as I looked him in the eyes and said how pleased I was to meet him. "And I must introduce our good friends Marie and Franco Alix," I said as I motioned for them to meet. We went around with further introductions and when the general pleasantries concluded, I asked Liv if she was still happy living in Chicago, as I had last heard, and how she and Harry had met.

"Yes, I've still got my condo on the Gold Coast, but Harry lives in New York City. As you can imagine, I've been spending more and more time in New York with Harry. I just love New York, it's like Chicago on steroids and without all the Midwesterners!"

"Have you heard that our old friend Nick opened a successful James Beard awarded restaurant on West Broadway?" I asked.

"Oh yes, Harry and I have dined there several times. It's just lovely. He must be raking it in, even *we* have to wait weeks for reservations," Liv added turning to look at Harry.

"Liv just means that I'm pretty well connected in the City, as my family has worked on Wall Street for generations. We can usually get past any Maitre d' on short notice," Harry said simply with stereotypical East Coast entitlement.

Midwesterners, I thought to myself, are not the worst of the lot. Sam, most likely sensing my thought, changed the subject by saying, "Liv, I have to say you look just wonderful. I can see life has treated you well. Lauren and I are so pleased to hear of your engagement. Tell me, when do you and Harry plan to tie the knot?"

"We're getting married in just a few weeks, March 15th, at the newly re-opened Rainbow Room. We've just finished all the paperwork and this is our last getaway before the wedding stress begins." Turning to Harry, Liv continued by saying, "We just have to invite Lauren and Sam now that you've met them. Lauren is from my hometown, my first best friend ever Harry." Turning back to us, "I still can't believe we've run into you here. Estes Park was my idea. I never thought we'd run into people we knew in this small town in the middle of nowhere."

"Of course. No question about it, Liv. Any friend of yours is a friend of mine. We'll make sure you receive an invitation," said Harry graciously.

"That's very kind," I said. Then, "Liv, I take it you will be moving to New York then?"

"Oh yes. I love the City. Harry's family has an enormous estate called Trommeter on the Gold Coast of Long Island. I swear it's like the Great Gatsby there; it takes fifteen minutes to walk from the kitchen to the front door. I guess I'm just drawn to anywhere called the Gold Coast, but Long Island's Gold Coast is the real deal, isn't that right, Harry?"

We all laughed politely and Harry had the good sense to look slightly abashed.

"Would you care to join the four of us for dinner tonight? We've just decided on Bistro Vendôme back there, around the corner," I asked Liv and Harry.

"I'm afraid we couldn't. Harry has some romantic plan for me this evening, don't you lover?"

Pursuing, I continued, "Perhaps we can meet up again for drinks at the Stanley tonight, after dinner then? I just have to hear more about what you have been up to all these years Liv."

"We'll most certainly stop by the bar, Lauren. Do you think you will be there around eleven or so?" said Harry.

Leave it to the French to be nonplussed. "That is some kind of childhood friend," said Marie. "I simply cannot wait to meet more of your old friends, Lauren."

"I know, right? Liv has always had attitude. For some reason I'm drawn to friends like that. You know, you and Franco aren't exactly wallflowers either."

"Tout à fait!" replied Marie.

"Sam, Franco, let's go in here," I said calling up ahead to them. "Marie, you'll just love this little jewelry shop."

We entered the small, warm shop, with Franco, Sam and Olive following. The store clerk, a grey-haired, outdoorsy type of man, greeted us. The floor was filled with custom-made, curved, well-lit display cases filled with shining rings, timepieces, necklaces and baubles. The walls displayed art glass pieces in all manner of color schemes. Marie and I walked around slowly while the men and canine perused the wrist watches.

"Lauren, look at this lovely piece." Marie was pointing out an emerald cocktail ring that was cut on the bias. The clerk immediately appeared and opened the cabinet to let Marie try it on.

"It's beautiful and green; your color, Marie. That unusual cut makes it look art deco. I love the cut of that stone. It's so retro but contemporary at the same time. It looks like it would fit right in at Liv's fiancé's Great Gatsby home," I said joking.

"Cocktail rings are meant to be daring," said Franco from behind me. "Marie, it looks wonderful on you. May I purchase it for you as a memento of our trip here to Colorado?"

I immediately stood aside, hoping that Franco would insist, regardless of what Marie might say next.

"Oui, Franco. Je suis amoureuse."

I turned to find Sam and Olive smiling at me from the far end of the shop. I walked over to them and patted Olive.

"I think Franco is buying Marie an emerald cocktail ring," I said to Sam. "Isn't that exciting? It's really pretty too."

Sam and I stayed clear until Marie walked over to show us her new gift. It truly was perfect for her. The color, the cut, the size; unique just like her.

"I'm glad you will forever have a memory of this vacation with us in Colorado, Marie. It looks beautiful on you," I said as she held her right hand out to show us.

"Oui. It's a beautiful, what do you say, souvenir," summed up Marie while Franco transacted with the salesman.

When we exited the shop, Marie pulled her cigarettes from her hand bag and lit one up. I asked her for one as well. The ring was perfect on her smoking hand as she lifted it to her face and I told her so. Then I whispered to her that I knew exactly what she could get for Franco as a souvenir. We slowly continued up the Riverwalk and as we approached the town's most authentic western store, I nudged her gently and said they have the best hats here.

She smiled and called for Franco and Sam to follow us inside. This store, called Shepler's, had a large selection of western wearables. Everything from sheepskin coats, to personalized silver belt buckles, cowboy hats and boots; it was a mecca of ranch to city accoutrements. Sam, Olive and I walked over to the ladies boots. Sam knows that I always have an eye open for the perfect boots to wear with jeans, and that I particularly like the Lucchese brand, which Shepler's, I immediately noticed, had a tremendous selection of. I eyed a cognac-colored pair of leather pumps that were finely stitched with the perfect heel and striped toe box. They were not boots at all, but rather sophisticated heels with a slight western feel, due to the stacked wooden heel and fine exposed stitching. The style could be dressed up or down.

"Try them on," encouraged Sam gamely.

I asked the clerk for two sizes and sat down, patting the seat next to me for Sam and Olive to take a load off. While we waited, we saw Franco trying on hats with Marie nearer the front door of the shop.

When the sales lady returned she opened both boxes for me and helped me slip on the smaller size first, which, of course, were a bit too small.

"I swear my feet have gotten larger as I've aged Sam," I said and I tried on the larger pair.

"Thankfully almost nothing else has," replied Sam loud enough for the saleslady to hear.

As I stood to walk around the store in the beautiful Lucchese western-styled pumps, the sales clerk asked Sam if she could give Olive a dog treat. I walked to the front of the store to show the shoes to Marie. She and Franco both verbalized their approval, so I decided the pumps would need to come home with me.

Franco, on the other hand, was not so sure about the hat he currently had on his head. I thought it looked terrific. I do love a man who can pull off a cowboy hat in appropriate situations, and Franco's tall frame and square jaw certainly could, but he had a point when he said that he didn't want to have to deal with it on the plane ride home.

"Perhaps a western belt with a nice silver buckle would better suit this situation, Franco," I said while glancing at Marie.

"Yes, Franco. Let's look at those. Wouldn't it be wonderful for you to have a real cowboy belt to wear in France? Everyone in our warehouse will call you J.R. Ewing!"

"And that's quite a compliment, Franco," I added. Then, "Plus, Sam told me you own some race horses. I imagine a big silver belt buckle will go over very well at the *hippodromes.*"

I returned to Sam, who was chatting amicably with the sales lady, and told them both that I had decided on the shoes.

"Good," said Sam. "I like them as well."

A few minutes later, I traded Sam my shopping bag for Olive's leash and we went in search of Marie and Franco who had momentarily disappeared from view in the large store.

When we found them, Franco was giving a different clerk his initials and pulling out his wallet. Marie smiled broadly at us and announced that Franco had decided on a finely tooled black leather belt with a silver oval buckle that would be engraved with Franco's initials. The clerk added that the shop would be happy to deliver the finished belt to the Stanley before we departed in three days.

Marie and Franco held hands as we continued toward the end of the Riverwalk. We then turned to the right and headed back to the hotel via Main Street. Main Street held more utilitarian shops than the touristy and luxury goods retailers located on the Riverwalk. We passed an independent coffee shop called the Mountain Sun, an Ace Hardware shop that looked like it was still circa 1950 inside, a townie bar advertising open mic night and cheap drink specials, the ubiquitous tourist t-shirt shop, a liquor store and a pet shop called Free Range. Olive deserved to go in and I asked if anyone minded if we popped in this shop as well.

"I'd love to pick something up for my little Vivi," exclaimed Marie. "I do miss her terribly, you know," she said leading our pack inside.

The shop's resident dogs, two huge and well-behaved Alaskan Malamutes greeted Olive as we entered, and ignored us. Olive, always social yet a bit submissive, licked each of their mouths in a sign of respect.

The pet store was filled with the cutest dog toys, collars and leads, jackets and treats, which all looked handmade to me. There was virtually nothing made out of plastic. The store also carried a selection of feline, aviary and small rodent supplies.

"What a lovely shop," I said to the clerk. "Are you the proprietor?"

"My partner and I own this place. We've run Free Range at this location for well over a decade now. I bake many of the treats for both cats and dogs, which you see here, and my partner sews. She makes most of the apparel and collars that we sell. Where are ya'll from?"

"My husband and I, and Olive here, live just down in Denver. Our friends are visiting all the way from the South of France, though."

"My, my. Such a long way to come. What brings you to our little corner of the world?"

"Frankly," I replied, "We wanted to show our friends here the *true* Rocky Mountain experience, not the homogenized version one finds at the popular ski destinations."

"Good for you." Turning to Marie and Franco, the clerk continued, "Estes has quite a history you know. Homesteaders and mining, and now tourism and Rocky Mountain National Park. Plus, between the ghost sightings up at the Stanley Hotel and the bear sightings here in town, I'm sure you'll find your stay here lively."

"Another person that mentions ghosts!" said Marie. "We didn't experience anything of the kind last night in the hotel, but perhaps we still will."

"The last person who talked of the Stanley ghost, Jarvis, it was, he said there was something particularly fearful about the original elevator in the main lobby," I said.

"Correction," said the co-owner, "It's not *just* the elevator. The ghost stalks the whole hotel, but the elevator is where the body was found."

"The body?" said Franco.

"Yes. A woman was murdered at the Stanley, back in the nineties, you know. She had been poisoned and collapsed and died alone, locked in that elevator during a power outage. Shortly after the sightings purportedly began."

"Who was she and who poisoned her?" I asked.

"Just a tourist, no one of particular note," replied the shopkeeper. "But her murderer was never uncovered. Quite a tribulation for the hotel at the time."

Sam who had been perusing the merchandise, and not listening to our conversation, called to me, saying, "Lauren, look at this awesome winter coat for Olive. It's high-tech, with polar fleece on the inside, Gortex on the out and reflective stripes for nighttime, too. Bring her over, let's have her try it on."

I excused myself and walked Olive over to where Sam was holding up several of the handmade dog jackets. Olive was shy to try on the jacket that Sam liked best in front of the Malamutes. We didn't often dress her up in clothing, but once we velcroed her inside of it, it was charming. A true Colorado coat for our Colorado mutt.

"My partner makes those," said the proprietor, who had walked over to us. "Aren't they great? Very popular too. She calls them "Ruff Wear." It looks like it fits perfectly. Do you like the color?"

The jacket was red with black trim and the reflective piping was silver. A perfect match for our tri-colored Olive. Olive quickly adjusted and once she saw that the other two dogs didn't poke fun at her, she pranced around the shop relishing the attention she was garnering from us humans.

Our visit to Free Range concluded with one hundred-dollar dog coat and one bargain bag of handmade dog cookies for Olive, and an embroidered collar with mod midcentury patterning in orange and cream and a squeaky plush elk with felt antlers for Vivi. Oh, and a delicious ghost story.

Chapter 21

"THAT WAS A most satisfying dinner," proclaimed Franco as we all drove back to the hotel in the rental later that night.

"I enjoyed it as well, Franco. The wine you selected was wonderful. What was it again?" I asked from the backseat.

"One of my favorites. It was a light red Gamay from family winery Pasquier-Desvignes Lauren. Just think, that bottle has made its way through our warehouse and export distributorship all the way to that restaurant here in Estes Park, Colorado. It carried our export label. I looked. And it's still sold at a fair price too!"

"You and Marie should be proud, Franco. In my book, that is no small feat, running such a successful company in such a competitive industry."

"Oh, it is. You have no idea. Small bottlers, of questionable origin, always trying to undercut us. I have to stay on my toes all the time. And Marie asks why I work so much!"

"Franco, I just want to spend more time with you and quite frankly we have staff who have worked for us for two generations now, who are quite competent to take care of the daily business."

Sam interrupted this oncoming conversational train, to agree with Franco by acknowledging to Marie that he often worked more than I would like for him to as well. He explained to all of us that he feels justified, however, as it keeps him challenged and quite frankly allows us to enjoy luxurious getaways and to be very comfortable. He concluded this rebuttal by reminding us that if he didn't work so hard, as Franco also does, the four of us would never have met.

"I appreciate that, Sam. I really do," responded Marie, "and I do love you, Franco, even though you know you don't have to work anymore and that you're simply a workaholic who is happier away from our home. Perhaps you are not French at all, but really an American industrialist."

Franco was silent for a moment, then said, "It may very well be, and soon I will have the western belt to prove it!"

We were all laughing as Sam pulled into the guest parking lot just to the side of the front lawn of the Stanley's main building. As we got out of the vehicle Sam asked if we all still wanted to go into the Crimson Room again that evening.

We were all game. Sam locked the car and turned to tell me he would go back to our suite to check on Olive and to take her outside for a short walk. He then announced to Marie and Franco that he would meet us in the bar in thirty minutes or so, before walking off in the opposite direction toward the Lodge outpost.

Marie, Franco and I walked up the beautifully lit front steps and Marie said she was going to stop on the veranda to smoke a cigarette.

"Would you like for us to wait with you, Marie?" I asked.

"Non. I will enjoy the night view from here and will join you inside shortly," she responded.

I checked my wristwatch. It was almost eleven p.m. I hoped my friend Liv would be in the bar, or at least arriving soon. We hadn't had a proper conversation yet, after running into one another so unexpectedly.

"Well, it's just you and me Franco, for a little while at least. Thank you again for dinner. What may I get you from the bar?" I asked him as we crossed in front of one of the large stone fireplaces in the lobby, just beside the Crimson Room's entrance.

"Let's look to see if your friends are here first, Lauren. You must be anxious to reacquaint yourselves."

I looked all the way down the onyx bar, but did not see Liv or Harry. I did, however, recognize Jarvis and Kip. They were holding court with a small group of people, perhaps other guests, who appeared just as delighted with their stories as we had been last night.

"I don't see Liv, Franco, but I see Jarvis and Kip. Shall we say hello to them and then find a table? The bar looks full tonight."

He nodded and let me lead the way. As we walked the length of the bar, I continued scanning for Liv. I nodded my head politely at the silent silver-haired couple, whom I noticed with satisfaction were sitting at a small table opposite the bar, their shoulders and heads close, speaking with one another in hushed voices.

"Kip, Jarvis! How nice to see you again. Did you both have a good day?" I asked when we had passed the couple's table and after they saw Franco and me approach.

"We did. We were just telling our new friends here about all the elk, big horn sheep and sundry wildlife we saw up in the park today, and how Jarvis here almost killed me by driving us off the road on our return to the hotel here, by trying to avoid hitting a real cowboy who was actually riding his horse right in the street, in the middle of town."

Before any of us could respond, Jarvis exclaimed, "I did *not* drive us off the road and almost kill us! I simply ran up on the gravel shoulder a bit. The cowboy was wearing black leather chaps and a cream-colored felt cowboy hat, you see, and I just love that look. I was simply distracted momentarily by his chaps, and his horse, Kip."

We laughed. What a pair, I thought to myself before realizing the pun and then stated the same fact aloud and thankfully garnered a laugh from their small crowd. Jarvis jumped up from his stool, offered me his seat and pulled over another from against the far wall for Franco to sit on. The bartender asked our assemblage if anyone needed anything. Franco requested a Stella beer and a gin and tonic for Marie, and I ordered a bottle of San Pel water, a glass of Rombauer Chardonnay and a perfect Manhattan for Sam. Introductions were made around the group by Kip who included a descriptive nicety about everyone. Mine was "the statuesque Lauren from Denver, who was unfortunately already married" and Franco's was "the dashing Frenchman, who was also unfortunately married, but not to Lauren," which garnered another chuckle from the group. I tried to pay attention to all of the introductions but my mind wandered wondering if Liv would show up tonight.

I caught a few of the new names. Richard, the non-gambler from Las Vegas and Susan the oil painting artist from Indianapolis, Indiana. I tried to focus and asked Susan if she could describe her preferred painting style. After it took her a few minutes to describe what I heard as "abstracts using oil on canvas," I asked her if she had by chance crossed paths with a contemporary painter who I knew, also from Indiana, and who had just opened a gallery space in the Broadripple neighborhood of Indianapolis.

Just then a commotion ensued from the front area of the bar. Heads turned, including ours, and there entered Liv and Harry. Even from way down the bar, I could tell that Harry was completely drunk.

I jumped up and rushed forward to Liv's side. She dropped her arm from around Harry's waist and greeted me warmly. Harry stood there with us for a moment, said 'ello to me and then proclaimed that he needed a drink. Liv and I watched him wander over to bar and jostle a sitting patron to the side. Liv looked at me and said, "Sorry. Harry's had a bit too much. We have been celebrating, but since we're staying here and not driving anywhere, I guess I should let him have one more."

"We've all been there Liv. No worries. I'm just glad you're here. Let me excuse myself from the group I've been talking with and let's get a quiet table together. Is that alright?" I said as I took her hand and led her to the far end of the bar to meet Kip and Jarvis and the group.

I picked up my water and wine and introduced Liv to everyone before asking Franco if he minded if Liv and I sat at a table further from the bar to catch up with one another. Nodding, he said he would keep an eye open for Marie and Sam.

"You remember Harry, don't you Franco? He's just down at the front end of the bar ordering drink. I'm afraid he's had one too many, would you mind keeping an eye on him as well?" Liv asked matter-of-factly.

Before Franco could answer her, Jarvis said, "We certainly will, my dear. Is he by chance an actor by trade? He has the looks for it."

"No, he's just a spoiled trustafarian with a day job to keep up appearances, I'm afraid. But he's all mine. Don't get any ideas of taking advantage of him in his current state," Liv replied before smiling broadly, swinging her long hair and pulling me away to an empty table at the far corner of the room.

After we made ourselves comfortable at a little two-top near the back windows of the Crimson Room which overlooked the outside sculpture garden, I asked Liv if she would like to share my water. She replied yes, that she felt a headache coming on and would certainly need to be the sober one tonight.

"Liv, Harry is gorgeous. His eyes are beautiful, perfect summer blue, and I just love his dark hair and the dimple on his chin. He reminds me of a modern-day Cary Grant. You two make a beautiful couple. Wherever did you meet? How long have you know him? Are you crazy in love?" I asked, sounding just like the teenager that I was the last time we had seen one another.

"Ah, let's see, in Chicago at the East Bank Club, about one year ago, and yes, as much as I ever have been," Liv replied.

"I'm so happy for you. I can't believe you're finally getting married, Liv. This is your first, right?" I asked. Then, "You know, I saw Robyn in Denver just a couple months back. She told me that she had had dinner with you and Harry in New York. At least I assume it was Harry. Robyn described the man you were with as drop-dead gorgeous. She said that she had loved seeing you again and had greatly enjoyed meeting Harry. She also relayed what a nice couple she thought you two were."

"That was a fun evening. I enjoyed seeing her, too. Robyn is surely doing well for herself, in spite of working in the non-profit sector. Yes Lauren, Harry will be my first husband. I never thought I wanted to get married, Lauren, but he's such a good catch and he pursued me relentlessly." She grinned lasciviously.

"You should be pursued relentlessly, Liv. You're so beautiful, even more so than when we were young, and you're a smart cookie, too. You could always have had any man that you wished, I guess it's just taken you a while to figure that out, Liv. But I'm glad you have now. Speaking of which, what were the romantic plans for you tonight that Harry mentioned this afternoon?"

Just then, I saw Sam walk into the bar. I saw him recognize Harry, who had propped himself up by leaning heavily against the bar. Sam walked straight up to Harry and began speaking to him. I couldn't hear what he was saying.

"Hold that thought, Liv. Sam has just arrived and he's talking to Harry. Come to think of it, where is Marie?" I looked around. Marie was not with Franco, who was still sitting on the far end of the bar talking with Kip and Jasper and their group. "Do you see our friend Marie anywhere in here, Liv?"

"No, but here comes Sam with Harry."

"Hello ladies," said Sam.

Harry did not speak; he just sauntered around our small round table and planted a sloppy kiss on Liv's mouth.

"Harry, you taste like whisky, you handsome devil," she teased. Then, "You remember Lauren."

"But of course. The school friend of my love." He looked at me with glazed eyes, smiled and swayed slightly.

"Liz was just about to tell me about your romantic evening tonight Harry," I said.

Realizing Harry was a bit too drunk for my taste, Sam said, "I think Liv and Lauren want to catch up, Harry. Shall we retire to the bar and leave these beautiful ladies to their own devices?" He bent down to kiss me, and asked "Is this my drink?" pointing to the Manhattan on our table.

"Sure is. Thanks, Sam. Jasper, Kip, Franco and some other nice people are just over there. Have you seen Marie? She's not in here yet and she just stopped to smoke a cigarette out on the veranda before Franco and I came in."

"No," he said. Then "I'll ask Franco if he knows where she is," before he turned and led Harry over to Jasper and company.

"So what exactly did you do tonight to get Harry so intoxicated with love?" I joked.

"It was amazing actually. Harry and I took a private helicopter ride at sunset, with a fully equipped bar on board, and toured Rocky Mountain National Park from the sky. He planned the whole thing. It was amazing; they picked us up and dropped us off right on the meadow below the swimming pool, here on the hotel grounds. After it got too dark to see the park, we flew toward Denver to view the city skyline at night."

"Wow, that is impressive, Liv. Sounds wonderful. And he planned this as a surprise for you?"

"Yes. I had no clue. He just told me to wear flat shoes." She pulled her long leg out from underneath the table showing me the snakeskin d'Orsay pump currently on her foot. "Which I definitely did *not* do, as I simply expected to go out for a nice dinner."

"You're too much Liv, I love it!" Then, "Tell me that shoe means the hotel has found your missing bag."

She jolted. "No. I'm quite sure someone stole it, but they won't get anything really valuable in that suitcase, just my *unmentionables*. There was nothing very good in that bag."

Strange, I thought, considering how last night her missing bag had seemed so very important to her. "Well, I'm glad nothing valuable, like those fantastic shoes, was lost, Liv," I said out loud.

"How are your parents?" she asked me next, rather abruptly.

"They're fine. I don't see them as often as I would like. My mother still lives in the same house I grew up in, the same one we would have sleepovers at. My father is enjoying retirement. They're both still healthy, thankfully. What about your family, Liv?"

"Scattered all over the country, I'm afraid, but I am an aunt now you know."

"No I didn't know. Your little sister has a baby?"

"Yes, three in fact, and divorced already, too."

"Time flies, doesn't it, Liv?"

"Sometimes not fast enough…"

Laughter erupted from Kip and Jarvis' motley crew perched at the bar. Sam was clearly sharing a story with the group. Sam is always extra demonstrative while telling tall tales. Marie had still not arrived.

I looked back to Liv. "Did you say you're having a large wedding, Liv? Sam and I really appreciate your offer to include us, but I don't want you to feel that you have to invite us."

"It'll be quite small actually, only around 100 people, Lauren. Harry's parents passed away when he was quite young and with my family so scattered, it'll mostly be friends and business associates of Harry's and mine. Some real interesting people, some big ballers too. You and Sam really should come. It'll be convenient, right in the City at a beautiful little historic Chapel and the Rainbow Room is just about a dozen blocks away."

"Did you just refer to your guests as big ballers, Liv?" I said laughing at the pedestrian expression.

"You know what I mean Lauren."

"I do. Congratulations, Liv. I'm happy for you and it's great to see you again. I mean it. I've missed you Liv."

"And I you," she responded. "How did we ever lose touch anyway?"

"It was just the age, so many changes for both of us after high school. Moving away to different colleges, then more moves around the country for work. We simply lost touch."

"I hate to cut our visit short, it really is wonderful to see you, but I'm starting to feel a headache and I really do need to get Harry into bed. Look at him over there, he can barely stand up."

"I understand. I want to get into bed soon myself," I said teasing her.

We both stood up and I reached toward Liv to give her a big hug. "It really has been wonderful to see you. I am happy you are doing so well, Liv. Perhaps we can have lunch tomorrow, while we are both still here at the Stanley together."

"I'd love that Lauren. Lunch will be perfect. Harry and I always go running in the morning and that'll give me time to shower and change at the spa after my massage."

All heads turned in our direction as we stood and walked toward Harry, Sam, Franco, Kip, Jasper, Susan and the rest of the group. It was Liv who drew the attention, just by moving, just by being so very striking with her outstanding good looks. Just like in school, I thought.

"Harry, say goodbye to your new friends," she said before grabbing him around the shoulder. "Please excuse us. We need to go to bed."

Everyone said good night. Then I asked her quietly in her ear, if she would like for Sam to help her get Harry upstairs to their room.

She said no, it was not necessary, then sauntered out of the Crimson Room with Harry hanging on her side.

Chapter 22

SATURDAY MORNING THE first sound I heard was Sam whispering to me that he was taking Olive outside for a walk and would be back soon. He gave me a dry kiss on my check and then I heard the door close in our front room. The bedroom was still dark and I must have quickly fallen back asleep. I've always been a sound sleeper; the type of person that needs to set two alarm clocks if I have to wake up particularly early.

What seemed like a few minutes later, I was roused from sleep again by the feel of Olive jumping up into the bed beside me. I sensed her staring at me behind my closed eyelids. I rolled onto my side to face her and I felt the rhythm of her tailing wagging. I smiled and opened my eyes. She sat there looking at me with a long pink string hanging from her mouth.

"What's this?" I asked Olive.

She remained silent like dogs do, so I sat up to better understand what was going on. I took the string from her mouth, but only had hold of one end of it. The length of the string ran across the floor and into the bright sitting room off our bedroom. I got up and still holding the pink cord with my hand, followed it into the other room where Sam sat on the couch in front of the fireplace. The draperies were open and the room was full of light. Sam smiled broadly at me but did not say a word. Olive was by my side as I continued to follow the string leading to the coffee table in front of Sam. There, at the end of the string, lay two coffee cups and in between them a small red box which was tied with the other end of the pink string.

"Mister Hendrick," I said. "What's this?"

"A gift for my beautiful wife," replied Sam simply.

I sat down beside him and gave him a big smile, trying not to imagine what my hair looked like or how poorly my breath likely smelled. I picked up the red gift box and untied the pink ribbon from around it. It was a jewel box! Lifting the hinged lid, I saw a beautiful thin rose gold necklace studded with small diamonds that were scattered around the length of the long chain. It was beautiful; just my taste.

"How do you know me so well, Sam? I love it," I said as I put it over my head and let it hang over my nightgown. "It's beautiful. Thank you."

"I love you," said Sam. "I saw it in the jewelry store yesterday and could not resist going back to get it for you. It looks as wonderful on you as I imagined, even with that wild morning hair. Lauren, what do you do to it when you're sleeping?"

Ignoring Sam's running joke about my morning hair, I turned to Olive. "And what a good delivery dog you are, Olive. That was so clever of you to wake me with the string from the other room," I said to our sweet dog who was now trying to squeeze between Sam and me on the couch.

"I've ordered breakfast for us, Lauren," said Sam tickling Olive behind the ear.

"How did I get so lucky?" I asked as I leaned over Olive to kiss Sam warmly. Like clockwork, exactly two sips of coffee later, there was a knock on our door. Sam rose to answer and a tray was rolled in by the white-jacketed room service attendant. He asked Sam if he should place it in between the two chairs located by the window and Sam said yes.

Our breakfasts smelled wonderful when the silver plate covers were removed. Sam had ordered a meaty Denver omelet for himself and a traditional breakfast of scrambled eggs and bacon for me. There was also a small plate of fresh fruit and two still-warm scones in a basket. We ate and I looked down to admire the sparkle of the diamonds in my new necklace in the sunlight in between bites.

"Did you see Marie or Franco while you were out this morning?" I asked.

"No. I ran into no one except Stephanie, the Stanley's manager. Oh, and I saw that artist from last night in the lobby, Susan, I think her name is."

"Yes. That's right. Susan. She seemed nice." I took another bite of the freshly cut fruit and then said, "That was so strange, Marie disappearing last night. I wonder if she became ill and went back to their suite? I'm surprised she didn't just come into the bar to let us know though."

"Franco didn't seem concerned. Plus I think we would have heard from him if she had not been in their room last night when he retired."

"That's true, Sam. Maybe, I'll just try ringing their room right now to check in," I said as I walked over to the desk. I picked up the handset and dialed their room number, 515. It rang a few times and Franco picked up, saying bonjour.

"Bonjour, Franco. It's Lauren and Sam. How are you this morning?"

"Very well, Lauren. And you?"

"Thanks, Franco. We're just fine. We're eating breakfast in our sitting room at the moment. I just wanted to phone to make sure Marie is ok."

"Oh, she is fine. She came back to our quarters last night and fell sound asleep. She was still sleeping peacefully when I returned from the bar."

"I'm so glad to hear that. May I speak with her?"

"I'm afraid she's indisposed just now."

"Oh, ok. What would you two like to do today, Franco? I think I'm going to try to persuade Sam to go for another trail ride today. Do you think you would like to join us for that? Marie said she might be interested in riding with us while we're up here."

"Actually Lauren," said Franco, "she's not feeling tip-top today. I think it is what you said, altitude sickness. We discussed going to the spa today and relaxing under the expert hands of trained masseurs. I think that would be best for her."

"Yes, that sounds perfect. Well, enjoy yourselves and we'll look forward to sharing dinner again tonight."

I replaced the handset and sat back down in front of the remainder of my breakfast. I took a bite of my scone and looked at Sam. He peered back at me with one raised eyebrow and a mouth full of omelet. When he was done chewing and had swallowed, he asked "Are they ok?"

"I *think* so," I replied honestly. "Franco didn't actually let me speak with Marie, she was in the bathroom or something, but he said she was sound asleep in their room when he went back last night."

"That's good," said Sam.

"He also said that they weren't going to join us riding today. They will be going to the spa instead as Marie is still not feeling tip-top."

"Are we going riding today?" Sam asked me.

"I'd like to. The weather looks nice and who knows when we'll have another chance."

"I thought you were having lunch with Liv today. It's already almost ten thirty."

"Oh my gosh, I almost forgot. I haven't had enough coffee yet," I said then took another large swallow from my mug. "But will you go riding with me today Sam? I'd really like to. Just for a couple hours? I'll call Liv and see if she can do a late lunch. After this breakfast, I won't be hungry for a while anyway."

"Yes, but please call Liv now to make sure she is willing to have lunch later. Realistically, it'll probably be two at the earliest before you'll be able to meet her."

I walked to the phone again and this time dialed zero for reception. I asked to be connected with Liv and Harry Ross' room. The clerk found it under his name and quickly connected me. The phone rang and rang. Finally an out of breath Liv answered with a terse "Hello".

"Liv, it's Lauren. Good morning! Can you speak? Are you in the middle of something?" I asked.

"I'm fine. I'm just getting around. Um, Harry is out running. I decided not to join him today. It's funny: he's the one who got sloshed last night but I'm the one who feels hung-over; if I sound weird I blame it on the booze."

"Wow. I'm impressed. Not with you, Liv," I joked, "but with Harry. You do sound hung-over."

"Yeah, Harry's like that. His brash confidence carries him through almost everything. He just wills himself not to be hung-over, I think. Like he wills himself to be popular and wills himself to be a scratch golfer. He's his own best friend. You know the type?"

"He's a confident man, most successful men are. But you are too, Liv. You would never be accused of being a shrinking violet. It sounds like you're a good pair."

"Yes, I suppose we are," she responded.

"Actually I'm calling about lunch today, Liv. Sam and I want to go for a horse ride and I'm wondering if we can do a late lunch? We can call it tea. Maybe around three?"

"That'll be fine, perfect, in fact. I've got some calls to make and I need to get to the spa for a facial and pedicure. Three will be perfect, Lauren."

Hanging up the phone, I turned to Sam and said, "All our friends are going to the spa today. We're free to go riding!"

Arriving at the stable, Sam and I were pleased to learn from Geoff that we were able to take the same two horses out again for an unguided couple-hour ride. Sam sat atop Charles and I was happy to be back on Pablo. We decided to ride the same trail as the day before yesterday, but hoped to make it a little further out on the trail this time.

"It's nice being here in Estes during the off season, Sam," I said as we trotted through the open field a few minutes later. I was feeling more confident, being on the same horse again and on the same trail, and was proud of myself for keeping up with Sam and Charles at a quick clip. "You know, during the tourist season up here this trail would be busy and we would never have been able to get these horses out so quickly, by ourselves and on the fly, like we have this trip."

"It's like I always say Lauren, everything is better during the shoulder season," replied Sam.

"I thought you just said that because everything is less expensive in the shoulder season."

"That too."

"Sam, look, it's snowing!" I exclaimed giddily as we approached the steep part of the trail on the far side of the meadow. It had just begun to snow and the effect was magical. Out here alone, just Sam and me on our rented horses, no sounds but our voices and the rhythmic gait of Pablo and Charles's hooves on the earthen ground. The snowflakes were very light and small, glittering in the sun which was still shining. Who doesn't love snow in the sunshine? The only thing better, I thought, is when it briefly rains during sunshine and creates a rainbow.

We slowed the horses to a fast walk as we entered the more densely forested ascent. In this narrow section of trail it was darker and the snow was not yet heavy enough to break through the foliage. I was in heaven. I had the best husband in the world, who that morning had just surprised me in a very thoughtful way with a new necklace, this trip with our new friends Marie and Franco was fun and going well, and we were in the beautiful Needles mountain range riding horses in the snow and sunshine with no one else around us.

Sam and Charles slowed to a stop before me and I gently pulled Pablo's reins so as not to rear end them. Quick as a whip, Sam jumped off of Charles.

"What's up?" I asked as I watched him drop the reins and march ahead. We were located just before a switchback, I noticed. It was the steep switchback with the rough-cut stone steps and wooden hand rail on the inside of the curve of the trail.

Just then I saw what had prompted Sam's abrupt dismount. There was a large dark mass laying at the bottom of the steps. As I looked closer toward the bottom end of the steps, Sam bent down before the dark pile and obscured my view of it from atop Pablo. "What is it, Sam?" I called.

All of a sudden, before he turned toward me or answered, I knew. It was a body. Someone had fallen down the steep, hard steps. My stomach lurched and I tensed, my mouth undoubtedly hanging open as I processed what I thought I was seeing.

"Oh my god." I dismounted Pablo and thoughts of Marie entered my head as I scrambled up to where Sam was bent down in front of the dark motionless lump. "Is it Marie?" I squeaked in a strange voice that sounded an octave higher than normal in my ears.

"Stay there, Lauren," said Sam.

"No. What's going on? What is it Sam?" I asked as I caught up to him. He was bent down, on both knees, with both of his hands on what I could now clearly see was a limp body.

"Oh my god."

It was face down. I couldn't see the face, which was probably for the best. Standing just behind Sam, I could see dark, almost black hair, under a black knit cap on one end of the black outfitted body: the other end was wearing red, black and white Nike trainers.

Sam's hands were around the person's neck.

"Are you checking for a pulse?" I asked, stating the obvious.

"Yes, but I don't feel anything. He feels cool."

"Is it a man?"

"I think so. I'm going to roll him over now. Perhaps you should stand back?"

There was a pool of dark liquid in the dirt next to the head, which prompted my Basel reaction and I tasted a sourness in the back of my throat. I stepped back, then turned and walked the few yards back to Charles. I picked up his reins and turned again to watch Sam roll over the body. Sam struggled a bit. I could tell even from here, that the body was completely limp and since the legs were not straight out, Sam had to straighten each of them before he could completely roll over the motionless person. I saw him look into the face. It was a man, I could tell from the nose. Thank goodness it wasn't Marie. Why would Marie even be out here, I wondered? What a ridiculous thought.

Sam moved his hand from the body's torso and then brushed the eyes shut. He called back to me, "He's dead, Lauren. No doubt about it. Looks like he just tripped down the steps and hit his head here. It's Harry, Lauren."

"What?" I said. "Liv's Harry? No way." I dropped the reins again and took a deep breath as I walked back toward Sam and the body. Even with the eyes closed, I could now tell that Sam was correct.

Chapter 23

"I CANNOT BELIEVE this. They just got engaged," I said to Sam.

He said nothing, just stood up.

"I can't believe this. We just met him. He was fine last night, drunk, but fine. I cannot believe her fiancé is dead before us, and we just found him like this. This is insane."

"Let's try to use the word *tragic*, Lauren. We need to phone for the police right away." Harry reached into his coat pocket and pulled out his phone. "No signal," he said. Then, "Did you bring your phone?"

"No, I didn't," I replied as I looked down at Harry's unmoving body. The snow was just beginning to break through all the limbs and branches, and was landing softly on Harry's black running outfit. He was still wearing his white ear buds. The one on his right ear still in place and the one from his left dangling in the bloodstained, moist dirt near his neck. Liv is going to be devastated, I thought, as I looked at his attractive face. It looked as though he had fallen down on his side as there was a large raw gash on his left temple that was still red with dark blood. It wasn't actually a lot of blood. It was hard to believe someone could be dead with so little blood loss. His left shoulder, arm and leg were all dirty with dust from the trail.

"Do you want to ride back to the stable to phone for help, Lauren? I can wait here."

"What do you think happened exactly, Sam? It looks like he hit the ground on his left side."

"Well, last time we saw him he was good and snookered, as you said. Frankly, I'm surprised he went for a run this morning at all. He must have been hung-over and he probably just tripped on these stone steps, running down them, and hit his head just hard enough and in the right place to kill him."

I made a wide circle around Harry's body and began to climb up the stairs. I guess I was just curious to see the view from the top and to see, for myself, what steps that can actually kill a fit, healthy man like Harry looked like.

"Come on, Lauren. We need to get to a phone to call the police."

"Just a minute, Sam. I just want to look around. It's not like there's a chance to save him anymore."

As I reached the top, I was almost out of breath. The steps were steep, twenty-two in all, and each of varying heights and slightly different widths.

"Oh god, if you fell from up here. I can totally see how it could kill you. He must have bounced down too. Ugh, it looks painful. Sam, come up here and check out this perspective."

Sam climbed up and we both peered back down on Liv's fiancé's still body.

"Maybe you shouldn't have rolled him over, Sam. So the police could have seen exactly how he landed."

"Yeah, you're probably right, but I felt like I had to make sure he wasn't still alive. I couldn't quite tell at first. I'm sure it'll be ok, I'll be sure to tell the police how and why I moved him."

"What a tragic accident. I can't believe this, Sam."

"Come on, Lauren," said Sam and he moved to the far side of the stairs and began to walk down the trail on the far right.

"Sam, I don't want to ride back by myself. Let's go together," I said as I carefully began to descend the steps. Then, "Why do you suppose he ran down these stairs instead of taking the trail?"

"I don't know, Lauren. Maybe he thought it was better exercise, balance with his eye-foot coordination, or maybe there was someone else on the trail side, blocking it."

As I was almost halfway down, still a good fifteen feet or so above Harry's dead body, I saw something strange; a fresh little indention, a gash around the side of the wood toward the base of one of the vertical beams holding the rough hand rail.

"Sam, come here, look at this," I called.

"Come on, Lauren. We need to get the police up here. Let me help you up on your horse so we can ride back to the stable together."

Ignoring him, I bent down on the step, being sure to keep my left hand firmly on the handrail, and looked at the gash more closely. It was very thin, but appeared fresh. It was on both sides of the square post as well as on the back side. The corner closest to the top of the stairs also had a slight chip. I stood up and looked to my right. There, almost straight across on the far side of the trail, was a rather good-sized, mature pine tree. I carefully walked over to it. Toward the base of the large trunk, which must have been eighteen or twenty inches in diameter, I saw something else peculiar. A small hole. I bent down again. There, about ten or so inches from the ground was most certainly a hole, and it also looked fresh. I could just barely see a bit of the yellow-green tree trunk innards. It did not look like a clean hole that a nail would make, but rather a rougher hole of the type a screw, with threads, would create. Thoughts of trip wires entered my head.

"Sam, really. Please come back up here. I've found something strange, something you will not believe, if you don't see it for yourself," I called down to him.

"Oh alright." I watched as he dropped Pablo's reins on the ground once more and told both horses to "stay" as if they were dogs. I could tell from his body language and the way he literally stepped over dead Harry to climb back up to where I was that he had lost his good humor.

"Look at this, Sam," I said pointing to the small hole in the trunk.

"Hmm." He said nothing else, but bent down on the trail in front of me and peered at it.

"What is this? And why isn't it all dried out?"

After a moment, "It's a screw hole, Lauren. Why it's here I don't know."

"Sam, it's about ten inches up. Couldn't someone have screwed a little i-hook in here to make a trip wire across the trail and over across the stairs?" Turning my head, I looked past the trail back to the stairs.

"And look there, Sam. That railing post has a fresh indention on it that looks like it could have been made by a thin wire." I stood and walked across the trail again and back to the opposite post on the far side of the steps. Sam stayed where he was but stood up and watched me.

"Look, Sam. Someone could have run an almost straight wire from that tree to the base of this post here," I said.

"Oh Lauren, you and your conspiracy theories. You exasperate me. Can we go now? You can show this to the police, but we need to go get them first." He left and walked down toward our horses.

I looked back toward the tree trunk. It didn't appear to have a wire mark around its circumference and I couldn't see the little hole from here. I decided to move away lest I ruin any evidence.

"Coming, Sam," I said. Knowing when it's best not to antagonize Sam further is an invaluable skill I've been trying to master in our many years together. Sam is very tolerant, but when he's had enough, he's had enough.

I took one last look at Harry, who now had a light dusting of snow on him, and walked over to Sam and Pablo. I gave Sam a kiss on the cheek and he let me use his bent knee to mount Pablo. "You know Sam, I wouldn't want to find a murdered body with anyone else."

Sam swung his leg over Charles and said, "Lauren, he was not murdered. Who on earth would want to murder him? He was up here in Estes Park for a pleasure trip only with Liv, his soon-to-be wife. He just fell. He may have still been drunk for all we know. It's a tragic accident. Tell the police everything, of course, but please don't upset Liv any more than she will be already with your wild theories of espionage, intrigue and murder."

"You're right, Sam."

We rode back to the stable mostly in silence. My head swam. I have never in my life seen a real dead body before outside of a funeral home. The snow continued to fall and we trotted back along the same trail. It wasn't terribly cold and the sun was still shining. It was almost noon when we finished up the last section of trail that led directly to the stable.

"I just had a terrible thought, Sam."

"Another one?" he replied testily.

"Yes, another one. Do you think any animals will get to his body before the police arrive?" I had read stories of how quickly wildlife can locate and feast on lost hikers once they had bloodied themselves.

"No. I don't imagine that will happen, Lauren. Unless of course he was left there overnight."

We jumped down off of Charles and Pablo and tied them to the hitching post directly in front of the stable's office door.

"Back so soon?" called Geoff as he lifted his head from the computer he was working on.

"I'm afraid we have a problem, Geoff and we need to use your landline right away," said Sam.

"Are the horses ok?" said Geoff, getting to his feet. Then looking at us both closely, "Are you both ok?" His horses first, tourists second, I noted. Good man, I thought.

"Yes and yes, Geoff. We and your horses are all fine, but we need to call the police."

With a look of surprise in his eyes, he picked up the handset from the office's cordless phone and handed it to Sam. "Is there anything that I can help with?" he asked and then looked at me.

"I'm afraid we've found a dead body out there in the Needles, if you can believe that, Geoff," I said. It was strange, I have never uttered those words before, and I was surprised to discover that it was difficult for me not to smile. What *is* wrong with me, I thought.

Sam said, "Quiet please," while holding the receiver to his ear.

Geoff and I both turned to watch what Sam would say next.

"Hello. Yes, this is an emergency. My name is Sam Hendrick. My wife and I have just found a dead body."

Sam then turned to Geoff and calmly asked what they phone number was where we were. He repeated the number slowly to the person on the other end of the line, after Geoff called it out.

"Yes, I am sure he is dead," Sam said next. Then a long pause. Next he proceeded to inform the emergency operator of his current location at Sombrero Stables, again asking Geoff for the exact street address.

Then it became interesting, as Sam tried to explain that yes, he did know the deceased but that he had just met him the day before. He didn't really know him well. That he and I were out riding horses, just since about eleven am today, and that we had come across the body, *already dead*, lying on a trail. Sam then repeated into the phone that the body was lying at the bottom of some stairs on a trail near Sombrero Stables, and that he was dead when we found him.

"Yes, I checked the pulse myself," said Sam next. "His name is, err, was Harry…" Sam turned to look at me and I said "Ross." "Ross" said Sam into the phone. "Harry Ross from New York." Another long pause. "Yes. My wife and I can wait here. Yes, we can lead you to the scene of the accident." Pause, then "So the Larimer County Sheriff will be here in a few minutes? Ok. Good. Thank you. Goodbye," said Sam, then handed the phone back to Geoff who was standing there with a blank look on his face.

"Well, this is a first," said Geoff as he replaced the handset into its receiver.

"For us too, Geoff."

Chapter 24

"GEOFF, MAY I have some water while we wait?" I asked.

"Sure thing. I've got some bottles in the fridge in back," he said. "I'll be right back."

Turning to Sam, who was sitting next to me on one of the stable office's metal folding chairs, I said, "How long did they say it would take for the police to arrive?"

"The emergency operator said the sheriff will be here shortly. I assume this Needles wilderness area is under county jurisdiction, so they're calling in the Larimer County personnel instead of the Estes Park police."

"I can't believe we found a dead body, Sam. This is too weird; it's surreal actually. Poor Liv."

Geoff returned and handed us each a bottle of water, then asked, "Where'd you leave the horses?"

"They're just out front, Geoff, tied to your hitching post. They are both great horses. Very obedient and docile. Frankly, I'm sorry our ride was cut short by all this. Can I go ahead and pay you now, before the authorities show up?"

"No need. You weren't gone long. Speaking for Sombrero Stables, I wouldn't feel right about charging you for a trail ride that ended like this. Let me just get the horses out into the corral so they can drink some water too."

As the door closed behind Geoff, I felt like a whiny child but couldn't stop myself from saying out loud, "What is taking them so long?"

"Just relax, Lauren." Sam looked at his wrist watch, chuckled and then said, "They probably figure since he's dead already, it's not as urgent."

"Sam, I'm still thinking about that little hole in the tree trunk. Do you realize that there's also a fresh scratch on the handrail post almost exactly opposite from that tree?"

"Yes."

"That is a huge coincidence, don't you think? I think someone planted a trip wire on those stairs and Harry was intentionally sabotaged. Perhaps he got into a fight with someone last night while he was drunk?"

"Don't get ahead of yourself, Lauren. That's a very incriminating thing to say. Just tell the police, I mean the sheriff, what you saw, and let's let them handle it." We were silent for what seemed like ages. Then Sam said, "Funny what wild thoughts you have sometimes, Lauren."

Was he beginning to believe a trip wire was possible and that Harry was intentionally felled and left to die out in the wild by himself? I replied, "Funny how my wild thoughts are right sometimes, Sam."

Geoff returned to the office and announced to us that two sheriff's vehicles and an ambulance had just pulled off the main highway. Before the office's exterior door closed behind him I could just hear the far-off scream of the sirens. It was just after one. The sheriff had taken almost a full half hour to arrive.

A few minutes later an entourage of five men in uniform burst into the office where Sam, Geoff and I waited.

"Someone reported finding a dead body from here?" bellowed a portly middle-aged man wearing a gun, a cowboy hat and a tan and brown sheriff's uniform complete with a gold badge just like one sees on TV.

Sam stood. "Yes sir. My name is Sam Hendrick. This is my wife Lauren. We're visiting for a few days from Denver."

No handshake. Just business. "My name is Sheriff Smith. I'll be handling this report. Where are you two staying?"

"At the Stanley Hotel, Sheriff."

"Ok. Where's the body?"

"It's out on the main westerly heading trail from here. At the bottom of some stone steps. Maybe four miles away from here."

Geoff, who had been standing and watching from behind his check-in counter, corrected Sam. "Those steps are only three miles out. I know exactly where they are."

"And you are?"

"Geoff Hanson. Assistant manager here, sir."

"What happened to John?"

"He moved to Aspen at the end of last season, from what I heard. Never met him," replied Geoff.

Turning to the two deputies beside him, Sheriff Smith told both the tall skinny one and the shorter slim one, who looked like they could be brothers, to get the ATVs out of their trucks. Both men turned and exited the office without a word. Then to the two EMS personnel, dressed in casual black uniforms, he asked, "How do you boys want to get up there?"

The older EMS staffer replied, "We've got a sled for the body. My partner Joe here, will hook it to the back of one of your ATVs. We'll just hitch a ride up with you, if that's all right."

Sheriff Smith replied in the affirmative and Joe nodded and walked back outside without a word. Geez, this was just like TV.

"Ok, now, who is the deceased?" the Sheriff asked Sam.

I couldn't resist chiming in. "His name is Harry Ross. He's visiting with his fiancée from New York City. Sam and I used to know his fiancée, but we had just met *the deceased* yesterday."

"Where is this fiancée now?" the Sheriff asked.

"I believe she's at the Stanley's Spa. They are, were, staying there as well."

"What is her name?"

"Liv Ross or Rogers. I'm not sure if she's taken her husband's name yet. They were just engaged recently, and we just ran into one another, unexpectedly, up here in Estes. Her maiden name is Liv Rogers."

That prompted Sheriff Smith to open the cover of the net book he had been holding. He swiped the screen a few times then pulled out a stylus and appeared to make a few handwritten notes on the tablet's screen. When he was finished he looked back up to Sam and me and said, "So you two were out riding horses on the Valley trail here and just came across the body lying right in the middle of the trail, at the bottom of some steps?"

"Yes, sir," I said.

"Did you touch the body? How did you know the man was dead and not just injured?"

Sam replied, "I saw something lying in the trail ahead of us, Sheriff and stopped our horses. I jumped off, approached on foot and quickly realized that it was a man, lying face down. I put my hand on his neck. It felt cold and he didn't move. Then I turned him over to be completely sure he was not just passed out. That was when I recognized him as Harry Ross. He was, I'm sorry to say, completely and totally dead, Sheriff. It appeared as though he had been out running and had tripped and fallen down the stone stairs on the trail and hit his head. We found the body at the base of the staircase and he had a rather large gash on the side of his head, which was bloody. His leg was also twisted at a rather unnatural angle. Aside from that Sheriff, we didn't touch anything."

"Alright Mr. Hendrick," said Sheriff Smith. He them turned to Geoff and stated flatly, "Not a word about this Geoff, until we can notify next of kin."

"Yes, sir," replied Geoff.

Turning back to Sam, the Sheriff said, "Mister Hendrick, if you have no objection, I'd like for you to show us where the body is located."

"Sheriff, may I come along too?" I asked.

"Do you really want to Ms. Hendrick? There is no need, really."

"Yes, Sheriff."

With a glance toward Sam, he took a breath and replied, "Ok, then. Let's go."

I winked at Sam, who just shrugged his shoulders, as we followed the Sheriff outside to the two waiting ATVs.

We just barely fit. I was sitting next to Sam in the back seat of the vehicle carrying the Sheriff and the taller of his two deputies who was driving. The other ATV followed behind us carrying the shorter deputy, the two EMS men and pulling a funny looking trailer which looked like an extra-large Thule roof-rack but on big nubby wheels.

It was still snowing lightly. The ATVs were loud and bumpy as we drove up the first section of trail toward the open field. I have ridden in an ATV before, many Coloradans have them, but I generally prefer the peace and quiet of horseback riding or simply hiking with our dog while out in nature. Both vehicles stopped at the far edge of the beautiful valley where the trail became narrow as it entered the forest again.

"Is this the trail the body is on?" bellowed Sheriff Smith.

"Yes, Sheriff. Maybe a mile up from here."

"Is there another way in, Deputy?"

"Nothing wide enough for the ATV to my knowledge sir," replied his partner who was driving.

"Damn. I hate these accident calls up in the mountains. Getting too old for them." Then turning toward us, he yelled over our heads toward the ATV behind us, "We're gonna have to hike in from here. Get your stretcher and equipment boys."

Up we walked. All seven of us. I felt the worst for the two EMS guys, who had opened their sled, pulled out a typical stretcher and were now carrying it by hand, loaded with a couple of cases of medical equipment on top, up the first narrow switchback. None of us spoke until the Sheriff asked Sam how much further he thought it was.

"We'll traverse to another switchback and then the body will be maybe a quarter mile further. It's essentially at the third and last switchback on this side of the ridge, Sheriff," replied Sam.

We prodded on and I reached for Sam's hand. I was determined to think through how I could most effectively show the Sheriff what I now firmly believed was the evidence of a trip wire, which had most certainly led to Harry's tumble and his ultimate demise.

Fifteen or so minutes later in our upward climb, Sam dropped my hand, and sped up to Sheriff Smith who was toward the head of our pack and announced, "It's just up there, Sheriff."

And so it was. Harry's body was just as we had left it, but now completely covered in a dusting of snow. He black shape had been transformed into an almost invisible white lump, camouflaged by the light snow now covering the earthen trail and the stone steps too. I was glad Harry had still been a very visible black lump when Sam and I had first seen him. Like this, we may have accidentally trampled right over him on Charles and Pablo.

Sheriff Smith instructed Sam and me to stay a few feet back. The EMS boys laid the stretcher on the ground next to Harry's body and immediately bent down to check for vitals. The Sheriff was moving in a close circle around the body looking at the ground and then up at the steps and then at the body.

"You say you moved the body, Mr. Hendricks?" he called to Sam.

"Hendrick, sir. Yes." He took a step forward, but the Sheriff held out his hand, his thick palm out, to stop him. "He was turned face down, Sheriff," continued Sam, "and his leg was bent at an awkward angle, underneath him. I simply straightened his leg, his right one I believe, and then rolled him over, so that I could make sure there was no life."

"I understand. That's no problem, Mr. Hendrick. Cut and dry to me. Looks like the fellow was out running, slipped coming down these steps and fatally hit his head on the stone on the way down. Boys, take a look around while I hear what our medical team has to say."

The older EMS man said, "He's dead, Sheriff. I'd say by a good several hours. Looks like blunt force trauma to the cranium suffered in a fall."

"Ok. Thanks, Joe." The Sheriff then bent down to the body and essentially frisked it. He didn't seem to find anything, except a tiny MP3 player and what looked like a dark green room key card from the Stanley in Harry's sleek microfiber jacket pocket. I assumed he was looking for a wallet or ID. "Get him outta here. We'll be right behind you." Then turning to his deputies, he said, "See anything, boys?"

The taller of the two called out "no" from the top of the steps and the other said "nothing" from where he was currently standing in the middle of the trail next to the stairs.

"Sheriff," I said.

"Yes?"

"My husband and I did notice something that we wanted to point out to you."

"Ok. What is it Mrs. Hendrick?" he asked.

"I think the victim may have been tripped. I, I mean we, saw a screw hole in that tree there," I said pointing. "And over there on the hand rail post almost exactly opposite the tree, there seemed to be a thin scratch in the wood, the sort a wire pulled tight might make."

The Sheriff was quiet. He looked at me quizzically, then looked at Sam, who nodded his head solemnly.

"I can show you, Sheriff."

"Stay there, ma'am," he replied. Then turning to his deputies, he said, "Take a look at those trees. We're looking for a screw hole and some damage to a handrail."

The deputies followed orders without a further word and Sheriff Smith walked over to where Sam and I had remained standing.

"I'll need to get your information. I have a quick form here on my tablet you can fill out," he said opening the tablet. He swiped at it, tapped the screen a couple times and then handed it to Sam. He then looked at me and said, "How did you come to find a screw hole, as you call it, in a tree out here while riding horses?"

Why did I, all of a sudden, feel nervous? It was the look on his face. I kept my voice even and told the Sheriff everything. He stood quietly and listened. His face remained neutral and I took that to be a good sign. A sign that he was taking my theory of a trip wire seriously. When I was finished he did not say a word to me. He simply turned back to his deputies and asked if they had found anything of the nature described. The taller one, on the stairs, called back that he did see some scratches on one of the posts. Sheriff Smith then turned back to us and extended his hand for his tablet back from Sam. He then turned back to his boys and yelled, "Do you have your scene tape and cameras? Mark anything you find and take photos. Make sure the date & time stamp setting is on."

The Sheriff turned back to us and flatly asked, "Why would someone want to trip this man?"

"We don't have any idea, Sheriff," replied Sam quickly, before I got a word in. "He's a businessman visiting from New York on a pleasure trip with only his fiancée with him, to our knowledge."

"But he's also, I mean, he was also rather wealthy, Sheriff, to our knowledge. And, he was really very drunk last night when we last saw him. Perhaps he had a row with someone?"

"Did you see him argue with someone last night?" the Sheriff asked me.

"No, we didn't, but we only saw him for about half an hour around midnight at the Whisky Bar in the Stanley."

"Don't worry, ma'am," said the Sheriff. "It was most likely an accident, you said yourself he was very drunk last night. As you probably know, the effects of alcohol linger quite a long time in one's system up at this altitude, especially for lowlanders. Rest assured my team and I will check every avenue, including speaking to," he looked down to his tablet, "Miss Liv Rogers. All I ask is that you both don't leave town without notifying my office. Now then, let's get back down to town, so I can notify the fiancée."

Chapter 25

SHERIFF SMITH OFFERED to give Sam and me a lift back to the Stanley with him. I was glad to be in the front seat of the Sheriff's vehicle. Sam, however, was in the back seat looking a touch uncomfortable as most of the tourists on the Stanley's grounds turned to look at us as we passed by in the marked SUV. It was just three o'clock as we pulled up to the main entrance of our hotel. I had told Sheriff Smith that Liv and I had a late lunch date at the Crimson Room restaurant at three.

"Good. Save me the trouble of locating her," he said. Then, "Let me do the talking Mr. and Mrs. Hendrick, but it'll probably be good for you to be there for support, after. This is never easy news to break."

We three walked into the lobby together and then up to the restaurant's host stand. Taking off his cowboy hat, Sheriff Smith asked the young lady on duty if there was a woman by the name of Liv already waiting.

With an unmistakable look of curiosity, the hostess affirmed and led us toward a small table in the rear of the rather empty restaurant where Liv sat alone with a glass of red wine in front of her. She was looking down toward her phone. When Liv's head lifted and turned in our direction, I immediately noticed a look of shock in her eyes, then seeing Sam and me just behind the Sheriff, her facial expression turned to one of surprise with her perfectly groomed eyebrows raising high on her forehead and a tight-lipped grin below.

"Ma'am," said the Sheriff pulling out the chair located directly across the table from Liv. "My name is Sheriff Smith. Are you Liv Rogers or Ross?"

"Yes," she replied.

The Sheriff sat down and adjusted his gun. I said, "Hello Liv," as Sam pulled over two chairs from the next empty table for us to sit on.

"What's going on?" Liv said looking from me to Sam and then to the Sheriff.

"Do you know a Mr. Harry Ross, ma'am?" Sheriff Smith asked her flatly.

"Why, yes. He's my fiancé. We came up here together, but I don't seem to know where he is right now. I was just texting him, but he hasn't responded."

"I'm deeply sorry to inform you Miss Rogers, that it appears he's had an accident just outside of town in the Needles wilderness area, my jurisdiction, and has passed away."

I reached over and put my hand on Liv's thin forearm. She looked at me with wide eyes, but with a blank expression. This is terrible I thought to myself. The news is not registering for her yet, she's probably thinking, for a very long few seconds, that this is some sort of a mix-up or terrible joke. I held her gaze and nodded my head slowly.

A moment later all hell broke loose. Liv completely lost her composure. She jumped up, swatted my hand off of her arm and in the process knocked over her wine glass, which splashed onto Sam's jeans and wailed loudly, "No, this is some sort of mistake! Harry is out running and will be back any minute."

"Please sit down, Liv," I said calmly and reached to hold her hand. She stood there looking alarmed and turned on Sam and me.

"I don't know what is wrong with you, Lauren," she screamed. "This is not funny at all."

"Please sit down Miss Rogers," said the Sheriff.

A minute later she complied. The moment her bottom hit the seat, she exclaimed, "Oh my god," and the floodgates opened. She sobbed and wailed and I rubbed her back, feeling devastated for her.

"Ma'am, I am genuinely sorry for your loss. This is the worst part of my job, but I hope it will make you feel better to know that he most likely died quickly and without a lot of pain."

Wow. I felt sure the Sheriff was lying when he said that and I was surprised at his empathy for telling Liv that Harry's death was quick and painless. I'm no expert but Harry's fall had looked to me like it had hurt, a lot. Like the Sheriff I would never say this to Liv however.

Liv continued to cry and sob. Her face was red and shiny when she pulled it out of her hands after Sam offered her a stack of tissues, which he had garnered from the hovering hostess.

"I'm so sorry Liv," I said as I reached to hug her.

"Why are you even here?" she said glaring at me through her wet eyes, brushing off my embrace.

"Mr. and Mrs. Hendrick have told me that they are friends of yours, ma'am. They called 911 after finding the body this afternoon while out riding on the trail."

"What?" shrieked Liv. She turned to Sam and me and asked with disbelief and tears streaming down her face, "You found Harry?"

"Yes, Liv," said Sam in his most gentle and soothing voice. "I am so sorry. It was an accident. He had fallen while out running and Lauren and I just found him lying on the ground. We are very sorry to have to tell you this Liv, but he was already gone when we found him."

"Oh my god," she cried again.

After a couple of minutes, Sheriff Smith said, "Miss Rogers, I need your contact information."

Liv blew her nose and cleared her throat. She gave the Sheriff her mobile phone number and home address in Chicago, which he tapped into his tablet.

"And how long are you planning to stay here in Estes Park, ma'am?"

"We were planning to fly back to New York Sunday Sheriff."

"New York? You just gave me a Chicago address," said the Sheriff.

"I have an apartment in Chicago. Harry lives in New York City. I was going to stay with him in the City until after our wedding."

"I see, Miss Rogers. Can you give me that address as well?"

She read off an address on West 57th Street and the Sheriff typed that in as well.

"Is there someone in the deceased's immediate family whom you can notify to come here to identify the body and complete the paperwork?"

"Yes. Harry has a brother. I will call him right away."

"Thank you, ma'am. What is his name?"

"Nick Ross."

"Ok. Nick Ross from New York," said the Sheriff rising from the table. Then as he pushed his chair in, he handed Sam his card and then one to Liv. "Again, I am very sorry for your loss, ma'am. Please don't leave town until his brother or another relative arrives. If no one can come, let me know immediately. I need to have the body identified by a relative within 48 hours, but 24 is better. Please have Nick Ross call my office when he gets here, Miss Rogers, and if there is anything I can do to help you, please call me."

Sam and I walked Liv to her room. At this point in her shock, she was completely silent.

As she used her key card to open the door to room 525, her and Harry's suite on the opposite corner of the building from Marie and Franco's, I said, "Liv, may I come in and stay with you for a while? I don't want to leave you alone right now."

"Yes. That would be nice," she replied as she walked inside.

I turned to Sam, gave him a kiss and said, "Will you check in with Olive and call Marie and Franco and make plans for us for dinner tonight?"

"Of course. Do you want to stay in the hotel this evening?"

"Yes. That's probably best, Sam. I'll try to encourage Liv to join us too, but if she doesn't feel up to it, I'll make sure we get some room service sent up here to her before I leave. I'll be back to our room to change by about five or so."

"It's nice of you to stay with her, Lauren. Please make sure she calls Harry's brother and please don't say anything about your suspicions. Now is not the time. You told the Sheriff everything. He'll handle it."

"Ok, Sam. I love you."

I closed the door and walked into Liv and Harry's suite. It was immaculate. I've always liked neat people and obviously Liv was still as fastidious as I remembered. Harry must have been as well. Liv had plopped herself onto the couch, her shoes and handbag dropped on the floor where she sat. She had the grim look of realization or possibly resignation on her face.

"How about I make us some tea?" I asked and turned to the bar. "Or would you like something stronger, Liv?"

"Tea is fine," she said quietly without looking at me.

After the tea was brewed, I sat down next to her on the couch and said, "Liv, this is just terrible. I am so very sorry about Harry. What can I do to help you?"

"I don't know Lauren. He must have been hung-over, to fall and die, die out running today. I shouldn't have let him go. I know I didn't feel well enough to go running with him, and I drank much less last night. Why did I let him go?"

"You can't blame yourself Liv," I said. But a wild thought went through my head; who else would have known he would go running on that trail and intentionally string a trip wire across it.

"Do you know the steep stone steps that he fell on Liv? Did you two run that same trail yesterday?" I asked.

She turned to me. "Yes. I mean no. I don't know, Lauren. What difference does it make?"

"I was just wondering Liv. Forgive me, I don't know what to say. I'm in shock too, I think."

She gave me a strange look then and stated vehemently, "Please go, Lauren. I need to be by myself and I need to call Nick, Harry's brother, to tell him the news. I'll be fine. I just want to be by myself right now."

"The one thing about a murder case; if you just let people talk long enough, sooner or later somebody will spill the beans."

Nick Charles

Chapter 26

It was summer in the city, hot and humid, but the nights were glorious with every restaurants' outdoor tables booked days in advance. Windows were wide open everywhere mixing the noise from indoor conversations and laughter with that of the street; revelers walking along the sidewalks, taxi horns blowing, bicyclists weaving through the street traffic and handsome cabs filled with wide-eyed tourists visiting Chicago from around the world. It was the night that I fell for him. The night that I knew I would say "yes" should he ask me to marry him. It was our sixth date.

My doorman phoned to tell me Harry was in the lobby. Harry had arrived exactly on time. The doorman inquired if he should send him up or ask him to wait for me. I told him to send Harry up and took one more look in the mirror while he rode the elevator up to my floor. I liked my reflection. I looked happy and relaxed. My snug Leger dress was perfect for a summer night, low cut and short and showed the slim figure I worked so hard for. Upon hearing his light rap on my front door, I smiled at my reflection and opened the door for him.

Damn, he was handsome. I've always been drawn to a certain esthetic of man, a clichéd look which amounted to tall, dark and handsome with a healthy wallet. Harry was all of this and more. He was funny, congenial and smart to boot. Even though he was a few years my senior, he didn't have ex-wives, or children from other women, or any of that baggage.

"Harry, do come in," I said as I pulled him through my doorway playfully and into my foyer. Once inside, he did not release my hand and instead, pulled me into his arms. He took a deep breath of my hair from near my ear and used his free hand to turn my chin up so that our eyes locked. "I love you, Liv. I have never known another woman who has intrigued me so well," he said looking directly into me, our noses a mere inch apart. Before I could respond, he moved his hand from my chin around to the back of my neck and pulled my mouth gently onto his. His kiss reached my toes and I believed everything about him.

We sat on my couch and talked while drinking aperitifs which I had prepared for us. I had dimmed the lights and lit a couple of candles which rested in the crystal holders that I had picked up at Bloomingdales as a wedding gift for a co-worker and had loved so much that I had gone back to the store the next day to purchase two more for myself. My window, facing Lake Michigan, was tilted open and we could just barely hear the constant rumble of traffic from Lake Shore Drive far below over the Charlie Parker jazz that I had playing from my phone over a Bluetooth speaker placed on my bar.

"The merger I have been working on will conclude soon, Liv," he said. "The redundancy has been negotiated and the new shared office space outfitted. The C-level and Officer responsibilities and remuneration packages have all been worked out and agreed upon. It'll soon be time for me to get back to New York and out of their hair, Liv."

"Do we have to talk about this now, Harry? I've been so happy getting to know you. I don't want at all to think about you leaving me, now that I've grown so very fond of you."

"That's why I want to discuss this now, Liv. Frankly, I've known women in other cities over the years and it's always been conciliatory when the time came for me to return home, to New York, to look and wait for my next business acquisition opportunity."

"What are you saying to me, Harry?"

"I'm saying, Liv, that I've never felt so strongly about another woman. That I love you dearly, and that I want you to consider moving back to my home with me." He placed his drink down on my coffee table, reached over and placed my glass down beside his. He took my hands in his own. "You won't have to work, if you don't want to, Liv. If you feel about me the way I do for you, I would like very much for you to come home with me. I have enough for both of us, a penthouse in the city and a large estate on the coast, on Long Island, but I am alone, Liv. My parents died when I was quite young and left me rather well off. I do not have to work, you know, it just fills my days. Noblesse oblige and all that. I don't have many close friends and my only family, my brother, who also lives in New York, has his own life. I want to share my life with you, Liv, if you're willing."

Ten days later I flew to New York with Harry. He hadn't yet proposed, so I kept my apartment in Chicago and simply moved in with him with three suitcases filled with my best clothes. I felt giddy and impetuous, like a happy school girl with not a care in the world. Harry treated me well. We had fun together and enjoyed each other. I met some of his business partners. I met a few of his friends. I met his brother.

In the elevator riding down from Liv's suite, I decided I'd stop at the front desk to inquire if anyone had seen Harry last night or this morning. What Sam didn't know wouldn't bother him, I rationalized. To my great pleasure I found Stephanie, the assistant manager, standing behind the front desk counter with nary another guest in sight.

"Hello, Stephanie. How are you today?" I asked.

"Very well thank you, Mrs. Hendrick. How is your stay?"

"I'm afraid we've had some bad news, Stephanie, but nothing owing to the Stanley. I wonder if you know the guests in room 525 by sight, Stephanie. Liv and Harry Ross?"

She looked down toward her computer underneath the counter. When she looked back up at me she had a sly grin on her face and a twinkle in her eye. It's hard to be inconspicuous when one is exceeding beautiful, I thought.

"I have seen the Rosses," she said. "A very attractive couple. You know them?"

"Yes, Liv is a longtime friend of mine and Harry Ross is her fiancé. I wonder, did you happen to see them last night or this morning?"

"I did see Mr. Ross yesterday. I probably shouldn't say this," she lowered her voice. "He was a bit, how do you say, under the weather. He tripped over that chair there on his way into the bar. I noticed because there was a man sitting in the chair at the time, who consequently spilled his drink."

"I understand completely, Stephanie. I think we saw him shortly after you did and in the same condition. Did Mr. Ross and this other man have any sort of argument about the spilled drink?"

"No."

"Okay. And that's the only time you saw either of them yesterday or early today?"

"Well, I saw your friend, Ms. Ross, come and go through the lobby a few times today. She was always by herself. They're both very attractive you know, it's hard to miss them."

"Indeed Stephanie. Liv is one of those fortunate women who keeps getting better looking. Oh, by the way, may I use your phone to call the Spa?"

"Certainly," she said. She dialed, then passed the phone over to me.

"Stanley Spa. This is Jules. How may I help you?" said the voice on the line.

"Hello Jules. My name is Lauren Hendrick. I'm a guest of the Stanley and I'm looking for a friend who is also a guest at the hotel. Can you tell me if a Liv Ross or Liv Rogers has been there today?"

"Let me look. Just a moment."

"Take your time," I said.

"No Liv Ross or Rogers had an appointment with us today, Ms. Hendrick."

"Would she possibly have come in without an appointment, perhaps just to use the sauna or whirlpool without a treatment?"

"No, I don't think so, as she would have had to leave her name and room number and I do not see anything today under either name."

Thank you very much, Jules." I handed the phone back to Stephanie and said thank you to her as well.

As I walked outside and down the sidewalk to the Lodge building where our suite was located, I didn't like what I was thinking, so I forced myself to change my line of thought. Liv had absolutely nothing to gain from harming Harry. They were not married yet and she would certainly not have anything to gain monetarily from his demise prior to their legal marriage. Plus, and more importantly, I was once very, very close friends with her. She was a smart, educated and beautiful woman. She was driven yes, but to murder, no way.

I didn't have my room key, so I knocked on our door and immediately Olive barked from inside which lightened my mood. Sam opened the door. I gave him a big hug and then kissed Olive on the head.

Freshly showered and dressed, Sam and I sat at a lovely window table opposite Marie and Franco at dinner that night. I had asked Sam to relay the story of Harry's demise out in the mountains to our French friends, who sat opposite us speechless until Sam finished telling them both what had all transpired in the eighteen or so hours since we had last seen them.

Marie's reaction amounted to shock: Your friend's fiancé whom we just met yesterday is dead? Franco's riposte was more indignant: Why do tourists always die in America?

Later over scrumptious Tres Leches and berry compote desserts, I asked Marie and Franco, "Did either of you, by chance, see Liv at the Spa today?" Sam kicked me under the table. He had not said a word to them of my suspicions of a planted trip wire having led to Harry's death.

"No," said Franco, "but I saw her in her exercise clothes in the lobby and then enter the elevator when I came down this morning for some cigarettes for Marie."

"You did?" said Marie.

"Yes. I tried to make eye contact with her to say bonjour, but she was "in the zone" as they say, all flushed and out of breath from running, it seemed. She did not look in my direction."

"What time was this, Franco?" I asked.

Marie gave me a strange look and Franco said, "It must have been around seven, or rather just before, as I woke early this morning and wanted to make a business call in the lobby so as not to wake Marie."

"But Franco, why would you be making a business call at seven in the morning on a Saturday?" inquired Marie.

Franco puffed his chest a little, I noticed. He remained silent. His Adam's apple bounced up and down slightly; a tense unintentional gesticulation. He didn't appear to appreciate this line of inquiry from Marie. What have I started now? Interpersonal relationships can be so complicated, I thought, especially with couples. Ask any married couple an innocent question which has nothing to do with the parties asked, and a whole different bone of contention is often unearthed. But now I was curious why he was making business calls on a Saturday too, as I had seen his reaction.

With all six of our eyes on him, Franco's options were simple. He'd have to answer or avoid. He pushed his chair back from the table dramatically as if preparing to retreat but then thinking better of it, he turned to Marie and stated as flatly as a man with a melodic French accent can flatly state, "Marie, you must learn to trust me. Without trust a marriage has nothing, but since you must challenge me in front of our friends, I will tell you that this business call had to do with *my* horses. I was getting a report from Henri." He turned to Sam and me, "Henri is my primary trainer." Then he continued, "One of my fillies had bucked her shins just before we left on this trip and I wanted to know how her training run had gone today."

"How did she do today, Franco?" asked Sam after a moment.

"Very well indeed, thank you, Sam. Henri reported her to be in excellent shape, fully recovered. She timed one minute for five furlongs."

"That's very fast. How old is she?"

Before Franco could answer, a loud coughing erupted from behind me. I saw Franco and Marie's eyes dart to a somewhere behind Sam and me in the restaurant. The coughing quickly changed to more of a desperate gagging sound. I turned in my chair and recognized the quiet, older, silver-haired couple whom I had noticed in the hotel a few times before. The man was choking! His face was a deep red and he was flinging his arms wildly around him. Before I could process what I was seeing, the din in the restaurant became still as all eyes moved to this man who needed help. The woman with him jumped up, ran around the table and began to slap him quite hard on the back. I think I heard Franco say, "Here goes another one." The manager ran over then and lifted the man from his seat. He was still retching in the most uncomfortable way. The man-ger wrapped his arms around the man's chest from behind and began to squeeze and lift him in a sort of Heimlich maneuver. Everyone in the room was silent, watching this terrible scene in a sort of deer-in-headlights way. Thankfully, a few moments later the manager's abdominal thrusts worked and the man's gagging changed to a strong cough after a piece of what looked like rare beef flew from his lips and landed on the floor beside their table.

Sam and I turned our heads back toward our table so the couple wouldn't notice us staring, and Franco lifted his glass and said, "To one less dead tourist in America!"

Chapter 27

SAM RETURNED TO our suite after his early stroll with Olive, holding a newspaper instead of a scone, on Sunday morning. "Lauren, it's snowing like crazy out there."

I was standing in front of the gleaming marble bathroom vanity finishing my makeup. I bent down and patted Olive. The tips of her soft ears were still cold from the outside air. Olive loves the snow and looked a bit sad to be back inside already. I added a third coat of mascara and some Burt's Bees to my lips and walked out into our main sitting room.

Sam was on the couch reading the *Daily Camera* newspaper and I sat down next to him and said, "Good morning, Mister Hendrick. Have I told you today that I love you?"

"I love you too, Lauren." He didn't look up from the paper.

"Shall we order breakfast up, Sam, or should we eat in the downstairs breakfast room?"

He ignored my question, still reading. Then passed the newspaper to me and pointed to a small piece on the inside front cover titled "Body Found on Trail in Needles Wilderness".

> Larimer County Sheriff's department Saturday removed the body of a man found on a backcountry trail. "His body was brought out yesterday midday on a wheeled litter by Estes Park Sheriff Smith with assistance from Larimer County Search and Rescue," Cari Miller, a Sheriff's department spokeswoman said in a new release Saturday. The release didn't say if the death was considered suspicious. Miller couldn't be reached for comment. The man was found on an established horse trail on the east side of Needles Wilderness area. His identity will not be disclosed until next of kin are notified, Miller said. The Sheriff's office did not release any other information as of press time Saturday.

"We should check on Liv this morning, Sam. To make sure she's doing ok, under the circumstances."

"I agree. Let's stop by her room on the way down to breakfast," he said. "If she's not in, we'll leave a note for her with the front desk."

"Let's bring our coats. Olive's too. I think I'd like to walk into town for brunch today, if that's ok, Sam. Remember that little diner we've eaten at before, which we both really liked? They had amazingly good waffles with fresh fruit. Let's go there."

Dogs, especially sweet and mellow ones like Olive, often lighten one's mood and can spread cheer to people like Liv experiencing difficult times, I thought as the three of us rode the elevator down and walked over the Stanley's main building. I hoped Olive would be a nice distraction for Liv, should we find her in and distraught.

Sam was right. It was snowing outside. The hotel grounds had turned into a scene from a Hallmark made-for-TV Christmas movie. At the Stanley, with fresh snow covering the grounds, it could have been 1926 as easily as 2016 if one didn't look at the automobiles or at the people.

As we walked up the front steps and entered the lobby, I saw Jarvis and Kip sitting in the huge leather chairs flanking the left fireplace. They looked comfortable and relaxed, each in heavily textured woolen sweaters. I pulled Sam's hand in their direction and we strolled over to greet them.

"Good morning gentlemen. We're glad to see you both again. Have you met our dog, Olive?" I heralded.

"And a good morning to you!" replied Jarvis jovially. Then he extended his hand to Olive, who pattered over toward him eager to meet a new human.

Kip asked if we cared to sit in the empty chairs opposite and join them. I love being on vacation and having no real agenda which allows for impromptu social interactions. Plus, I'm one of those people who has always enjoyed meeting and getting to know strangers. Sam's also quite a talker and I could tell he enjoyed Kip and Jarvis' general aura of optimism, so we accepted their invitation to sit and visit.

"We missed you in the bar last night," said Jarvis as he scratched Olive's ears. Olive had made herself comfortable on the floor between them.

"We had rather a big day yesterday and went straight to bed after dinner," said Sam. "Did we miss much?"

"Not much at all," replied Jarvis, "just some gossip about your friends frankly; the very attractive couple whom we met with you on Friday night."

"Do tell, Jarvis," I said with slight trepidation, but with a smile on my face.

"Well apparently, the man who was sitting next to us last night at the bar is dating the petite brunette hostess who works in the restaurant. She told him that the Sheriff had come into the restaurant yesterday afternoon with a couple that she described as looking much like you two. She then told him that the three of you went straight over to an exceedingly beautiful blonde lady, who was sitting by herself at a table, to tell her that her that husband was just found dead. I certainly hope this story had been grossly exaggerated," concluded Jarvis.

"I'm afraid not," said Sam. "Liv and I stumbled across a body while we were out trail riding yesterday and it turned out to be our friend Liv's fiancé, Harry. It seems he had been out running by himself and had tripped on some rock steps on the trail. He fell and hit his head hard enough on the stone to, unfortunately, kill him.

"Oh my word. Please excuse Jarvis' rather blunt inquisition. We had hoped it was not true," said Kip.

"It's ok, Kip. It's a small town and a very small hotel, word is bound to get around," said Sam.

"We actually need to go upstairs to check on Liv," I said. "It's all rather unreal, frankly. The Sheriff told us Liv will have to call a relative of Harry's, his brother probably, as he and Liv were not married yet, in order to officially identify the body."

"It's simply too sad. Such a wonderfully attractive couple, on the very verge of marriage. We are so sorry," said Jarvis rather eloquently.

"Thank you," I said. "I have to admit, the only reason I'm not a complete mess over this is that we had only just met Harry here this weekend ourselves. I do feel very badly for Liv though. I can't imagine what she must be going through. By the way, had either of you seen Liv around yesterday yourselves?"

"No, not yesterday. Isn't that right, Kip?"

"That's right, Jarvis." Then turning back to face me, Kip said, "You know the first time we saw your friend Liv was before we met the both of you. I think it was Thursday or maybe Wednesday. I always get my days confused when we vacation. No matter. Your friend Liv was walking along Main Street in town. I remember because she had the loveliest outfit on with very high heels but she was carrying a large paper bag, like a grocery store sack. We noticed because she is so lovely looking and because the shopping bag she was carrying just didn't match her outfit at all." He smiled sadly as if in condolence.

"She is a very beautiful woman. And strong too. She'll survive this, I'm sure. I do feel deeply sorry for her though. Harry was to be her first husband."

"On that note, we'd better go up and check on her," said Sam.

"Please don't let us delay you further," said Kip standing.

Jarvis stood too and extended his hand to me saying, "It has been a pleasure to meet you both, Lauren. Again, we are most sorry for your friend's loss. We'll be in the bar again tonight, if you would care to join us there after dinner."

"Thank you Kip. Tonight I think Sam and I will need a drink, or three. We'll plan to see you there, with Marie and Franco in tow too, hopefully."

Sam, Olive and I rode the elevator up to the fifth floor. Sam was silent. I was thinking about the grocery bag that Kip mentioned Liv was carrying. Why would she have been buying groceries while staying at the full-service Stanley? She and Harry were probably health nuts. They probably needed to purchase fresh pressed green juices or sport drinks like Muscle Milk, I reasoned, since they had flown here.

We exited the elevator and turned away from Marie and Franco's suite to the opposite corner of the fifth floor toward Liv's suite. The hallway was quiet and we didn't hear anything from behind 525 as Sam lighted rapped on the door.

Olive looked up at me expectantly as we waited. "I hope she's ok," I said. "Perhaps we should just leave a note for her downstairs, if she doesn't answer."

Sam knocked again and as we were turning to leave, the door slowly opened.

"May I help you?" said a middle-aged man with a precise, fresh haircut and a five o'clock shadow above his thin upper lip and on his chin and cheeks. He had dark blond hair with just a hint of grey at the temples and was wearing an attractive, trim corduroy jacket with dark denim jeans and glossy leather

Chelsea boots. He gave the appearance of an orderly man; a man who took good care of his shoes.

Sam said, "We're here to visit Liv Rogers. We're friends of hers. Is she still checked into this suite?"

The man stood back, opened the door a few inches further and with a quizzical, surprised look said, "Yes, this is her room. I'm not sure she's up for visitors. May I tell her whose calling?"

"Please do," I said. "It's Lauren and Sam. We'd very much like to see her, if possible."

He nodded, asked us to wait a moment and shut the door softly on us. I looked at Sam. He looked at me and shrugged his shoulders.

"I wonder who that is?" I said mostly to myself as we waited in the hallway like unwanted Greenpeace solicitors.

Several minutes later, the door opened again. Fully this time. The corduroy jacketed man, stood back to let us enter and said, "Forgive me. Liv didn't mention she knew anyone here and I wasn't sure if she was receiving due to the unfortunate accident with my brother Harry yesterday."

"We won't stay long. We just wanted to check in on her and make sure she's ok," said Sam extending his hand toward the man.

He shook Sam's hand and said, "My name is Nick Ross. Harry's brother. I flew in immediately when Liv called to give me the news. I just can't believe it."

"We're very sorry for you loss Nick," said Sam. "This is my wife Lauren, a longtime friend of Liv's. Oh, and this is our dog Olive."

"Please come in and sit down," he said. "Liv is just in the bedroom. Said she'll be out in a minute."

Nick proceeded to busy himself at the bar, with his back to us, asking over his shoulder if we cared for anything. He looked nothing like Harry. Harry had definitely inherited the chiseled cheekbones, aquiline nose and thick dark, almost black hair. By contrast, Nick was of the same approximate build, at least six foot tall, but the resemblance stopped there. Nick appeared rather nerdy while Harry gave a dashing impression.

Liv's suite, I noticed next, was still exceedingly tidy, none of her or Harry's possessions were visible anywhere and not a newspaper, phone or pair of sunglasses lied about. The suite was neat as a pin, even in light of the tragic event which had just befallen Liv the previous day. It was just as her childhood bedroom room had always been, I thought. Some traits never change.

"I'd love a cup of tea, Nick," I said, "If it's not too much trouble."

"Not at all," he responded, his back still to us.

"Nick, is there anything that Sam and I can do to assist you or Liv? I realize you don't know us at all, but I've been friends with Liv since childhood and I'm sure you've heard that it was us who found your brother yesterday. It was such a shock, and so tragic," I said looking at Sam when I used his word, "and I feel, we both do, that we want to help you and Liv in any way."

Nick turned and I realized how similar to Matthew McConaughey he actually looked. Not the McConaughey who found stardom in *Dazed and Confused*, but the AIDs riddled character he played in *Dallas Buyers Club.* He had the look of a middle-aged man who ran too much and didn't eat any carbohydrates. Nick had sharp facial features resembling a bird, with teeth a little too large for his mouth and thin lips. He did not carry enough weight on his frame to look particularly strong, or even attractive.

The door behind us opened then, so both Sam and I stood up. Liv looked docile, her usual air of confidence had disappeared along with her usual erect posture. I immediately walked over to her and gave her a hug. She said nothing, but hugged me back. After a moment, I led her to the couch where Sam and I had been sitting.

"Liv, I hope you don't mind us stopping by, but we had to check in on you to see how you're holding up. Is there anything Sam or I can do?"

"I'm ok, I guess," she said sitting down. "You've met Nick? He's Harry's brother. He just got here. He flew straight out from New York, when I called."

"Yes, Liv."

Sam said, "It was good of you to arrive so quickly, Nick."

"Of course, what else could I have done?" replied Nick simply as he sat in the chair opposite the couch.

Liv gave Nick a strange look, her eyes at half mast, and then averted her eyes from his completely. She crossed her legs and coughed. She seemed nervous to me, but most likely it was grief. I picked up her hand and to lighten the mood, introduced Olive to her. She wasn't having it. She ignored Olive completely and simply said, "Nick, you know we'll have to go soon, to identify Harry's body at the hospital's morgue."

To his credit, Nick stood, walked over to where Liv sat and put his hand on her shoulder and said, "You don't have to come with me Liv, if you're not up to it. They need only me."

Liv placed her free hand on top of his, which still rested on her shoulder and said, "I know Nick, but I think I need to see Harry for myself. A part of me still believes this is all a big mistake and it's not really him."

Nick patted her shoulder before removing his hand. He looked at Sam and me and said, "What do you think? Should I let her go? Will it be too much for her?"

I looked at Liv then and asked her directly, "Wouldn't you prefer to remember Harry as he was Liv? I'm sure Nick can handle it. Wouldn't you rather stay and have some breakfast with Sam and me? We'd be happy to keep you company until Nick returns."

The head strong Liv that I remembered well, erupted. "No, Lauren. I want to go with Nick. Has it even occurred to you two that you're wrong and it was not Harry at all that you saw yesterday? You had just met him. You didn't know him at all."

From what Liv had previously told me about Harry and his small remaining family, I didn't assume Harry and his brother had been very close as adults. In fact, I was sure she had said the brothers were not. So I didn't expect that Liv and Nick had been close or even knew one another very well, so when Liv then jumped up off of the couch and ran over to Nick, dropped to her knees before him and began to cry into his lap, I was startled at the intimacy of her grief.

Nick patted her head and said, "Liv, of course you can go with me. Don't worry. This will all be over soon." He looked at Sam and me and shrugged his shoulders, while her face was still buried in his lap, as if he was surprised and a bit embarrassed by Liv's outpouring. "There, there Liv," he said and patted her head again.

I stood and walked over toward Liv after a moment. Nick looked at me rather helplessly as he was still pinned underneath Liv in his chair. I bent down and said, "Liv, we all love you. Of course we won't stop you from seeing Harry. I'm so sorry that it was Sam and I who found him and that we were with the Sheriff when he informed you of this horrible accident. Stand up now Liv," I said gently pulling on her shoulder.

She stopped crying and lifted her head. Nick sat motionless in the chair and looking embarrassed. I tugged on Liv's shoulder a bit more and said, "Liv, Sam, Nick and I are all here for you and are very, very sorry for your loss. Please come sit down and dry your eyes."

She obeyed and I handed her the cup of tea Nick had prepared for me which I had not yet touched. She took it from my hands gently and I could see that her face was wet with tears and that her eye makeup was smeared and running. I turned and walked into the bedroom from which she had exited and called over my shoulder, "Let me get you a tissue."

Chapter 28

Liv's bedroom was dark, so I opened the draperies. It was still snowing and it looked as if it was beginning to accumulate several inches outside. I turned to enter the ensuite bathroom and noticed that the bedroom was just as neat as the sitting area, with absolutely no personal effects lying around on any of the polished surfaces. The closet doors and dresser drawers were all closed completely. I walked into the bathroom and turned on the light. This suite had the same large marble bathtub as ours, but as this was the original building of the Stanley and not the newer construction of the Lodge outpost, where Sam and I were staying; there was a large functional picture window above the bathtub which our bath lacked. I could almost envision the original claw foot tub that had once been in the same spot. There were no bottles or cosmetics lying out on the vanity top by the double sinks. The only evidence that anyone was actually staying in the suite were the two toothbrushes and a tube of Rembrandt resting inside a water glass and the zippered Louis Vuitton cosmetic case placed neatly on the marble surface between the sinks. I picked up the tissues housed in a modern stainless holder and brought it back into the sitting room with me.

I pulled out a few tissues and handed them to Liv. She looked at me then with what I saw as fright in her wide, mascara-smeared blue eyes.

"You're very strong," I said to Liv. "You will survive this," I said, "but I am so sorry you have to go through it Liv. You don't deserve this tragedy."

She shook her head sadly then and wiped her eyes with the tissues. She said nothing so I sat back down and Olive jumped up beside me on the couch, on the opposite side from where Liv sat.

"Do you have a vehicle to get to the hospital Nick?" asked Sam. "I'd be happy to drive you or let you borrow ours."

"Thank you, but I'm all set. I flew into Denver and rented a SUV at the airport, so I have that here."

"Liv, do you want for me to phone your mom or your sister or your brother, anyone? I'll do it, if you don't feel up to it."

"No, don't do that Lauren. I'll tell them myself when I'm ready," she snapped. Then, as if realizing that I had meant no harm, she softened her gaze toward me and said, "I'm sorry I'm being so terrible Lauren. I'm just fucking upset and I think I'm half out of my mind too."

"Of course you are Liv. Lauren understands how upset you are," said Sam.

"That's right Liv," chimed in Nick next. "These people just want to make sure that you're ok. We all know you are grieving."

"You should be too, Nick," said Liv with ice in her voice.

"I am, Liv. I am. I lost my brother. Let's not forget that I've known him even longer than you."

Sam and I looked at one another. That was a pretty heartless thing to say we communicated to one another wordlessly.

"I just wish I would never have met any of you," cried Liv into her tissue, then she began to sob in earnest, shoulders heaving and gasping for air.

I didn't know what to say. Thankfully, I've not had too much experience with grief myself or even with grieving friends or family. I just wanted to try to make Liv feel better, but I had no idea how to accomplish it.

Minutes went by without any one of us saying a word. Nick looked like a skinny bird, his face in profile looking outside toward the falling snow. He tapped his right heel quietly, rhythmically on the carpet. Liv had her beautiful head bent down, her face mostly hidden behind tissues. She was calming down. Her sobbing subsided of its own volition. Sam was looking at me. When I returned his gaze, he motioned his eyes toward the door as a signal that he was ready to exit. I agreed and nodded slightly. I simply did not know what I could do to make my friend feel better.

"Liv," I said, "when will you be leaving the Stanley, and where will you go?"

"I'm leaving tomorrow. Our flight is direct back to JFK, so I'll just go back to Harry's home and stay there until everything's taken care of, I guess."

"You needn't worry, Lauren," said Nick. "I'll be on the same flight with her and make sure she gets to my brother's house safely. She can stay there as long as she wants. There won't be much for her to do, as far as Harry's estate goes, as they weren't married yet, but I'll make sure she's well taken care of. I know how much my brother loved Liv."

"Liv, would you like for me to fly out to help in a week or two? I'd be happy to help you pack or just keep you company, or anything."

"I don't know, Lauren. I can't think that far out yet."

"Ok. I understand. Well, let me make sure I have your phone number so I can call you and check in," I said pulling out my phone. I scrolled to Liv's name in my contacts list. Her record was accompanied by a photo of her that had been posted on Facebook a few years ago. She was smiling while sitting outside on a park bench. I tapped the picture to make it larger on my screen and showed it to her. "Look at the photo I have of you on my phone Liv. I'll bet you haven't seen this in a while."

She looked at it and after a moment, seemed to recognize the old photo. She smiled half-heartedly and said that the photo had been taken by her brother when she had last gone home to visit him and his family in the Midwest several years ago.

She gave me her phone number and I typed it in and told her that now she knew; whenever she would call me that was the photo of her I would see. She laughed just a little and I hoped we both felt better even if just for that brief moment.

Sam stood and Olive jumped down off the couch. "Liv, Nick, we'd like to invite you for dinner, just in the restaurant here in the hotel, since you'll both be leaving tomorrow. Would that be ok?"

"Yes, I think I'd like that, wouldn't you, Nick?" replied Liv.

"If you think you're feeling up to it, Liv."

"Wonderful. For fear of sounding like your mom, Liv, it'll do you good to have a decent meal and it'll make Sam and me feel better to at least do something for you before you leave. Shall we meet in the restaurant at seven for a drink and eat around seven-thirty?"

"Yes," said Liv simply while looking at Nick.

"Good. We'll see you then," I said bending down to hug Liv again. "I'm going to text you with my phone number here in a minute, Liv, so you'll have it handy. Call me anytime Liv, even while you're still here, if you need anything at all. Sam and I are here to help and support you any way that we can."

After leaving Liv and Nick in the far northern corner of the Stanley's fifth floor, we walked the length of the quiet hallway toward the far southern corner, to Marie and Franco's suite. Sam knocked softly on door 515 and it felt like déjà vu from just a half hour or so before at door 525. This time however, the door opened swiftly and fully after our first knock. We were greeted by a smiling Franco with a friendly bonjour. He immediately invited the three of us inside.

Marie was reclined on the couch reading a book and laid it spine up on the coffee table as she sat and greeted us with a warm good morning and a cooing in Olive's ear. Unlike the suite we had just come from, theirs was lived-in, with various pieces of apparel hanging from the backs of chairs and used coffee cups and glasses on almost every flat surface except the floor. I noticed a dirty ashtray on the sill of a window and asked Marie if I might have a cigarette.

She practically beamed when she said, "Yes, of course, Lauren. I think I'd like one as well. Would you care for a coffee too?"

"Yes, please. The Nespresso machines that they have here are quite nice, don't you think?"

"Yes. Room service is getting quite tired of me calling up for fresh cream though, so they finally brought a whole carafe to me which I have in our bar refrigerator, so we're all set." She pulled the desk chair over next to the arm chair by the window and opened it a couple more inches. She offered me a cigarette from the package on the coffee table and then turned toward the bar to make our Americanos. Franco and Sam were sitting on the couch already and Sam called out for a coffee too.

"Let me check my cream supply," Marie joked while holding the half-full carafe up in the air for us to see. "Yes, I think we've got enough for you, Sam."

When the Americanos were made, she took a cigarette for herself and joined me by the open window.

"What are we up to today?" she inquired after we had both admired the sparkly snowflakes that were blowing inside through the open section of the window before us.

"Sam and I were going to head into town with Olive. There is a diner that makes a wonderful, very traditional American breakfast of waffles, eggs and bacon. We had planned to leave a while ago, but just stopped in at Liv's suite to see how she's doing this morning and then decided we'd better stop in to visit you two also."

"How is she doing?" inquired Marie.

"Not great. In the short time we were there, she vacillated between crying in her soon-to-be brother in law's lap and being angry. Probably just grief. I certainly can't imagine how I would react in her situation. We met Harry's brother. He was in her suite when we got there. He couldn't be more different looking than Harry. Seemed nice enough though. His name is Nick"

"Liv was crying in his lap?"

"Yes, I thought it a bit odd too. Liv had told me that Harry and his brother weren't particularly close and I didn't think Liv had known Nick very well. But again, she was pretty agitated, so anything is possible I suppose. They have to go to the morgue, which is located the Estes hospital, today."

"Oh, my. I hope I never have to identify a body of someone I know, let alone love," said Marie earnestly.

"Me too."

We sat quietly smoking for a few minutes. The men were talking on the couch, but I wasn't listening. The tobacco tasted wonderful, probably because we were smoking indoors, such a taboo luxury these days.

"Harry's brother lives in New York too?" asked Marie upon snuffing out her cigarette in the Stanley branded ashtray which she must have asked housekeeping to provide.

"Yes, I believe that is what Liv told me."

"He certainly arrived quickly," she stated.

"Yes, I suppose he did. He seemed like a nice man, not as attractive as Harry, but nice and neat. Liv must have phoned him yesterday afternoon after being told a family member would need to identify Harry. Nick even said that Liv could stay in Harry's home as long as she wanted and that he would make sure she was taken care of, which I thought was very thoughtful as they weren't married yet and Liv probably isn't on the deed or anything. Who knows what he exactly meant by that, but I suppose that is what Liv will have to figure out."

"That is generous. Many wealthy families fight, what's the expression, tooth and nail, over estates when a relative passes. They want to keep the wealth inside the family. Maybe this is better for your friend? Can you imagine the family's reaction, if Harry's total estate was left to Liv and he died only a week or so after they had married? I'd bet she'd find herself in court by some long-lost relative."

"I shudder at the thought, Marie, but certainly there would have been some type of prenuptial agreement these days, don't you think?"

"Yes, I suppose so. I'm being quite pessimistic though aren't I? Perhaps I need to get some breakfast into my tummy to lighten my mood?"

“Spoken like a true French woman,” I joked, ”but a grand idea. Does an American diner breakfast in town sound appealing? Shall we gather our coats and hats and all take a walk through the snow down to Main Street?”

I nudged Sam when the check arrived for breakfast. He looked at me. “Please leave a generous tip Sam, since they let Olive come inside and sit with us under the table.”

“Don’t I always?” was his response with a smile.

Marie said, “It’s nice they let her in. It’s far too cold outside to have Olive wait on the sidewalk. Dogs are always welcome in restaurants in France; always have been. I can’t imagine not having my Vivi with me and I certainly wouldn’t want to have to leave her outside, by herself.”

“I’ll bet you miss her. Who’s taking care of Vivi now, while you and Franco are here?”

“She’s at home. Our housekeeper is watching out for her. I spoil her terribly and Maeve does not. Little Vivi will have lost a kilo or two in my absence surely.”

“I think I spoke with Maeve briefly when I phoned you?”

“Yes, you probably did. She is with us full-time and is almost a member of the family at this point. I think I’ve had her twenty years,” said Marie.

I lowered my voice, so Sam and Franco wouldn’t hear me so clearly, “Marie, did I ever tell you that I was really worried about you back then, when you were so sick suddenly after marrying

Franco and I hadn't heard back from you in weeks. You know how silly I can be, with my conspiracy theories and such. You sounded so unhappy at that time and then you were so ill all of a sudden, and when you stopped writing to me I was worried you were being poisoned!"

Marie parted her lips into an almost perfect O shape in mock horror and patted her heart, then said, "Lauren, you're simply too much! Who did you suppose was poisoning me?"

"I thought it was probably the help. Maeve or someone," I lied. And then, by way of excuse, "I was watching *Miss Fischer's Murder Mysteries* series on Netflix at the time."

"Well as you can see, I'm just fine now Lauren, but I am touched, in a strange way, that you were so concerned."

"May I let you in on another one of my theories Marie?" I said quietly, grinning conspiratorially.

"We're all set, ladies," said Franco as he, Sam and Olive began to slide out of our booth.

I made the universal one finger in the air sign to Marie, meaning to-be-continued, and we also slid out of the booth and allowed our husbands to help us on with our coats.

"Let's walk around a little before we head back to the Stanley. Is that alright with everyone?" asked Franco.

We all agreed and pulled our hats and gloves on as we exited the Main Street Diner into the still falling snow. It wasn't terribly cold outside and with my stomach full of waffles and strawberries, it felt warmer than it had when we had entered. After we had walked about halfway down the block and Marie had taken a couple of puffs from her cigarette, I touched Marie's arm to slow her stride a bit allowing the space between Olive, Sam and Franco in front of us on the sidewalk to grow.

"Marie, you're probably going to think this is crazy, and I admit it's just a conspiracy theory from my apparently wild imagination, but when Sam and I found Harry's dead body yesterday, we looked around a little before we rode back to the stable to phone the police."

"Yes," she said cautiously.

"Well, he was in his running clothes, and he had been really drunk the night before, but it's hard to imagine such a healthy man, who was in such great shape, to trip accidentally right on the top of those stone stairs." I hesitated.

"Yes," Marie said again, this time with her eyebrows raised in expectation of the point of my story.

"Well, after Sam checked his pulse and we were sure there was nothing we could do for him, I walked up to the top of the stairs that he had tripped down and I saw a little hole, it looked like a screw hole, in the base of one of the tree trunks. The hole looked fresh and was about a foot above the ground, so I walked over to the opposite side of the steps and there was a handrail post almost exactly straight across from that tree." I stopped and looked at Marie. She was smoking and looking at me intently, or perhaps patiently. I continued, "The post opposite the tree had rub marks on it, also fresh, also about a foot off the ground."

"What do you mean, rub marks?"

"It looked like the kind of indentation into the wood, that a wire would make that had been tied around the post and then pulled tightly, like by someone hitting and then tripping on the wire which had been strung between the two and falling forward with a hundred and eighty pounds or so of weight."

"So you think someone ran a wire across the stairs? From the tree across to the handrail?"

"Yes, exactly," I said.

"But who? Why? And even if there were a wire across the stairs, how do you know it wasn't for something else, at a different time, I mean?"

"I don't know, Marie."

We walked a little further in silence and I began to think about where someone would get wire. The men and Olive, still ahead of us, looked back and waved as they opened a green door and entered into a shop up the block.

"Do you want to go in?" I said to Marie as we approached the painted green door of the home furnishings store.

Marie snuffed her cigarette out on a trash bin on the sidewalk and said in one breath, "Yes, let's go in. Did you tell this to the police?"

"Yes. I told the Sheriff. Sheriff Smith. I pointed to the handrail and the tree, he didn't want us walking around, and told him almost exactly what I just told you. Just for the record, Sam saw it too, before we called the police. He agreed the hole looked like a screw hole, perhaps from an i-hook, which would be perfect to use to discreetly string a wire. He saw the rub marks on the post too."

"What does Sam say, Lauren?" asked Marie as she motioned for us to sit on one of the grey leather sectionals available for sale in the store.

"He said to tell the Sheriff and let him do his job, so that's what we did."

"Lauren, just for the sake of argument, if there was a trip wire, and it was actually meant for Harry and not for someone or something else, who do you think would do such a thing?"

"I have no idea," I lied again. "But Harry was a rich man. Money, revenge or love are almost always the cause of premeditated murder."

"What are you ladies talking about?" asked Franco as he sat down on the sofa next to Marie.

Before Marie could say anything I blurted, "I love murder mystery stories, Franco. I often make up little espionage tales to entertain myself. I was just…"

"Lauren, you're not telling Marie and Franco that Harry was intentionally tripped yesterday are you? I thought we agreed to let the Sheriff handle it."

"What?" said Franco turning to Sam, who then rolled his eyes heavenward and sat down next to me on the demonstration sectional.

Chapter 29

It had been decided. Everyone: Marie, Franco and Sam too, had all agreed. It was suspicious that Sam and I had seen what looked like the evidence of a trip wire where Harry had fallen and died. With looks of unabashed disdain, it had also been decided unfathomable to mention that my friend and Harry's fiancée, Liv, might be the culprit. All had agreed on the walk back to the Stanley from town that Sam and I had done the right thing in telling the authorities what we had seen, but that was all that we (meaning I) should do. It was just too serious an accusation to hypothesize who might be responsible for such a malicious act, which quite frankly, all agreed, was most likely an accident and that the hole and indentation we had seen had been left over from something or someone completely unrelated.

Upon returning to the hotel, Sam and I excused ourselves to our suite where I was, all had also agreed, to phone Sheriff Smith to inquire about his investigation but nothing more. Sam and Olive settled in the bedroom for a nap and I closed the bedroom door behind me, after pulling the drapes shut and kissing both of them. I picked up the Sheriff's business card along with my cell phone from the desk in our living room and then pulled out a bottle of Perrier from our bar while I thought about what I wanted to say to the Sheriff. I sat down on the couch and then got up again. I went back over to the desk to get the hotel's branded notepad and ballpoint pen. I carried them back to the couch, took a deep breath and dialed the office number printed on his thin, flimsy card.

"Sheriff's office," said a man's voice.

"Hello. My name is Lauren Hendrick. I'm calling for Sheriff Smith," I said clearly and slowly. It sounded loud in the Sheriff's office. I could hear quite a bit of talking in the background.

"Just a minute, ma'am," said the voice before a click and then the silence of being on hold.

While I waited I got up again to get the bottle opener and a clean glass from behind the bar. I sat back down, poured some Perrier into the glass and took a large drink. I waited another couple minutes, wishing that I had one of Marie's French cigarettes, and then heard another click before Sheriff Smith announced himself on the other end of the line.

"Hello, Sheriff. This is Lauren Hendrick, from yesterday. I just wanted to phone to ask if there is anything further that my husband or I can do to assist in your investigation."

"Thank you, Mrs. Hendrick," said the Sheriff. "Everything is under control. We have a positive ID on the body. Your friend, Liv Rogers and the deceased's brother, Nick Ross, met me at the hospital morgue a couple hours ago. I'm afraid you were correct yesterday. The body is positively that of Harry Ross."

"You were there with them you say, Sheriff? How did Liv take it, if I might ask?"

"As well as can be expected. Naturally, she was quite upset. She began crying and had to leave the room."

"Did she and Nick Ross tell you that they will be leaving Colorado to go back to New York tomorrow?"

"Yes, Mrs. Hendrick."

"Well, I'm just curious, I mean..."

"Yes?" asked the Sheriff impatiently.

I cleared my throat, "Have you learned anything more about a possible trip wire?"

"I'm afraid, Mrs. Hendrick, I cannot discuss this case with you, except to say we, and I, will continue to investigate all leads and evidence at the scene."

"Do you think Sheriff, that there *had* been a trip wire planted from the tree to the handrail post in this case?"

"I can't discuss my findings with you Mrs. Hendrick. Will that be all?"

"Well, I guess so, yes."

"Goodbye, Mrs. Hendrick."

"Sheriff?" Think quickly, Lauren, I said to myself. "Sheriff, did you find out where Liv Rogers was yesterday morning, around the time of death? I think she usually runs, I mean ran, along with Harry, but she told me she was going to the Spa here at the Stanley yesterday instead, but she didn't."

"How do you know she didn't?"

"I called the Spa myself to ask."

"Mrs. Hendrick, I interviewed Ms. Rogers myself and I cannot discuss this further, except to say you'll need to stay out of it. This is a matter which will be handled thoroughly and solely by my office. Good day, Mrs. Hendrick."

"Just one more thing, Sheriff"

"Yes."

"Did you confirm exactly when his brother arrived here? It seems like he got here so quickly. Did he really just fly in today?"

"Yes, ma'am," said the Sheriff.

I waited for more to no avail. Then said, "Did you check his plane ticket or boarding pass? He told me, us, that he took a commercial red-eye from New York then rented a SUV from DIA just this morning."

"Yes, Mrs. Hendrick that has been confirmed. Now I really need to go."

"Ok Sheriff. Just so you know, Sam and I will be departing to go home to Denver tomorrow also. I assume we are free to leave?"

"Yes, ma'am." Was that snark in his tone?

"You have our home contact information. Please do let us know if you have any further questions for us."

"I will," said the Sheriff. "Goodbye."

Damn it, I thought as I hung up. The conversation had not made me feel better. I was not at all convinced that the Sheriff had really looked into the possibility of a trip wire. He said he had interviewed Liv, but she's so beautiful and had been crying, how thorough an interview had it been? The only certainties

Sheriff Smith had imparted were that the body really had been that of Harry Ross, and that Nick Ross had only flown into Colorado today. Was the Sheriff really investigating this like a murder case, or was he hoping for a cut and dry accidental death case involving an out-of-town tourist who was not known locally and would therefore be forgotten quickly?

"Well, I'm not convinced," I said aloud to myself and stood up. I pulled on my coat and grabbed the keys to the G-class. I left a note for Sam that said I had taken the car to go into town, noted the time, three-forty p.m., and signed Love, L.

As I walked through the parking lot, I looked for Nick's rental SUV, but as I did not know the exact make or model and because most of the vehicles in the lot and in Colorado in general were SUVs, I didn't spot it. Many of the parked vehicles also carried discreet rental car company emblems, so I walked back inside, into the Lodge lobby.

Molly was sitting at the small front desk and smiled when she saw me return. "Did you forget something, Mrs. Hendrick?" she inquired politely.

"Actually, yes, Molly. A friend of mine asked me to get his sunglasses from his SUV. I have the keys, but can't remember the car since it's a rental. His name is Nick Ross. He's staying in the main hotel but taking a nap right now. Can you look up the make or model of the car he registered with?"

"Let me check," she said as she began typing.

I crossed my fingers inside my coat pocket.

"Yes, here it is. Nick Ross. Looks like an Escalade with the license number YVM-2247."

"This is the Nick Ross, who just checked into the hotel *today, this morning,* right?"

"Yes, that is what it shows here, Mrs. Hendrick."

"Thank you so much, Molly. I'll be able to get his sunglasses now. Appreciate it," I said as I turned and headed back outside to the parking lot.

As I walked down through the first aisle of the guest lot in front of the hotel, I was pretty impressed with my detecting skills. That had gone far better than my call with Sheriff Smith. I had reconfirmed with the hotel that Nick had just checked in today and soon I'd be able to make sure he had only had the vehicle from Denver since this morning too. As I rounded the first aisle and made my way back toward the hotel in the center row of the lot, I looked up toward the top floor corner windows of the hotel. Marie and Franco's room was dark and Liv's had a light on but I couldn't see anyone or anything inside. As I rounded the third aisle I saw a black Escalade with a Colorado plate that began with YVM. I couldn't remember the numbers that Molly had said, but the first letters had been YVM. This Escalade was dirty enough to have been driven up here in the snow from Denver and it showed a little Hertz sticker on the driver's side of the windshield. I pulled out my phone from my handbag and typed a note: Escalade, Hertz, YVM-2247 from the plate. I peered inside the vehicle but didn't see anything personal or of particular note, just a Starbucks cup in the holder between the two front seats. The tinting on the back seat windows was darker and I wasn't able to see anything on the backseat bench or floorboards.

After I got myself inside our rental SUV, just one row over from the Escalade, I googled Hertz DIA and dialed the airport location's office number that popped up on my screen. I asked the woman who picked up the line if a Nick Ross had rented his Escalade yet, as I was waiting for him.

"Let me look," she replied. Then not more than two seconds later said, "Nick Ross checked our vehicle out this morning at six sixteen a.m."

So Nick had not arrived to the Stanley until this early morning. That was good news, I supposed as I started the Mercedes. I turned on the windshield wipers and set the defrost to high. I didn't feel like getting out and scraping the snow off the car. Once the front windshield was clear enough to see through and the back was almost clear enough, I put the SUV in reverse using the little paddle-shifter on the steering column, pulled out and headed the five minutes down into town and toward Main Street.

If I wanted to purchase a rather long length of wire and i-hooks, and maybe a screwdriver and pliers to twist the wire nice and tight, I would go to a hardware store to get them, so I parallel parked on Main Street near the old-school Ace Hardware store that Marie, Franco, Sam and I had all walked past on our first day in Estes Park. Surely however, if the trip wire had been intentionally strung across the trail to kill Harry and not for some other reason, I wouldn't buy these things so nearby. I would have garnered my materials a long time ago, from several different stores in different towns clandestinely and then secretly carried the items up with me.

As I fed the parking meter with some quarters from my handbag, I turned toward the old-timey storefront with its wood façade and hand-painted red Ace sign, which was swinging slightly over the sidewalk in the breeze. The store really did look like it had not changed one iota since 1959. The store door pulled open as I approached and a man wearing a baseball cap with a trout embroidered on it paused to hold the door open for me to enter. As I said thank you to him I noticed the bag he was holding; a sack made of kraft paper which was the same size and shape as a paper grocery sack, just like what Kip and Jarvis had described seeing Liv carrying.

I wandered through the quiet store. Its narrow aisles were piled high with all manner of gadgets and tools. But why would Liv purchase these incriminating items so close by, I thought as I perused? Then it hit my waffle and coffee-filled head. Her suitcase had been lost at the Stanley. She had been making a scene at the front desk about it when I had first seen her with Marie. Now I understood why she had been so aggrieved about the loss of her bag and why, when I had asked what was so important inside of it, she had shrugged it off with her simple answer of toiletries. With renewed vigor, I marched up to the two cash registers near the front door.

"Are you finding everything alright?" asked the clerk in a red vest working the checkout lane nearest me.

"I am, thank you. But I have a quick question," I said lowering my voice and leaning toward him across the counter. "I know this is a very random question, but did you happen to sell a rather large amount of thin wire and some i-hooks to a woman here the other day?"

A deep V formed between the clerk's bushy eyebrows as he recollected. "No, can't say that I did, lady, but it's hard to remember all of our customers. She from around here?"

"No, she wouldn't have been anyone you know, but she is very pretty, tall, slim, well dressed and with long blonde hair."

"Wire, you say?"

"Yes, a rather long amount of it, maybe forty or fifty feet?"

Turning his head, he called over his shoulder, "You see a pretty blonde lady buying wire here, Chuck?"

I looked at Chuck hopefully. He cocked his head, shrugged his shoulders and said, "Yeah, there was blonde in here day before last. Bought a mess of picture hanging material."

I bounded toward Chuck. "Really, like on Thursday?"

"Yeah, it was probably Thursday," he semi-confirmed.

"Was she pretty, with blue eyes, well-dressed and about yay high?" I asked, holding my hand up to about five foot nine, a couple inches above my head.

"Sure was. I never saw her before. Looked like she was from out of town."

"And she bought a lot of wire and maybe i-hooks and pliers?"

"Sure did. I told her the wire she was buying would hold an elephant, but she said the frames on her art were really heavy."

"What else did she buy?"

"Oh, the usual stuff. Some i-hooks, thought those were too big too, and some pliers and a small hammer, oh and wire cutters too."

"Oh my gosh," I said aloud.

"Know her, do you?" said Chuck to me as he looked at his colleague, who had also come around to Chuck's check-out aisle to hear what my fuss was about.

"Yes, I think so. Can you tell me, Chuck, how did she pay?"

"Paid cash. I remember because almost no one pays cash anymore 'cept the old-timers and because well, as you said, she was quite a looker."

"Yeah, that's definitely her," I said. Then, "Chuck, one more thing: has anyone else come in to ask about her?"

"No," he replied with a quizzical look over toward his colleague.

I thought for a moment, then turned to the other clerk as well and asked them both very clearly, "Has anyone else come in yesterday or today to ask about someone buying wire?"

Both men shook their heads from side to side.

"Ok, then. Thanks. I appreciate it." I spun on my heels to depart and heard Chuck call out, "Why you asking about this, lady?" I ignored him, exited the hardware store and walked back toward the Mercedes through the still-falling white snow.

As I drove back up Main Street, I saw the snow-covered Stanley Hotel looming largely, with its massive grandeur, high above town. It was starting to get dark out, even though it was only four in the afternoon, because of the cloud cover. The G-class' headlights turned on automatically and I suddenly now felt sure that Liv had set the trip wire which had killed her fiancé. But why? What could she possibly gain? They hadn't been married yet. She had seemed to me to really love him, or at least she seemed genuinely happy to be marrying him. Was her soul so black she was capable of such a heinous act as murder, or had she just planned to injure him for some reason of her own design?

I followed the blue directional sign on Main Street and turned east down Howard Street toward the Sheriff's office. I drove a couple miles away from town up a rise opposite the Stanley, all the while intending to tell Sheriff Smith everything I had just learned from Ace Hardware, the helpful place. How appropriate and true their tagline.

As I parked just past the small single-story red brick building which housed the Larimer County Sheriff's office, I wondered what good could come from this. The Sheriff had already told me to let him do his job. Sam, Marie and Franco had all agreed that the soundest course was to let the authorities do their job. Nothing was going to bring Harry back from the dead now. This was real life, not some mystery story I was reading. Incriminating Liv with such a serious charge wouldn't change a thing. Except, perhaps, how Liv would forever feel about me.

Chapter 30

"Don't you just love Depeche Mode, Lauren?" asked Liv rhetorically as we drove south together in the night toward Florida with their music blaring. We were in Liv's car, an economical red Honda Civic which we had deemed in better mechanical shape than my Chevy Nova, for our spring break road trip to Florida. Liv was driving and singing along to the music. I was smoking and looking out the window at the dark, flat land. I agreed with her and added that we should be grateful to MTV for enabling so many British bands to break in the US. Liv and I had become disenchanted with the stale misogynistic lyrics of the popular American hair bands of the era. We had musically turned our allegiances to the UK with the dawn of MTV.

We had decided to drive through the night to save our meager spending money and allow us a bit more time in our destination city of Miami. We had agreed to drive her car in shifts and to both stay awake all night making sure the other did too. So far the trip had been uneventful except for a restroom and coffee shop break at a truck stop just off the highway a few hours back. There we had seen and heard man and woman arguing in a booth of the attached 24-hour diner. We didn't pay much attention to what they had been yelling at one another about, and neither did the employees. The scene was slightly surreal, the way we all ignored them, as if this type of verbal domestic altercation were commonplace and to be expected in places like 24-hour truck stop diners.

As Liv and I walked through the attached convenience store, the man in the booth garnered our full attention and that of the staff by yelling "You're nothing but a dirty whore" loudly at the woman as he stood. She retaliated, also loudly, by calling him a "jackass" and then a "big fat loser who (she) never wanted to see again". He took this as his cue, grabbed his jacket from the booth's bench and with one final, loud "Bitch" stormed out of the truck stop diner and got into his parked car just outside the door.

"I'll bet she runs after him," I whispered to Liv from our position just behind the Doritos. "No way. What self-respecting woman would chase after a man like that? Look, even his car is a beater and I'll bet he stiffed her with their bill too."

Memories and snippets of conversations swirled through my mind as I made an illegal U-turn in front of the Larimer County Sheriff's office. What if you're wrong, said the voice in my head. You'll hurt a dear friend.

I drove straight back to the Stanley having decided once and for all to let the chips fall where they would without any further interference from me. I would console and support Liv as best I could and would immediately put these dubious thoughts and cynical suspicions about her out of my head forever.

It was four-thirty when I returned to our suite. I heard Olive scratch at the closed bedroom door. I opened it to let her out into the living room with me and saw that Sam was still sleeping soundly. His breath was heavy and rhythmic and the dark room smelled like him. I love Sam's smell. Olive's too, for that matter. Perhaps the secret to a happy relationship is as simple as making sure that one likes the smell of their loved one, I thought lightly as I patted Olive and walked over to the bar to get her the very last home-baked dog biscuit from her Stanley-provided stash.

As Olive finished her treat and drank some water, I picked up the phone and dialed 525 to reach Liv's room. She picked up on the third ring. Her voice sounded warm with sleep or perhaps, slightly lax with drink. Either way, I did not care. It was good to hear her and I told her so.

"I'm feeling better," she said. "I still cannot believe this happened Lauren, but I'm coming to terms with it, I guess."

"Yeah, that's pretty much all you can do Liv. Is Nick there with you? Has he been supportive, I hope?"

"Why do you ask? No, of course, he's not here with me Lauren. I barely *know* the man."

"I was just hoping you weren't alone is all."

"I'm alone and sad, but I'm fine, as I said. I just want to forget all this and go home tomorrow."

"Sam and I are leaving tomorrow too for Denver, Liv. Will you be going home to Chicago or to New York?"

"New York. It's where my stuff is, and Nick did say he'd fly with me and get me settled into Harry's condo for as long as I needed. I don't expect I'll stay there long, but I will need to call off our wedding, obviously, and pack my things."

The last word caught in her throat and I could hear her stifle a moan. "It's going to be difficult Liv, but you'll get through it. Are you sure you wouldn't like to come to Denver with Sam and me for a little while first, for some perspective perhaps, before having to inform everyone in New York?"

"Thank you, Lauren, I really mean it." Her voice sounded like a little girl's now, soft and breathy. "I know you want to help, but like I've always done, I don't want to hide or procrastinate from what has to happen next."

"No one could ever say you were lazy, Liv, but will you at least promise to invite me to help you in New York or come visit us in a few weeks so I can make sure you're ok?"

"Of course, Lauren. I can't think of a better situation to have a true, old friend by my side." These words were like music to my ears and it didn't hurt that her voice was again rich and full sounding when she had said them.

"Thank god it's our last night here, Liv. I totally understand you wanting to get out of Colorado, but there is the matter of one more dinner first. Can I tempt you to join Sam and our friends Marie and Franco for a quiet, early dinner here in the hotel tonight?"

Silence.

"Come on, Liv. You have to eat and we'll do our best to take your mind off of all this. I'll even walk you back to your room just as soon as you're finished eating if you want to be by yourself and retire early."

"Ok, Lauren. That would be nice. I'll ask Nick to eat with us too. I guess I need to get to know him better as I'll need his help taking care of everything back in New York. What time?"

"It's about five now. Does seven or seven-thirty sound better to you?"

"Let's say seven, Liv. I do want to go to bed early tonight. Tomorrow is going to be a long day. Remember, you promised to let me leave just as soon as I finish eating, Lauren," she laughed and then hung up.

Had Liv been a little drunk on the phone, I wondered as I tiptoed through our dark bedroom and into our bathroom. I hoped she was. I knew I'd be drinking if my fiancé had just died unexpectedly the day previous. I was glad she had agreed to join us for dinner. I felt confident we'd be able to take her mind off of Harry for at least for a couple hours. I was also hoping to reiterate my support of her and my offer to help her, in any way over the next few weeks and months. It was the least I could do, and I meant it. There was simply no way she had had any part in Harry's death. What had I been thinking? I switched on the bathroom lights and closed the door softly behind me before turning on the water so as not to rouse Sam. I would save that for after my bath.

Chapter 31

DRESSED IN MY tightest jeans, my brand-new cognac hued leather pumps and a low-cut, V-neck silk tee with my favorite Hermès wool tweed blazer on top, I felt beautiful as Sam and I strolled into the hotel's warmly lit Whiskey Bar. Even though we had been in the bar several times already during our visit, I was still impressed by the intentionally soothing incandescent glow cast upon the patrons' faces who sat along the glorious, up-lit natural onyx bar. The grain in the bar was so strong it almost looked like amber.

We saw Marie and Franco immediately. They sat next to one another about halfway in and we surprised them as Sam gently patted Franco on his back. He stood immediately, looked me up and down, then gave me a friendly hug and said, "Lauren, you look tall." I gave Marie a kiss on both cheeks, sat down next to her and replied, "Merci, Franco. I have my new Lucccheses on. I don't wear high heels very often, but aren't they fine?" I waved one foot out slightly behind our bar chairs for the men to admire. "Thank you again, Sam. I just love them.

It's so fun to buy a few things when traveling, isn't it?" I said to the group.

"Marie, you look lovely this evening as well with that amazing ring," said Sam smiling dashingly. "What did you both get up to this afternoon?"

"Oh, it was fun. Franco and I went to the game room over in your Lodge building. We met the nicest couple from Arizona and played a few games of snooker with them."

"Alas," said Franco, "We lost to them three frames to one. I think they may have been sharks." Marie and Franco laughed together good-naturedly at the memory of their snooker defeat and Franco reached to Marie's hand and gave it a squeeze. She looked at him adoringly. It was good to see, with this small gesture, how much they cared for one another.

"And what have you two been up to since we last saw one another?" asked Franco turning his attention back to Sam and me.

"I took a long, wonderful nap with Olive," replied Sam. "Speaking of which, what did you do while I was resting?" he asked me.

"Oh, I just read my book on the couch and watched the snow fall." Turning to everyone, I embellished my lie further with, "I'm reading the newest mystery book by Robert Galbraith. You know, the pseudonym that J.K. Rowling writes under."

"Isn't that the author of the children's Harry Potter series?" asked Marie.

"Yes, she also writes adult fiction, including crime mysteries, and very well, if I do say so."

"I didn't know that," said Franco. "Do you read many murder mysteries, Lauren?"

Sam and Marie grunted, rolled their eyes in unison and then laughed. Apparently two of the three of them remembered my penchant for detective stories well.

"I also phoned Liv this afternoon to see how she's doing," I continued. "I encouraged her to join us for dinner tonight. I hope you don't mind. She agreed but said she'll be wanting to make it an early night, however, and will go to bed just after dinner. She might bring Harry's brother too." I looked at my wristwatch. "They should be here in a few minutes, actually."

"We'd enjoy having them dine with us," said Marie graciously. "I don't like the thought of her up in her room all by herself after what has happened."

Sam waved his hand toward the bar's entrance behind me. We all turned to look as Nick gave us a solicitously broad smile and approached. He was not a typically handsome man like his brother had been. But he was a well-groomed one. The fact that he used a shiny pomade in his precisely cut short hair added to his rakish effect.

"Hello, Nick," said Sam extending his hand. After they shook, Sam said, "May I introduce our friends and traveling companions all the way from the South of France, Marie and Franco Alix."

After introductions and hellos were made, I asked Nick where Liv was. I was surprised they had not arrived to the Whiskey Bar together.

"I assume she'll be down in a minute. She called me late this afternoon asking if I would like to join you all for dinner. I do hope it's ok?"

"Of course Nick," I said as Franco nodded.

"She told me to meet here at seven. Perhaps I should have stopped by her room first and escorted her down. I guess this is an example of why I'm still single," he said in a self-deprecating, joking way.

Sam laughed politely as did Franco while Marie and I just gave each other a glance.

"I'm sure she'll be here soon. It's just seven now," said Sam.

"Nick, before Liv gets here, I just want to say again how sorry we all are for the loss of your brother. Perhaps it will be better if we don't speak of his accident at dinner, unless of course if Liv brings it up herself," I said and looked at everyone to gauge whether they agreed with my suggestion of tender-footing around the tragic topic this evening.

"Yes, of course. I also think that would be best, Lauren. It was a very strenuous day for her," said Nick with a touch of melancholy in his voice and lowered eyes. "You know we had to identify him today? I never in my wildest dreams would have ever thought I'd have to identify the body of my younger brother in a morgue."

Touching his arm very gently, Marie said, "This must be very difficult for you."

I looked at Nick's pronounced cheekbones and high forehead. Again he struck me as the type of man whom, in spite of his bird-like face and shiny shoes, naturally projects an aura of self-importance. A man who thought highly of himself and would not suffer nonsense from those around him. I thought back to Liv saying that Harry was not very close to his brother. Hadn't she alluded to the fact that his brother was not as driven or successful as Harry had been, that Nick had been the irresponsible one, a spendthrift? The fact that Nick wore, I now noticed, a Vacheron Constantin time piece, a wristwatch more precious than a Rolex, did match up to Liv's description. Just then his thin lips parted and he said, "Shall we all order a drink while we wait for Liv to join us?"

And so it was done. Nick picked up the check for our round despite Sam and Franco's protestations. Still standing but now holding a Sapphire gin martini in his hand, he raised his crystal glass and said, "To my brother Harry! There will never be another. May he rest in peace."

We each raised our cocktail glasses in appreciation of his sentiment and wordlessly drank in acknowledgement. After a minute passed, I excused myself from the bar and walked over to the hostess stand at the entrance to Crimson Room. The hostess was not at her post so I peered into the nearly three-quarter full dining room. I saw Kip and Jarvis sharing a table with the painter from Indiana that I had met with them the other night and another woman. Kip was again wearing a brightly patterned shirt and was pouring wine into the painter's empty wineglass. It appeared as though they had just sat down as there was no food on their table yet. Several parties over from them, near the inside wall under a large framed black and white photograph of a herd of elk, I saw an empty table set for six, seemingly waiting for us. The dining room was fairly quiet at the moment decibel-wise, in spite of the nearly 50 people seated inside. The effect of snow falling outside can sometimes hush people inside, I mused not for the first time.

A young man arrived at the host stand where I stood and said, "Welcome to the Crimson Room. May I help you?"

"Yes, please. My party has a reservation for seven this evening, but we'll be a little late. We're just in the bar waiting for one more. Will you be able to hold our table?"

"What name is your reservation under?"

"Hendrick. Six people at seven, but it might be seven-thirty before we're ready. What time is it now?"

Looking down at his tablet, he said, "Yes ma'am, whenever you are ready. We'll hold your table, no problem."

"Thank you." I looked down at my watch, it was nearly seven twenty. "So it'll be ok even if we arrive closer to eight?"

"Certainly, I've made a note. Take your time and enjoy your drinks. We'll have your table waiting."

I turned and went back to the bar and saw that Liv had still not arrived. As I sat down and picked up my drink, Sam asked if everything was ok. "Yes," I said. "The restaurant will hold our table as long as necessary." Sam kissed me while the others chit-chatted about their mutual love of the always reliable French Bordeaux. "Sam, it's almost seven-thirty, I think we should go and get Liv."

Nick must have overheard me. The studied look of nonchalance which he had arrived with was suddenly replaced by a rigid stance. He straightened, turned to me and said, "That's a good idea, Lauren. Why don't you and I run up to Liv's room together now and get her?"

As Nick and I rode the supposedly haunted elevator up to the fifth floor he was silent. His toned, overly slim body was still tense. His brow was furrowed and his deep set eyes seemed further recessed in his skull.

"Nick, when I spoke with Liv this afternoon, after you both returned to the hotel, she seemed sad but fine. Do you mind if I ask how she handled seeing Harry at the hospital morgue?"

"She completely freaked out Lauren. Caused quite a scene actually, crying and wailing, she even threatened to faint for a moment."

"Oh, dear."

"I was eventually able to get her to calm down, but it took much effort. I think it had been the sight of his grey, almost waxy-looking body in that cold room. It didn't look like my handsome brother at all. It was difficult for me too, I can tell you. But she practically went into hysterics until I could get her away and down to the main hospital waiting room." The elevator doors opened and as we walked toward the corner of the hallway where suite 525 was located, Harry continued, "I always think it's best to remember loved ones how they were, not by viewing their dead body. You know, I've never approved of open casket funerals for the same reason. I had hoped Liv wouldn't want to accompany me to the morgue, but as you heard she insisted."

I knocked on door 525 and he whispered, "It may have been too much for her after all, seeing Harry like that."

"Liv has always been a strong woman, Nick. It'll take time, but I'm sure she'll recover." I knocked again. "By the way, Nick, thank you for offering to let her stay in Harry's condo as long as she needs to, to get herself re-established on her own, without him." I struggled to keep my voice down so Liv wouldn't hear us and continued, "She told me she quit her job in Chicago when she moved in with your brother." I knocked again, louder this time. "Liv is smart and driven. She'll get another job quickly, but it is kind of you to make sure she's taken care of for what will certainly be the next few months."

"It's the right thing to do, Lauren. I know that. Please do not worry about your friend. She won't find herself homeless on my watch."

"Thank you, Nick." I reached into my clutch and retrieved one of Sam's and my personal cards. I handed it to Nick and said, "Here is our information, Nick, please do reach out if you sense that Sam or I can do anything to help Liv."

This time Nick knocked on the door. Loudly. We waited another millisecond and then both realized it was taking Liv far too long to answer. My heart raced and I must have looked strange because Nick next said, "We probably just missed her. I'll bet she's down in the bar already. Let me ring her cell phone."

He pulled out his cell from his front pant pocket, called and stood there looking at me. My heart was pounding loudly but I could just make out the slight sound of chirping from inside the suite. "I hear her phone ringing inside," I whispered to him. I peeled my eyes away from Nick's eagle-like stare and pounded on the door again.

When he removed the phone from his ear and said, "She's not answering. She must have left her phone here and gone down," I immediately asked him to call Sam. I dictated the phone number and he handed his cell over to me. I hoped and prayed Sam would answer even though he would not recognize the incoming number. It rang a couple times and I silently chastised myself for not carrying my phone regularly.

"Hello?" Sam said into my ear.

"Sam, it's me. Calling from Nick's phone. Liv's not answering. Please tell me she's down there with you."

"She's not, Lauren."

"Oh, no. I'm worried, Sam. What should we do?"

"Stay calm, Lauren. Where are you?"

"Nick and I are outside her door. We've been knocking and she doesn't answer. She's not answering her cell either, and I can hear it ringing inside."

Silence. "Sam?" I said.

"Get someone from the hotel to let you in. Tell them it's an emergency. We'll wait down here in case she shows up. I'll call this number as soon as we see her."

"Thank you, Sam," I said. Sam's cool head always grounded me and made me feel more in control of life situations which began to spiral. I told Nick Sam's plan of action as I handed his phone back to him. He agreed and immediately headed back toward the elevator with a quick gait, heading to the front desk. I remained standing at Liv's suite door and pounded on it again, loudly. Nothing. "Liv!" I called to the door. "Are you there?" Silence, except for the sound of my heart pounding in my ears. Then I heard a shrill squeak from my right side. I turned. It was the chamber maid's stock cart as she rounded the opposite corner of the long corridor.

"Ma'am!" I called as I jogged down the hall toward her. She looked up, surprised. "Ma'am, my friend in 525 needs help. Please, please let me in. Front desk has been notified, but it's taking too long. Please unlock the door for me."

"No understand," she said in broken English.

Damn. I took her hand and pulled her back down the hall with me, toward 525. "Por favor," I commanded, pointing toward the door's card key entry slot. "Emergency!" I said.

She looked me up and down and then pulled a card from the front pocket of her uniform. She inserted her master key into the slot, the light turned green and I grabbed her hand again and pulled her into the room with me calling, "Liv!"

I rushed in front of the maid into the pitch-black room. She must have flipped a light switch because suddenly a light behind me near the door switched on. Again, I called out "Liv, where are you?" as I stood in the center of the empty cream-colored living room. The room was still neat as a pin but Liv was not there. I saw a cell phone lying on the coffee table.

"Quedar por favor," I yelled back to the maid, who was still standing in the entry with one hand on the door knob. She gave me a quick nod and I flew into the completely dark bedroom. The bedroom door was open and I turned the wall light switch on. Again, Liv's bedroom was perfectly clean and neat, like I had seen it previously, but no Liv. Damn, I thought to myself. *Where* is she?

I looked around her bedroom and called out "Liv!" again. There was no one here. The suite sounded and felt empty. Then I saw something strange. On the dresser situated between two closet doors and under a large starburst mirror lay Liv's handbag and what looked like some cocaine next to it. I walked over and reached to turn on the lamp next to her purse on the dresser but thought better of it and immediately pulled my hand away from the lamp's light switch. Liv's Fendi was lying on its side and next to it was a cello packet filled with white powder. Next to that on the gleaming mahogany wood was a small pile of more white powder and a rolled-up bill. It looked like a twenty. Not possible, I thought to myself, Liv didn't do drugs. Never had, not even at university. I resisted the urge to touch anything but I bent down slightly so that I could see inside the top of her purse, which was lying on its side partially open. I saw what looked like a dark yellow plastic prescription drug container with a white childproof lid. Strange.

I wanted to open the closet doors but didn't want to risk leaving my fingerprints anywhere, so I turned and walked toward the dark bathroom where the door was open. The light was not on and I could just smell the moist air of a recent shower. I stepped into the dark room and my pump slipped out from under me. I landed with a thud on my rear. "Damn it," I shouted into the dark room. As I placed my hands on the cool marble floor to right myself I noticed the marble was wet. I stood back up and as I wiped my wet hands on my jeans, I noticed something opaque in the bathtub. The clear navy blue night sky was illuminating the huge jetted bathtub just enough for me to see that a body was in it.

My Basel response kicked in, as it always does in times of duress. My core temperature shot up and I began to feel dizzy. It was Liv in the bathtub, I was certain. I could make out her slender naked body and long, light blonde hair submerged in the water. I ran back into the bedroom and grabbed a pillow from the bed. I shook it furiously, while trying not to hyper-ventilate, and finally got the case off of the pillow. I pulled the pillow case over my right hand and used it to gently turn on the bathroom light switch. More pill bottles were strewn messily on the vanity counter and Liv was naked and still in the water. I didn't have to check. She was dead. Her usually beautiful bright blue eyes were dark and empty like holes boring emptily up toward the large picture window framing the ghastly scene.

Chapter 32

Liv didn't do drugs. In fact, she had always been adamantly against them. Clean living and a devotee of all self-improvement and health fads, she had always disapproved of even my cigarette smoking. She was not someone who would have voted for the legalization of marijuana in the state of Colorado. The drugs spread out messily in her bedroom and here on the bathroom vanity were not indicative of her at all. Could she have changed so much during the years in which we had lost touch?

I stared down at the two prescription bottles on the counter. I didn't see a real prescription label on either of them. Both amber plastic containers were blank, unlabeled. There were several pills scattered on the counter near the open plastic bottles. Some were large white ovals and there were also a few small, round, coral-colored pills. I had no idea what they were. I turned my attention back to Liv.

Liv wasn't the type to commit suicide. In fact, she had always harbored little tolerance for weakness in herself or in others. She was not someone who would give up easily. She was the type who was determined to live to one hundred years, at least. Could she have changed so much, on such a spiritual level, since we had been best friends?

I stared down at her slender limp frame in the huge bathtub. She was heart-stoppingly gorgeous, even dead. But I couldn't bear to look at Liv for long with the vacant black holes she now had for eyes. I began to feel dizzy again, then a sort of paranoia washed over me and I felt a strong urge to get far, far away from her motionless naked body. I heard voices in the distance behind me. I glanced out of the window, which was centered above the tub, but there was nothing to see, no one could have witnessed what had occurred in this bathroom. The window only afforded a view of verdant pines below the night sky and very faint lights from Estes Park far in the distance between the dense foliage. There was not much water splashed about the tub, just some on the marble floor where I had slipped as well as, some glistening drops high up on the window sill. Could the area have been wiped dry? I couldn't wrap my head around Liv committing suicide.

I looked over at the towel racks. A full supply of bright white towels appeared to be hanging on the racks. I touched a couple gently with my left hand, the hand not ensconced in the pillowcase, but the cotton felt dry. I walked back into the bedroom and used my pillowcase-covered hand to open one of the closets. Liv's clothes were hanging neatly inside, with shoes lined up like soldiers below. I didn't see any wet towels.

"Lauren!" I heard Sam yell loudly as a thunder of people burst into the suite from the front door. I turned and ran in the living room and into Sam's arms.

"She's dead. In the bathroom," I said pointing with my still pillowcase-covered right arm. I recognized Stephanie and the chamber maid who had let me in. Franco, Marie and Nick were also in tow, as well as what looked like two maintenance men. Stephanie said, "I'll call for the police," and picked up the phone on the desk as the two maintenance men walked into the bedroom and toward the bathroom.

Franco said, "I'm glad we're returning home tomorrow."

Marie looked at Franco haltingly, and then toward me still in Sam's embrace and asked, "Lauren, are you alright?"

Nick and the housekeeper said nothing as I nodded my head in Sam's chest. Sam said, "Lauren, why is there a pillowcase on your arm?"

Stephanie hung up the phone, "The police are on their way. They asked me to clear the area." She turned toward the bedroom and continued, "Let me just go get John and Ed."

I pulled away from Sam, just a few inches, and removed the pillowcase from around my arm and dropped it onto the back of the sofa. "I'm ok Marie, just shocked. Liv is dead in the bathtub. Drowned from the looks of it. I can't take much more of this either. I'm glad we're going home tomorrow too, Franco. Oh, and I put the pillowcase on my hand so that I wouldn't get fingerprints on anything Sam. I had to turn the light switch on in the bathroom."

"That poor woman," said Nick softly.

Stephanie and her male employees returned from the bathroom. She was paler than when she had gone in. She gestured her arms wide and motioned us all toward the suite's door and outside into the hallway.

Stephanie closed the door behind all of us and sternly announced, "I'll wait here for the police. You all, back to work and don't speak of this tonight. Mr. and Mrs. Hendrick, Mr. and Mrs. Alix and you, sir, Mr. Ross, right? I am very sorry. I'll take care of everything from here until the authorities arrive. Please go down to the dining room and order anything you like, compliments of the Stanley."

"Merci beaucoup," said Franco leading the way toward the elevator as he rubbed his belly comically. "I am famished."

I felt shell-shocked; similar to the feeling one gets when one hasn't slept in over 24 hours, as I held Sam's hand tightly and the five of us headed back down to the Stanley's restaurant. As we were led to the six-top table still waiting for us, Kip and Jarvis and the Midwestern artist greeted us.

"It's nice to see you all again," said Kip. When none of us responded with anything more effusive than forced grins, Jarvis accurately added, "You all look like you've seen the Stanley's famous ghost! Is everything all right?"

"We've had a bit of a shock actually, but I hope you won't mind if we don't get into it now," responded Sam as we all sat down at the table next to them.

I looked at the empty chair, where Liv should have been sitting, and heard Jarvis quietly say to his dining companions,

"I do hope it's nothing to do with their beautiful blonde friend. Look, she's missing."

Dinner passed uneventfully and solemnly at our table. I managed to eat a few bites of the comforting butternut squash ravioli which Sam had ordered for me. Only after Jarvis, Kip and their dining companions bid us each adieu and had departed from the restaurant, Nick broached the silence by saying, "I feel responsible, you know."

My head shot up from the bright-green sugar snap peas which I had been stirring around my plate, "Responsible?"

"Yes. I never should have allowed your friend Liv to go to the morgue with me to see Harry. She didn't need to be there. The Sheriff only needed my identification. I had no idea it would lead to her committing suicide." He whispered the word *suicide.*

I stared at Nick, and he held my glance unflinchingly until Sam said, "It's no one's fault Nick. These past few days have amounted to an unbelievable tragedy, by far the saddest that I have ever known." Sam put his hand on my thigh under the table and turned to me, "Lauren," he said softly, "Please don't be too sad. It's a tragedy, yes, but what happened to Harry and now with Liv would have occurred even if we weren't here, Lauren. It's just too bad you were the one who had to find Liv. To see her." Sam took a deep breath then continued a bit more loudly toward our table and companions, "I can't imagine what you think, Marie and Franco. Thank you for bearing with us through all this."

"We don't hold any of this against you. I'm sorry your friend has died, Lauren, but this sure will make a great story for all our friends back home," said Franco as Marie sighed deeply.

"This is unbelievable," summed up Nick as he also sighed solemnly.

Sam and I left our friends in the bar that night, our last in Estes Park, as I felt very tired and Sam agreed it would be best for us both to retire early. As we walked through the lobby and past the grand staircase, I asked Sam if he minded if we went back up to the fifth floor to see what the police were doing. He abruptly stopped walking and said flatly, "No, Lauren."

"Why not, Sam? She was my friend and I found her and I don't think she committed suicide, Sam."

I felt like a child being condescended to, as Sam took my hand and said, "No, Lauren. We're not getting any further involved in this. We're leaving for home tomorrow and the police or the Sheriff or whoever is in authority around here will deal with this. We, meaning you, are not going to interfere."

"But Sam"

He cut me off. "No, Lauren. We are not giving anyone any reason to detain us from traveling home tomorrow morning, Lauren. We have to drive Marie and Franco to the airport and I have to get back to work. We need to leave as quickly and quietly as possible, in my opinion."

Chapter 33

The alarm buzzed at six that Monday morning, but I was already awake. I had been lying in between Olive and Sam in the large, comfortable, king-size bed staring at the ceiling for an hour already. Sam was sleeping peacefully and automatically pushed the button on top of the nightstand clock to snooze the alarm. I gave him a kiss, brushed his cheek and whispered, "Let's get out of here and go home, Sam."

"Mmmm," he groaned.

"Mmmm," I imitated as I rubbed his thigh and then very slowly moved my hand up to his warm belly. "Olive, get down … off the bed."

We hit the snooze button five times that morning and left the suite feeling much better than when we had come in the previous night. Olive, Sam and I greeted Molly at the front desk of the Lodge's lobby and asked her to have our bags brought down. She handed Sam our folio and said, "The Sheriff has requested to speak with you, Mr. and Mrs. Hendrick, before you depart. He asked that you both meet him in the Stanley's Timber conference room."

I looked over at Sam and mouthed *uh-oh.*

"Thank you, Molly. We'll head over to the Timber room now."

As Olive relieved herself near a grove of Pine trees flanking the lake side of the snow-covered front lawn Sam said, "Let's make this quick. We'll tell the Sheriff we have to leave at eight-thirty to get the Alix's to the airport for their international flight home. I'm sure he won't delay us. We'll just answer any questions he has and not offer any additional speculation."

"But don't we owe it to him and to ourselves, morally, to tell him exactly what I saw when I found Liv?"

"Yes, of course. But please let him ask the questions this morning, Lauren, and then if you feel you have additional information that he does not address, you can phone him later from Denver, ok? We really can't miss the Alix's flight, Lauren, and I want to get back home."

We phoned Marie and Franco from the lobby telling them we were checked out but that we would be speaking with the Sheriff, at his request, and would meet them in the lobby in one hour to depart.

We walked up the wide, ornately carved grand staircase to the meeting and conference rooms located on the second floor. Olive led the way. Why do dogs always act like they know exactly where they're going even when they have no idea of their final destination? We followed her until we saw the directional sign pointing us left toward the Timber room. Sam said "Left side" to Olive, she turned, and we walked down the dimly lit carpeted interior hallway with Olive in the lead again.

We heard a man's voice and saw an open door which led into a small room containing a huge crystal chandelier, three uncovered, round banquet tables and one Sheriff Smith. He was sitting at the table closest to the window and had his back toward us while talking on his phone. There was a notebook and the tablet on the table beside him along with a black tray holding a silver coffee urn, cream, sweetener and several ceramic cups and saucers which the hotel must have provided for him.

"Sheriff Smith?" announced Sam as we three stood a few steps inside the room.

He turned and waved us over to the table where he was sitting and made a one-moment sign with the hand not holding his phone. The Sheriff had his same golden badge and tan uniform on. He looked much more tired than when last I had seen him. His posture was hunched with his shoulders pulled forward and his short hair looked rumpled. I wondered if he had been here all night as I picked up his upturned brown felt cowboy hat from the seat I wanted to sit on. I placed his hat, careful to keep it upturned, on to the far center of the table.

"That's it then," he said into his phone, still looking out the window. "Yes, let's try to keep this away from the media until at least tomorrow. Yes, we'll downplay the narcotics. Gotta go."

He turned in his seat to face us and slipped his phone into his shirt pocket. Without further preamble he said, "I understand you found the body last night here at the hotel?"

"Yes, Sheriff. Lauren went up to Liv Roger's suite to check on her when she didn't come down for dinner. I'm afraid

Lauren found her dead in her bathtub and then Stephanie, the Stanley's assistant manager, who was with us, phoned for the authorities immediately."

He glanced at me, dark rings under his wrinkled brown eyes. "Anything to add Mrs. Hendrick?"

"That's all correct, Sheriff, but a maid had let me into Liv's suite. The door was locked. I called out for her and she didn't answer. Her cell phone was on the coffee table, I noticed. I went into her bedroom, turned on the lights and noticed some drugs on the dresser, which concerned me because *Liv doesn't do drugs*. Then I went into the bathroom, which was also dark, with no lights on. I slipped on some water on the floor and fell down. When I got up, my eyes had adjusted to the darkness and I saw her in the bathtub motionless. I decided I better not get fingerprints on anything else, so I went back to the bedroom and put a pillowcase over my hand."

"So you were alone in the room at this time? Your husband, the maid and Stephanie weren't there?" he interrupted.

"Actually, the maid was still in the living room, but when I put the pillowcase on, before I returned to the bathroom, I called to her to go get help. I then went back into the bathroom, flipped the light switch on with the pillowcase and saw that it really was Liv in that tub and that she was certainly, absolutely dead already."

"Anything else, Mrs. Hendrick?"

Both Sam and Sheriff Smith looked at me intently.

"Well, I did notice more drugs which were unlabeled and messily spread out on the bathroom vanity. There was also water on the floor, which is what I slipped on, and some water splashed much higher up on the window sill, which I thought was odd."

"Why did you think that was odd?" the Sheriff asked, a bit grudgingly, I thought.

"Because, if Liv committed suicide alone by drowning herself in her bathtub why would she splash water way up on the windowsill? Also, why would the bathroom lights be turned off? Do people drown themselves in the dark? And lastly Sheriff, the drugs looked planted to me. To make her seem despondent and unhinged and capable of suicide. None of which I believe she was. Liv did not approve of drugs and I can't believe those were hers."

"Mrs. Hendrick, I saw Liv Rogers myself just yesterday at the morgue when Nick Ross brought her with him for the identification of his brother. From what I saw, Mrs. Hendrick, she was despondent and unhinged. She was not in a tranquil mood at all. She was *very* troubled by her fiancé's death, further aggravated most likely by viewing his body.

"Mr. and Mrs. Hendrick, it is not uncommon for those close to suicide cases to initially deny it," he continued while looking at Sam for substantiation. "No one ever wants to believe that someone they care about has committed suicide."

"You're right of course," said Sam to Sheriff Smith. "So if there is nothing else, we need to be leaving Estes Park very soon. We're driving our traveling companions directly to the airport in Denver this morning."

"Just one more thing, Mr. Hendrick, and I want to be very clear about this. Please look after your wife. You located two accident victims in very short succession..." He looked at me, his expression softening along with the bags under his eyes. "Which can be *very* difficult emotionally. You may not feel it now, but you are under duress and need to take care of yourselves. I recommend you both try to get back into your normal routines once you're back home."

"Thank you, Sheriff. I'll do that." Sam began to stand.

"I'm just curious, Sheriff, what is the coroner's official determination of Harry Ross' death? You never told us."

"Blunt force trauma to the head, as a result of the fall he took."

"But accidental?" I asked.

"Yes, Mrs. Hendrick, accidental death."

"And what about Liv? Has the coroner already made his report on her?"

"You'll be happy to know," he said with a slight smirk, "Coroner Del Geddes is a woman, Mrs. Hendrick, and *she* has confirmed that your friend died by drowning. She needs another day for more detailed testing, we *do* follow all procedures here in Estes Park, to determine the time of death and to process exactly which drugs were in her system, but Coroner Del Geddes told me that in her professional opinion, it looks like cause of death will be ruled suicide by drowning."

Sam stood up again and extended his hand toward the Sheriff. I stood as well and smiled politely as they shook hands.

"I am very sorry for your loss Mr. and Mrs. Hendrick. This really has been an unfortunate time for you. We've notified Liv

Roger's next of kin, so I won't need anything further from either of you at this time. I have your home contact information, should we be needing to reach you. Please drive safely back down to Denver."

Chapter 34

"So what do you think really happened?" Marie asked from beside me in the backseat of the G-class after Sam and I had relayed the details of our brief interview, if you could call it that, with Sheriff Smith that morning.

"Unlike Sheriff Smith," I said, enjoying my opportunity for promulgation, "I firmly believe that both Harry and Liv were murdered this week in Estes Park."

"I don't see how, Lauren. I mean, I was following your line of thought that Liv might have been responsible for Harry's accident, but I see no cause and effect now that Liv is dead too," retorted Franco gamely.

"Let's start at the beginning, shall we?" I said. "I welcome you all to question my observations and assumptions. Let me know if I'm really just crazy to think what I do."

"Happily," said Sam from the driver's seat.

"Let's start with Harry. We all saw him drunk, almost to the point of stupor, on Friday night. Liv would easily have been able to sneak out of their suite after she took him back, while he most certainly was passed out in their room. It was dry and not snowing that night so she wouldn't have left prints of any kind where she strung the tripwire across the trail. Plus, she and Harry had already been at the Stanley a couple of nights and since they usually went running together each morning, she knew the route he would take Saturday morning, when she had begged off joining him. Also, Liv would have had ample time to go back up there to the trail to make sure that he was dead and to remove the trip wire before it began snowing and before Sam and I found his body at around eleven on Saturday morning. Remember, she did not show up to her spa appointment that morning, in fact she hadn't even made a spa appointment according to the employee I spoke with there that day, even though she had told me on Friday night that she would be at the spa the next morning."

Marie spoke first. "That all makes sense, but how do you know she had the materials and those tools you mentioned, to make a trip wire in the first place? I'm sure I wouldn't know how to fashion something like that."

"Liv certainly didn't look like any handyman I've ever seen!" added Franco with his usual dry humor.

"I didn't tell of any you this, but on Sunday after our brunch at the diner in town, I went back down to Main Street on a hunch."

"Lauren!" exclaimed Sam surprised as he looked at me in the rearview mirror.

"I see that I don't have the only insolent wife here. I can't tell you how happy this fact makes me," laughed Franco.

It was Marie's turn to exclaim Franco's name, punctuated by a joking rap on the back of his head in the front passenger seat.

"Come on you all. I'm serious. Let me continue," I said. If this is how seriously my friends were taking a double murder, I was probably way off base. Regardless, I hadn't yet had the opportunity to lay out the whole clandestine plot as I saw it, so I continued, "I went back into town on Sunday because I remembered how upset Liv was when Marie and I first recognized her at the front desk on Thursday evening. She was very angry that the Stanley had lost one of her bags, right Marie?"

"Yes, that's right. I remember that. She was very insolent about a missing piece of her luggage."

"After Sam and I found Harry, I began to wonder if she was so upset because that missing bag of hers may have contained the hardware which she had brought along with her to fashion Harry's trap." Pausing, I asked the car, "So, where would you all go, if you lost the materials which you had brought along with you and needed to get more?"

"I'd go to a hardware store," said Sam first.

"That's right! And then I remembered Kip and Jarvis telling us they had seen her walking in town with an incongruous paper shopping bag, so I went to the local Ace Hardware store and guess what?" I paused again for dramatic effect. "One of the employees, a man named Chuck, remembered seeing her and more than that, he remembered her purchasing a lot of wire, i-hooks and needle-nose pliers among a few other things.

She told him she needed the stuff to hang paintings in her home. She paid cash too, Chuck said."

"That's proof Lauren!" said Marie excitedly.

"It's certainly sounding more incriminating." But with further thought, Sam added, "But it's only proof that a woman, any woman, purchased the same materials used to hang pictures *or* to make a trip wire. Lauren, are you sure you didn't ask this Chuck leading questions? You may have inadvertently given him a terrific yarn to pull. I don't want to sound mean, but a shop clerk gets bored, I imagine, and it might be fun to tease a nosy, but beautiful, tourist like you who's asking a lot of questions."

"Now *that* is pure conjecture Sam! I did not ask leading questions. I simply asked if anyone remembered a woman buying *wire* from their store in the past few days. Plus, don't forget the paper shopping bag. The Ace on Main Street is old school, they still use kraft paper sacks, not plastic."

"I have to agree with Lauren, Sam. There are far too many coincidences and really Liv had no alibi, which we are aware of, for where she was when Harry was out running and fell that morning. But I still see no cause and effect, Lauren," Franco continued. "Why would she want to kill Harry? What would she have gained from it? And, doesn't her suicide last night negate the whole murder conspiracy now anyway?"

"Well, here's where I really don't have any evidence. I was hoping the authorities, Sheriff Smith or someone, anyone, would research the lineage of the Ross family money a little bit. I was up almost all night last night thinking about this. You see, Harry and Nick's parents were very wealthy, according to Liv. Gold Coast old money wealthy. Their parents died young leaving the entire estate to the two brothers. Liv had told this to a mutual friend just a few months ago."

"Robyn?" asked Sam from the front.

"Yes and when we visited at the Hyatt while she was in Denver for work this winter, she told me."

"Ooo, you told me about your reunion visit with Robyn in an email, Lauren. But Liv and Harry weren't married yet. She wouldn't have inherited anything from him yet," said Marie.

"That's exactly right, Marie. Plus it would be much too obvious to kill your brand-new, rich husband."

She nodded her head in agreement, rolled down her window, lit up and said, "Go on."

"So let's say both Harry and Nick inherited large family trust funds. But Nick drained his dry already. He's irresponsible, plays fast and hard according to Liv. Perhaps made some bad choices day trading or just poor investments. He's also a spendthrift, if you will, and doesn't want to work for more. Thinks he's entitled."

"Don't you mean Harry?" asked Franco.

"No, I mean his brother Nick, who flew out here and whom we all just met after Harry died."

Silence fell over the G-class as the car took a sharp switchback and we descended into a small, snow-covered valley. There was a rustic cabin located very close to the bank of Boulder Creek on our right side, with smoke coming out of its chimney. Amazing that it was still inhabited, I thought, after the last flood.

"So you're saying that Nick was having a secret assignation with his brother's fiancée and used her, Liv, to murder his brother because it would have been too obvious for him to do it himself, since he stood to inherit his brother's trust?"

"Bingo, as we Americans say, Marie. At first I thought Nick must have been up in Estes Park all along, but the Sheriff confirmed that he only flew in to Colorado on Sunday morning and I double-checked with Hertz, his car rental company too. They confirmed he physically picked up the vehicle out at DIA early Sunday morning. I think he manufactured his own alibi by being out of state when Harry died, just in case someone recognized that Harry's fall was not an accident."

"But even if what you say is true, Lauren," said Marie, "why would Liv do such a thing? She was already engaged to the still wealthy and more handsome brother."

"That's a good question, Marie, but maybe she simply fell in love with Nick after meeting him through Harry. Perhaps she grew to care for him more than she desired Harry," said Franco. "Don't they say that love and money are the two most frequent motivators for murder?"

"Yes, at least that's what Hercule Poirot always says," I said laughing at my fond memories of the pedantic little Belgian detective. "Now, I realize that this is real life and not an episode of *Hart to Hart* or *Murder, She Wrote* or something, but let's just suppose that Nick wooed Liv ardently, after he realized that their marriage would effectively cut him out of his brother's inheritance.

"Sam, do you remember," I continued, "when we went up to Liv's suite to check on her yesterday morning before she and Nick went to the morgue and Liv started crying from the floor onto Nick's knee, in his lap? That was such an intimate thing to do, don't you think?"

"Yes, I did notice that. Plus I thought he was very quick to say that he would," Sam took his hands off the steering wheel and made quick air quotation marks with his fingers, "take care of her for as long as needed. I thought that was generous, yet a bit odd."

"Yeah, I think she lost it a little bit then, forgot their act probably, because remorse was setting in for her, for what she had done. Nick, on the other hand, was sticking with their script that he would take care of her, the grieving widow, so they could continue their clandestine romance. He probably convinced Liv to murder Harry after he'd gotten her to fall for him, by saying they'd get together publicly after an appropriate length of time for her grieving. That they, Liv and Nick, would live happily-ever-after after his brother's estate was bequeathed to him."

"You know," said Marie, "I never mentioned it, but I thought it unusual that both Liv and Harry were both so equally, splendidly beautiful."

"You did? Why?"

"Because in my experience, when one is really ravishing, like they both were, one tends to be quite selfish, egotistical.

A beautiful person generally relishes knowing that he or she is the more beautiful half of the couple. In every relationship, in my opinion, one half needs more attention than the other. A relationship with two equally big egos is rare to succeed."

"Quite right, Marie," pipped in Franco from the front seat.

"Yes, I also see what you're saying," I responded to Marie and realized that even though I had never consciously thought of it before, there usually was one more attractive, self-obsessed person than the other in most of the successful long-term love relationships that Sam and I knew of.

Continuing, I said, "So let's assume that Liv and Nick were having an affair and to provide himself with an alibi Nick talks Liv into killing his brother far away from where he is located at the time. He convinces her they can make it look like an accident. That nobody would suspect her because she didn't stand to inherit anything. Which is true if any of us were to ask Sheriff Smith. Nick probably helped Liv come up with the whole plan. But I think, he never intended to share his inheritance with Liv and he realized that it's not unfathomable for a young widow, or almost widow, to become so aggrieved that she could commit suicide."

"Ok, Lauren," said Marie as she rolled up her window, "so how do you think Nick killed Liv then? Did he drown her in her own bathtub?"

"Well first off, Liv did not do drugs. I would stake my life on that."

"Please don't say that, Lauren."

"You're right, Sam. Bad expression. But when I saw the drugs messily spread out in her bedroom and her bath, it made me suspicious immediately. Also, no one could have seen in or witnessed anything through the picture window above her tub. That window doesn't face the parking lot or any other buildings or windows, plus it's shielded by some healthy pine trees, so it's perfect from that perspective."

"What perspective, Lauren?" asked Franco. "I want to hear you say it."

"From the perspective of Nick holding Liv underwater until she drowned and planting drugs around her room to make it look like suicide."

Marie exclaimed, rather giddily, "Yes! And does anyone know where Nick was before he joined us for dinner at seven?"

"No, not to my knowledge but I want to ask the Sheriff that same question when I phone him in a couple days. I also want to ask him to check into Harry's will and who his beneficiaries are. Sam and I agreed not to tell the Sheriff about this theory this morning because we didn't want to take too much time and risk not getting you two back to the airport in time for your flight."

"I guess he could have drowned her," said Franco, "and then composed himself, changed into dry clothes and then met us for dinner. That would have given him the opportunity to be with us all when she was found and to act as surprised as we." He thought for a moment, then added, "But you know Lauren, you and Sam could be suspected of killing Harry and Liv yourselves. I mean you found *both* of their bodies."

Sam took his eyes off the road and turned sharply to Franco beside him. Before he had a chance to respond, I pointed out, "Franco, there was water splashed up high on the window sill when I found Liv and her bathroom lights were turned off. If Sam or I wanted to murder my friend, we certainly would have wiped dry the water. I mean when someone OD's in their bathtub and accidentally submerges and drowns, I can imagine a little water splashing on the floor right beside the tub, but way up high? That implies a bit of a struggle to me. Plus who drowns themselves in the dark, in a pitch-black bathroom? It had already been dark outside for several hours. I think Nick just turned the lights off automatically, without thinking about it. I know Sam and I would certainly have left the bathroom lights on, if we were staging a suicide."

"More importantly Franco, Lauren and I had absolutely no idea that either of them would be in Estes Park these past few days. Plus, neither of us was in love with either of them nor will inherit anything as a result of either of their deaths."

"But we appreciate your confidence in us, Franco," I said laughing. "Don't we Sam?"

Sam didn't laugh. He was thinking. I could see his furrowed brow in the rearview mirror. Finally he said, "I believe your double murder theory makes sense Lauren. I admit it sounds like it could be possible that Nick killed both his brother by using Liv to carry it out and then killed Liv herself, but as I've said before, it's the Sheriff's department, the local authorities, who will need to sort this all out. They are the professionals Lauren, and I'm sure they are taking this situation seriously, I mean how often does a small town like Estes Park have two dead tourists in as many days?"

"That's just it Sam. How experienced do you think Sheriff Smith is, when it comes to solving two premeditated murders?"

"This poses an interesting ethical question now doesn't it?" Marie said next. "To what length is one responsible to go, to inform unbelieving or inexperienced authorities to investigate what they are considering an accidental death as, what's the word, a homicide instead? And if the police choose to ignore this information which has been provided to them, can one still sleep at night, knowing that a murderer may get away with their crime?"

Chapter 35

We four discussed the ethical responsibility a citizen has to assist law enforcement authorities in their work the rest of our drive down to Denver's international airport. Franco was inclined to stay out of it, hypothetically, while Marie, Sam and I felt that it would be our civic duty to help the police catch a killer. The only issue we differed on, was to what extent one should continue to help. As in most philosophical discussions, no one's mind was changed on the duration of one's ethical responsibility to assist the police, in this circumstance.

Sam and I bid farewell to our French friends that day in late February and I believe we parted as better friends than when we had picked them up just six days prior. I was grateful for the strong feeling of friendship I now had with both of the Alix's, as I knew it would most likely be some time before Marie and I were in each other's presence again. Two thousand air miles and two murders will do that to a friendship.

Sam and I both quickly returned to our normal and pleasant household routines. I made breakfasts for Sam before he headed to his office in the mornings and then Olive and I would go out for long brisk walks, as we both needed the exercise and fresh air. Spring slowly arrived and tiny, delicate buds were just beginning to sprout from the trees lining the streets Denver. I always feel badly for those early spring buds, the color of a frozen margarita, because Denver almost always has a false spring with an additional snowstorm or two still to arrive in April and even May.

I had phoned Sheriff Smith's office about a week after we had returned home from our trip to Estes. I had been hoping the Sheriff would reach out to us, but when he didn't I picked up our house phone and left a message asking for him to phone me back at his convenience. It took him two days, but when he did I was prepared with what I hoped to impart to him regarding Harry and Liv's deaths. Not always brief, I succinctly outlined my theory of Nick Ross ultimately being responsible for the murder of both his brother Harry and of his lover Liv. Sheriff Smith listened quietly, but informed me that after his department's investigation and the coroner's autopsies of both of bodies, his jurisdiction had already determined Harry's death to be accidental and Liv's to be the result of suicide. I told the Sheriff that it would be well worth his time to simply request a copy of Harry Ross' will in order to verify who stood to inherit his fortune and also to investigate Nick Ross' whereabouts at the exact time that the coroner had determined Liv's suicide had occurred.

The Sheriff thanked me with a touch of annoyance in his voice and reiterated that both cases were officially closed. I hung up the phone feeling jaded, with a further loss of my faith in humanity. A sense which I often tried, with difficulty, to overcome or at least ignore.

In April a couple of weeks later, Sam and I had a mid-week lunch date. We were planning to dine together at a new restaurant that had recently opened in Denver's renovated Union Station. The restaurant served gourmet vegetarian dishes exclusively, so delicious they promised, that even carnivores would not miss the meat. It was a small coup that Sam had agreed to dine there. Sam was a sophisticated and open-minded man, but he did love meat and potatoes above all else.

I was wearing a new DVF wrap dress that spring day and was grateful that it was not windy outside as I walked the few blocks over to Sam's office. I also wore the lovely, long rose gold necklace that Sam given me at the Stanley. I adored both the necklace as well as the memory of how Sam had gotten Olive to present it to me with the long pink string.

I entered Sam's office building, a steel and glass skyscraper that was one of the newer commercial towers located in Denver as it had been built only shortly after the turn of the century. The building was not an architectural marvel, but was modern, clean, and its thirty-eight stories of office space were almost fully occupied. Waving to Darius who worked at the lobby level information desk, I walked to the express elevator bank to ride to the thirty-fifth floor where Sam's firm was headquartered. Jennifer, as usual, sat behind the reception desk and greeted me with, "Long time no see, Mrs. Hendrick. Mr. Hendrick told me you were coming. I understand you have a lunch date today. Please go on through, he's been looking forward to your arrival."

Jennifer had always rubbed me the right way. Friendly and personable, yet professional. She was an asset to Sam's company, I thought. He obviously agreed, as Jennifer had worked for Sam for over five years already. I thanked her and walked down the hall to Sam's door. It was open and I could see him typing on his laptop. His jacket was off and the panoramic city view was dazzling in the sunlight behind him. Even after all these years, Sam is such a handsome man, I thought. Definitely the more beautiful one in our relationship.

"Hi, Sam." I closed the office door behind me. "You surely look dashing today. Is everything going well with work?"

"AOK, Lauren. Thanks for asking. Do you mind having a seat while I just finish my thought on this report?"

"May I have a kiss first?"

"Certainly. I'd like nothing more." He stood up and walked around his desk to me. Sam looked me in the eyes, put his arms around me, and said, "You are my happiness, Lauren. I love you," before kissing me.

"Wow. Sam, clearly we should have lunch dates more often."

His desk phone rang then and he kissed me again, quickly, before reaching to answer it. "Yes, Jennifer?" he said before listening to her message. He walked around his desk, sat back down in his chair and said, "Yes, have him hold a minute and then put him through."

"Lauren," he said, "It's a Jack Beck from New York. He's with an insurance firm there. He told Jennifer he wants to talk with me about Harry Ross."

"What?"

"Yes. Let's see what this is about. I'll put him on speakerphone." Sam pressed a button on his phone. "Ok, Jennifer. Put him though."

"Hello, Mr. Beck. This is Sam Hendrick."

"Hello, Mr. Hendrick. Thank you for taking my call. As I told your receptionist, I'm with Thrivent Mutual Insurance Company of New York."

"Please call me Sam. I hope you don't mind but my wife, Lauren, is here with me now. I have you on speakerphone."

"Not at all, Sam, and please call me Jack. It's about a Mr. Harry Ross. My firm's investigation division understands from the reporting authorities located in Larimer County, Colorado, that you were the people who had found the body of Harry Ross this February in Estes Park."

"That's true, Jack, but what is this all about? Why are you asking?"

"Harry Ross was a client of ours. He had a rather large, very large in fact, life insurance policy with Thrivent Mutual. In short, my claims department has declined payment to his beneficiary pending an independent investigation as to cause of death. We are not satisfied that, well, that his death was accidental, as reported by the local coroner. Thrivent Mutual is opening an investigation on this policy claim with the New York District Attorney as we expect to be sued by the beneficiary for declining payment. I am calling to ask you, and your wife, if you would be willing to cooperate and assist us with our official inquiry into Harry Ross' death."

Apparently, the road to justice is long, winding and slow, but eventually, it does arrive.

As Sam always says to Lauren:
I can't wait for our next adventure.

Made in the USA
Charleston, SC
16 February 2017